STEALTHY RUNNER-UP

The junior senator from California took the Capitol steps three at a time—tricky going down, exhausting coming back up. His route took him down the Mall and out to the Tidal Basin, then back. He jogged past the cherry trees, now heavy with blossoms—the most magnificent blooming anyone could remember.

Suddenly a warning bell went off somewhere deep in the senator's brain. He had been subliminally aware of the other jogger, the man wearing the navy blue warm-up suit, and had subconsciously quickened his own pace to maintain a comfortable distance between himself and the intruder. But now the other man was closing the gap. Steadily. Deliberately.

The junior senator from California hadn't been an insider long enough to discover the brutal contrast between the beauty of Washington's glorious spring and the ugliness it could bring into a politician's life. He didn't know yet that spring could be a season of death. . . .

"An intriguing story, cleverly crafted, with plenty of twists and turns. The suprises keep jumping out at the reader."
—Leonard Goldberg, author of *Deadly Care*

FATAL ANALYSIS

Jack Chase

A SIGNET BOOK

SIGNET
Published by the Penguin Group
Penguin Books USA Inc., 375 Hudson Street,
New York, New York 10014, U.S.A.
Penguin Books Ltd, 27 Wrights Lane,
London W8 5TZ, England
Penguin Books Australia Ltd, Ringwood,
Victoria, Australia
Penguin Books Canada Ltd, 10 Alcorn Avenue,
Toronto, Ontario, Canada M4V 3B2
Penguin Books (N.Z.) Ltd, 182-190 Wairau Road,
Auckland 10, New Zealand

Penguin Books Ltd, Registered Offices:
Harmondsworth, Middlesex, England

First published by Signet, an imprint of Dutton Signet,
a division of Penguin Books USA Inc.

First Printing, May, 1996
10 9 8 7 6 5 4 3 2 1

PUBLISHER'S NOTE
This is a work of fiction. Names, characters, places, and incidents either
are the product of the author's imagination or are used fictitiously, and
any resemblance to actual persons, living or dead, events, or locales is
entirely coincidental.

"Whatsoever things I see or hear concerning the life of men, in my attendance on the sick or even apart therefrom, which ought not to be noised abroad, I will keep silence thereon, counting such things to be as sacred secrets."

—Hippocratic oath

Prologue

Spring had come again, and with it, hope. And it was a particularly glorious spring, a fact which would later be remarked on by many Washington insiders who would long remember the brutal contrast between the beauty of that season and the ugliness it ushered into their lives. But they were the lucky ones, the ones who could remember. For others that spring ended forever the possibility of memory. For them it had been a season of death.

At first light the junior senator from California was out for his daily jog. He took the Capitol steps three at a time—tricky going down, exhausting coming back up. His route took him down the Mall and out to the Tidal Basin, then back. After five years it was no longer much of a challenge—except for the steps at the end—but he always found new inspiration in the sights and sounds of the nation's capital awakening to lead the world into a new day.

And it *was* a new day. A spirit of change was in the air, and Senator Saunders was determined to be a major force behind that change. It was his destiny. He could feel it in the very depths of his being. And Fate had recently given his career a significant boost. The *senior* senator from California had just announced, quite unexpectedly, that he would not be seeking reelection. In only his second term Tom Saunders would become the state's senior senator!

Saunders jogged past the cherry trees, now heavy with blossoms—the most magnificent blooming anyone could remember. He must, Saunders ordered himself, bring the twins down to see them. If not today, tomorrow for sure. Take the girls out of school if necessary . . .

A warning bell went off somewhere deep in the senator's brain. He had been subliminally aware of the other jogger, the man wearing a navy blue warm-up suit, and had subconsciously quickened his own pace to maintain a comfortable distance between himself and the intruder. But now the other man was closing the gap. Steadily. Deliberately.

A reporter. That had been Saunders' first guess. It wouldn't be the first time a neophyte newspaperman, hoping for an exclusive, had sought to take advantage of the senator's well-known routine. A brief phone call from one of Saunders' aides to the young man's editor would quickly straighten things out: this was strictly private time for the senator. No interviews. No interruptions. No exceptions. There would be an effusive apology. No editor could risk being on Senator Saunders' blacklist.

Saunders stole a quick glance over his shoulder. No, this was no reporter. Perhaps a military man—somebody's adjutant wanting to cut an early morning deal for his boss. Again Saunders forced himself to run faster. The man in blue was big, muscular—at best a sprinter. No way he could stay with Saunders over distance.

But Saunders was wrong. The gap closed relentlessly.

For the first time it occurred to the senator that the other man's presence might have more sinister implications. Saunders began to feel a sense of urgency, then desperation. He looked around for someone, anyone. There was only the man in blue. Closer now. Saunders caught a glimpse of a police car headed west on Constitution. Too far away to be of any help.

"Senator."

Had the man spoken, or was it just his imagination? Saunders ignored him and pushed himself to run harder.

"Senator Saunders!"

There was no use pretending he hadn't heard that. Saunders gave a half turn and a slight wave, the type a harried senator might throw to a constituent as he rushed through the Capitol on his way to a meeting. The man in blue couldn't have been more than twenty feet behind him.

"Senator Saunders! I want to talk to you about your relationship with Maria Garza."

Fatigue. Sudden and numbing. For several long moments that was all Saunders felt. Before he had any conscious understanding of the man's words, Saunders knew only that his arms had suddenly become too heavy to lift, and that his legs would no longer move. He was suddenly old. The fears of a lifetime had rushed down upon him in a single torrent, and he was drowning.

A total stranger. Perhaps that was fitting. In years of almost constant apprehension, Saunders had never quite been able to put a face to this moment. In the end, the most highly anticipated, most inevitable event of his life had taken him entirely by surprise. He stood still, breathing heavily, saying nothing.

It was the stranger who finally broke the silence.

"I'm George Aikins of the *Los Angeles Times*." He offered his hand. Saunders ignored it. The man shrugged. "Do you deny having a long-standing relationship with Ms. Garza?"

It was a lie.

Not about Maria. His love for Maria was perhaps the greatest truth in his life. The second greatest truth. Next to his love for his daughters. The lie was the suggestion that this man was a reporter. He was not. He was a thug, a caricature of a modern gangster made all the more menacing by a facade of condescending politeness.

"No comment." Saunders' voice sounded weak, even to himself. To anyone listening it was a confession.

"Doesn't matter." The stranger's face and voice were filled with sympathy. "We have all the proof we need."

Of course they did. If they knew Maria's name, they had proof enough. So what was the stranger after? Money? Saunders was anything but wealthy. A story? This was no reporter.

"So what do you want?" Saunders asked. Hardly a defiant response.

"We believe—that is, my editor believes—that the people of California deserve a senator of higher moral caliber. He thinks you should withdraw from the election."

Saunders managed to summon a tone of indignation. "You can't possibly imagine that you could get me to quit the race just like that." He snapped his fingers in the air.

The man in blue's tone was matter-of-fact. "If you with-

draw, I can promise you that we will keep the story to ourselves. What you do as a private citizen is your business."

"But this is nothing short of blackmail!" The senator's
indignation was now quite genuine.

The big man simply shrugged once again.

"Go ahead and print your damn story. The people of
California have heard worse. I might lose a few votes, but
I'll still win the election." Saunders thought he sounded
convincing.

"My editor wasn't thinking about the voters. He was
more concerned about your family, those two little girls."
There was a smugness in the way the man spoke the
words, as though he knew the effect they would have on
Saunders, as though he had read the senator's mind.

Saunders felt the numbness return. The air felt suddenly cold and damp. He fought to suppress a chill.

On the scale of threats, some would have considered
this to be a mild one. The man had not threatened his
daughters with physical harm—though Saunders knew instinctively that the stranger was capable of any cruelty
necessary to accomplish his goal. Still, the man had
known exactly which button to push to achieve the desired effect. He could have threatened to go to the senator's wife. That would have gotten him nowhere. Senator
and Mrs. Saunders were husband and wife in name only.
They maintained the facade of marriage solely for the
sake of the twins.

But the man had gone straight for the jugular, the children. Saunders had seen what public reports of infidelity
could do to the children of a political marriage. He would

not have his own children taunted and ridiculed. The senator offered one last, futile bluff.

"How do I know you're who you say you are? How do I know you're with a newspaper at all?"

The man in blue shook his head slowly. A slight smirk crossed his face. "What possible difference would it make?"

The man turned and began to slowly jog away, clearly confident that he had accomplished exactly what he had set out to do.

The junior senator from California watched him go, fighting an impulse to run to his office and call the *Los Angeles Times* to see if they really had a reporter named Aikins on staff. The truth of the man's words still rang in his ears: *What possible difference would it make?*

Chapter One

"You know who runs this country now, don't you?"

Experience gained over the past several weeks had taught psychiatrist Jason Andrews not even to attempt an answer. None was required. None was expected. When a man who is arguably the country's most powerful politician talks, you are expected to listen.

Jason was thinking about writing a paper based on all the politicians he'd met at the clinic: "The Narcissistic Personality, an Acquired Disorder," an unexpected dividend of his year's sabbatical at the Marsden Clinic.

"It's the A-rabs and the Jews, that's who runs this country." The congressman was building up a head of steam. "And I don't mean *our* A-rabs and our Jews. I mean the ones that live way the hell on the other side of the world."

Paranoid schizophrenia was a diagnosis that sprang readily to Jason's mind. Some days it seemed as though the Marsden Clinic was the paranoia capital of the Western world.

"But I'll fix 'em. They're not taking over this country while Hiram Bates is around!"

13

Yes, paranoid schizophrenia—with delusions of grandeur. A very common combination.

"So what have we got left, fifteen minutes?" Bates consulted his watch. "What would you like to talk about, son?"

Jason Andrews was forty-two years old and a full professor of psychiatry at Harvard, even had a little gray beginning to show at his temples to enhance his credibility. He was well beyond taking offense at Bates' calling him "son," implying that Jason was still a little wet behind the ears. But the congressman's choice of words was far from accidental. Bates had tried to control the interview from the moment he came into Jason's office, a common enough phenomenon among psychiatric patients.

Still, Bates' behavior was a bit extreme. He'd launched into his world-affairs diatribe more than half an hour ago and had been talking nonstop ever since. In Congressman Bates' case, however, there was an extenuating factor. The man who had just won election to his twelfth term in Congress—the man who would undoubtedly be chosen to replace the recently deceased Speaker of the House—was drunk as the proverbial skunk. And it was not yet noon.

"It's your hour, Congressman. We can talk about whatever you'd like, or we can just call it a day." Jason waited, patient, noncommittal.

Bates was a great, sweating pig of a man. Probably had been physically powerful at one time but no more. Now he labored for breath, all that fat pushing in against his lungs. His slit eyes narrowed as he thought.

And Jason knew exactly what was going through Bates' porcine little brain. Bates had paid for this hour, and he was determined to eat up every last minute of it. Like it was the last bite of bread soaked with the last glob of gravy on his plate, Bates was going to swallow it if it killed him. And it just might.

These psychological interviews were a throwback to the time not long ago when the Marsden Clinic had been a sleepy little psychiatric research institute. But Arthur Marsden had nearly run out of money and was in danger of losing everything until an oil man named Charles Talmedge rode in on his white horse with a scheme to rescue the place. Almost overnight the politically adroit Talmedge transformed the clinic into a chic spa catering to the Washington elite. Congressmen, senators, Supreme Court justices, members of the administration—politicos of every conceivable stripe—all came together in this luxurious melting pot in the Virginia countryside. Some came just to get away from the city, but many took advantage of the clinic's sophisticated medical facilities to get their annual executive physicals. These psychological interviews were tossed in as part of the complete medical exam.

"What do most people talk about?" Bates finally felt obliged to break the silence.

"Almost anything you can imagine," Jason said. And that didn't begin to cover it. Only this morning Jason had spent an hour talking fly fishing with the Secretary of State. Yesterday a federal judge had come in—every bit as full of himself as Bates was now—and suddenly broken down and confessed a lifelong struggle against pedophilic tendencies. Jason had been drawn to the clinic by the opportunity to work with Psychoden, Marsden's latest drug discovery. But the appeal of having a Harvard psychiatrist on board to conduct these interviews was too much for Talmedge to resist. He'd talked Jason into doing them a couple of mornings a week. Jason had resisted at first, but now was glad he'd relented. This was fascinating stuff.

"Some people talk about problems at home," Jason continued, "or the stress of their jobs. In this short meeting the most we can hope to do is identify areas of concern and perhaps talk about how one might go about seeking further counseling—if that is needed or desired.

"You'd be surprised how many times we've identified substance-abuse problems in these little meetings and have been able to help patients begin to look for solutions. . . ." It was a calculated risk, raising the obvious, but Jason felt obligated to do it. The response was immediate.

"You think I got that kinda problem? You know who you're talkin' to, boy?" The old boar had seemed docile enough rooting through the garbage on his own, but the moment he felt threatened he turned and showed his teeth.

Jason had a theory about alcohol. In excess it tended to untether the underlying personality. Under its influence some became gregarious, others sullen. Hiram Bates was a mean drunk and, Jason suspected, a mean man underneath.

"I was only giving examples of the kind of issues we deal with. . . ." It was, in one sense, the truth. "Why do you suppose you're so sensitive about this?"

Bates took a deep breath and began the struggle to stand. He had sunk very deep into the couch, and a rocking motion was required to begin to overcome inertia. When he finally got to his feet, it seemed for a brief moment that he would overshoot and topple forward. He put his arms out for balance.

"I don't need some college boy to tell me what I am. I'll be gettin' back to Washington. This meetin' is over." All said in the same tone he would have used to end a committee meeting back at the Capitol.

Jason sighed. "There's a note on your chart that says to remind you to get your blood work drawn before you leave."

Bates smirked at the suggestion. "I seriously doubt that's gonna happen."

"Do you have someone to drive you back to Washington?"

"I can drive myself." The old boar showing the teeth again.

"No, you can't." Jason's voice was even but firm. "The clinic will be happy to provide a limo, at no cost."

Bates rejected the idea with a curl of his lip and a wave of his hand and started to leave.

"I'm warning you, Congressman, the state police have been very conscientious lately. I'd bet you won't get a quarter of a mile before they stop you."

The congressman turned, his tone dismissive. "I wouldn't put the odds very high on that."

"Oh, I would," Jason said. "I'd put them near one hundred percent."

"Don't threaten me, Doctor. I'm protected by patient privilege. I'll sue the hell out of you."

"Suit yourself. The newspapers would have a field day with that, wouldn't they?"

"Don't you have any professional ethics, Andrews?" The

room was filled with Bates' indignation and moral outrage. "What kind of man are you?"

"The kind of man who's not about to let you go out and plow your car into a busload of school children."

"I'm taking this to Talmedge. You're in deep weeds, boy."

"I've been in deep weeds all my life, Congressman Bates. It's where I feel most comfortable."

As soon as the congressman stormed out of his office, Jason called Security and told them to make certain Bates was put into a limo. Jason's impression of Security was that they were much more interested in keeping an eye on him than in taking suggestions from him. Still, he managed to convince them that it wouldn't do the clinic's reputation any good if Bates' car took out a busload of kids right outside the main gate.

Jason wasn't worried about Bates. Bates was a bully, and therefore a coward. Any courage the congressman found was straight out of a bottle. But Talmedge was a different story. And there was something about the whole damn clinic that made Jason uneasy, something he couldn't quite put his finger on. He'd had the distinct feeling, almost from the moment he first arrived, that he was, once again, comfortably up to his neck in the aforementioned deep weeds.

Chapter Two

The following day began very early for Jason, when he was awakened by a phone call from the University of Virginia Medical Center at Charlottesville. The man on the other end was a neurologist named Klein who apparently was an old crony of Marsden. When the clinic operator told him that Marsden was out of town, Klein had to settle for Jason—a disappointment Dr. Klein made little effort to hide.

Whether it was because the cobwebs of sleep hadn't yet cleared from his head or because of Klein's condescending attitude, Jason was having a very difficult time understanding why this man was bothering him at six o'clock in the morning.

"I've got a patient here, Dr. Andrews, that I'd like to refer to your clinic."

Now Jason understood. Some VIP—probably at the state level, maybe the governor—had a hangnail or something and no one in the entire commonwealth was going to get another minute's sleep until it got taken care of.

"The patient is a Caucasian male, about seventy years old," Okay, so it wasn't the governor, "who was brought in

19

to the Medical Center last night by the police. They found him sitting in his car, stopped right in the middle of a freeway off-ramp—lucky he wasn't killed. The guy didn't know who he was, where he was—complete amnesia.

"When he arrived here he had no neurological deficits. We did an MRI and a spinal tap, which were both within normal limits. We just finished an EEG, which I interpreted myself, and it's entirely normal. I just did another complete neurological exam—still negative. In summary, this is a classical case of conversion reaction, hysterical amnesia."

This last leap lost Jason completely. "You said the man is seventy years old, Dr. Klein. Common things being common, don't you imagine that he's just had a stroke, and that the MRI will be positive if you repeat it in a couple of days?"

There was a very long pause at the other end. Dr. Klein was not entertaining alternative diagnoses at this time.

"You know that ten-pound neurology textbook you carried around in medical school, son?" Why was everyone calling him "son" all of a sudden? "Well, *I* wrote it."

Oh, *that* Klein.

"I just don't understand, Dr. Klein, why you decided this was a conversion reaction." Or, for that matter, why you're calling me at six in the morning."

"Well, there's a little more to the story. When Mr. Williams—that's the man's name—was last seen, maybe two hours before the police found him, it was by his daughter. She'd just put her two-year-old son into the backseat and sent him off to the store with granddad.

When the police found the car, Mr. Williams was all by himself."

Suddenly Jason was wide awake and all ears. He now knew exactly what this early morning wakeup call was about. This Dr. Klein was a pretty smart guy.

"Anyway, Dr. Andrews, I figure whatever happened to that little boy is locked up somewhere in his grandfather's subconscious. I don't think Mr. Williams is faking. I believe whatever happened to his grandson was so awful that Mr. Williams' mind just can't deal with it—so his brain has simply closed up shop for now. In a few days, maybe sooner, he'll start to remember—and I sure wouldn't want to be Mr. Williams when he does—but while we're waiting for Mr. Williams' memory to come back, we're sure as hell not doing that child any good.

"Marsden's always bragging about his latest wonder drug. I just figured I'd give him a call and see if he thought Psychoden would be of any help in this case. But they tell me Marsden's out of town. . . ."

Jason didn't need to hear anything more. With Marsden unavailable there was no one else who could do what needed to be done. His first call was to Rachel Chandler, the Ph.D. neuropharmacologist—the *beautiful* Ph.D neuropharmacologist—who worked with Marsden in his laboratory. Yes, Rachel was willing to provide the drug if Jason would assume medical responsibility. In less than two hours, they were all assembled in Jason's office: Mr. Williams, his daughter and son-in-law, Lieutenant Briggs of the state police, Jason, and Rachel Chandler.

Mr. Williams, looking every bit of seventy years old, sat in a wheelchair staring off into space. His daughter,

Angela McCall, sobbed quietly on the couch. Bill McCall was trying to be strong for his wife, but he could hardly trust his voice to speak. Jason was trying his best to obtain genuine informed consent for the use of the experimental drug Psychoden, but he knew the family would accept whatever was offered. What choice did they have? Their two-year-old son was out there somewhere. Right now they would agree to just about anything.

It occurred to Jason that they were trampling all over Leonard Williams' Constitutional rights. Once Mr. Williams was under the influence of Psychoden, he would tell whatever he knew—no matter how self-incriminating it was. But Jason decided against opening the civil rights can of worms. For now he would do whatever he could to try to help little Billy. It was, very simply, the right thing to do. After that he'd let the chips fall wherever they might.

"Psychoden is a drug that has been developed by Dr. Arthur Marsden, the founder of this clinic, to use in a procedure called narcoanalysis—which is, essentially, drug-assisted psychoanalysis." Jason wanted his explanation to be as complete as possible without confusing the McCalls with a lot of scientific mumbo-jumbo. "The personalities and behaviors of human beings are shaped, for better or for worse, by the experiences of a lifetime. Some of these experiences are remembered. Others, often the most painful or even harmful past experiences, are repressed. But even though we can't remember those events, they still affect our behavior—perhaps detrimentally. In psychoanalysis we try to help the patient recall events, especially those occurring early in life, in order to help the patient understand and take control of his behavior. Psychoden helps break down the barriers to remembering. While on the drug, the patient is able to verbalize repressed events—whether that repression is conscious or subconscious. After the drug leaves the patient's system, the blocks to memory return. The patient does not even recall what he has said to the therapist. This allows the therapist to gently prompt the memories back into the patient's conscious mind over a period of time.

"In your father's case, Dr. Klein believes—and I agree—that he has been through an experience so terrible that his mind simply won't permit him to relive it. This is probably a very primitive survival mechanism. Understand, we don't believe your father is deliberately withholding information. We don't think he's pretending. He is totally incapable of recalling what happened. With the help of Psychoden, we expect him to tell us all he knows. After the drug is removed, he'll be back just like he is now. He won't remember what he told us. We won't be forcing him to confront what has happened until his mind is ready to deal with it."

The McCalls appeared to be hanging on every word. Jason had no idea how much they were truly comprehending.

"Any questions so far?"

"Will he tell us where Billy is?" Mrs. McCall had no trouble cutting through the scientific babble.

Jason made his voice as gentle as possible. "I think we can expect him to tell us what he knows. We won't know *what* he knows until he tells us."

A few moments passed before Mrs. McCall spoke again. Her question was eloquent in its simplicity.

"Will it hurt my dad?" Was she being asked to make some horrible choice—between her father and her son?

"Psychologically, as I've said, I wouldn't expect the drug to change him. He will most likely regain his memory slowly, over time, whether or not we give him Psychoden. The drug itself has, very rarely, caused some minor, transient side effects. We are not aware of any reactions that are either serious or long-lasting. But you should remember that Psychoden is a new, experimental drug, and it has been tested on very few people. There is always the possibility that a new side effect will occur.

"Oh, and the drug is administered with a tiny skin patch, like a Band-Aid. So there are no needles. No pain."

"If it was a member of your family"—Bill McCall spoke for the first time—"would you use the drug?"

It was a frequently asked question, and Jason tried not to feel the implied insult: that he could possibly consider recommending something to a patient that he wouldn't recommend for a member of his own family. "Under the circumstances, I would have no hesitation," Jason said.

His answer seemed to settle the question. The quiet was suddenly profound, which only served to increase the startling impact of what happened next. Without warning the door to Jason's office suddenly flew open, and two of the clinic's blue-blazered security guards burst into the room. Lieutenant Briggs was instantly on his feet.

"Talmedge wants to see you, Andrews." It was the larger of the two security men who spoke.

"I'm with a patient. I'll see Talmedge when—and if—I

have time." Jason could hardly believe his eyes and ears. This was an incredible performance even for Talmedge's heavy-handed crew.

"Now" was all the guard said in response.

Lieutenant Briggs edged slowly forward, now almost between Jason and the guards. From the look on his face you could tell he didn't figure he'd have any trouble dealing with these two goons that Talmedge had sent down.

Jason held his hand out to touch Briggs slightly on the arm. "It's okay. The sooner I deal with this, the sooner we'll be able to proceed."

The McCalls were on the edge of their seats by now. Only Mr. Williams was unaffected by the commotion.

Jason addressed the McCalls, barely able to control his rage. "I'm sorry, this will only take a minute. Mr. Talmedge runs the clinic, and I imagine he has some questions about procedural matters. I'll be right back." It was a promise that Jason was not entirely certain he would be allowed to keep.

"Doctor,"—Lieutenant Briggs had his badge out for the security men to see—"if you're not back in five minutes, I'll come to collect you."

Chapter Three

The elevator was wood-paneled and thickly carpeted. Soft music wafted from hidden speakers. Its occupants felt no sense of motion as they were transported to the clinic's top floor.

Ordinarily there was something vaguely pleasant about the ride, and, Jason was pretty certain, his usual solitary trips in the elevator appealed to something distinctly primal. But it was one thing to take his patients back to the womb, quite another to retrace his own origins. His mind did not wander happily in that direction. Especially not today, when the womb had turned rather acutely crowded and claustrophobic.

Jason had always had a problem with authority. It got him into trouble in grade school; it got him into trouble at Harvard. Whenever anyone tried to place limits on him, his natural inclination was to resist. This tendency had not been a positive force in his marriage. One could make the argument that the exact opposite had been the case. And this same inclination had not always pushed him in the direction of political correctness at Harvard. Again, *au contraire.*

Not that Jason regarded the two security men who shared his elevator as authority figures. What frosted him was that they regarded *themselves* as authority figures. They were overflowing with self-importance.

"How about those Bullets?" Jason gave them his warmest smile.

Then the door opened, and Jason left them to ponder the vicissitudes of professional sport *a deux*.

The eighth floor contained an improbable melange of offices and departments. At one end was Medical Records and a computer bank that would do the Pentagon proud. Then there was the clinical laboratory with all the latest analytical devices, and next to it the room where patients had blood drawn for various tests. The Blood-drawing Salon, as it was called, was certainly unique. It was done as a cozy den with soft furniture and the ubiquitous paneled walls. Patients could sit upright or recline. They were invited to wear headphones and close their eyes. The idea was to make the clinic's VIP clientele feel as relaxed as possible and get their minds off the impending needle stick. By all accounts the system worked well.

Adjacent to the "drawing room" was Talmedge's sumptuous suite. The outer office was manned by the obligate officious secretary, Ms. Rotweiler. Jason had actually almost called her that once.

"Dr. Andrews to see Mr. Talmedge." Jason paused thoughtfully. "I believe I'm expected."

"Go on in." Almost as a single woof. Jason had the distinct impression that if he turned his back on her, she would be tearing at his pant leg before he could say "psychoneurotic."

One look at Talmedge drained all the whimsy from Jason's mind. From the time they first met, Jason had felt an instant dislike for the man. Talmedge was one of those characters who was so smoothly political no one knew what his convictions were. Jason assumed he didn't have any. Supposedly Talmedge had been enormously successful in the oil business until the price dropped to eighteen dollars a barrel and he got squeezed. It had been a whole lot easier to be a brilliant oil man when the price was twenty-five dollars a barrel.

"What the hell is going on here, Andrews!" Talmedge was livid. He was practically screaming.

Jason shrugged—as though he didn't have a clue what Talmedge was talking about. Creatures that eat their young, Jason decided, probably bear offspring which look a lot like Talmedge.

"The first I hear you're up to something is when three police cars roar up to the front of the clinic, lights flashing, and they tell me you've authorized some kind of carnival demonstration of Psychoden. We don't need this kind of publicity. We don't want it. I won't have it!" Talmedge's usual oily veneer of calm was nowhere to be seen. His face was red, the veins bulging. His blood pressure had to be going through the roof. "Who the hell do you think runs this clinic anyway?"

"Arthur Marsden." Jason kept his voice low and firm. He would have wondered if he'd even been heard if he hadn't seen the rage cross Talmedge's face. Jason decided not to leave the naked challenge sit out there all by itself for too long. "They're looking for a little boy who is missing. I think we can help."

"I don't *care* what you think. I won't permit it. I won't let this clinic be used for a sideshow. People come here because we're dignified and secluded. No one wants to be around this kind of publicity."

"Look. We've got a chance to help find this boy. We're already involved—couldn't back out now if we wanted to. It would be unforgivable if something happened to him while we're up here arguing."

"I'll decide what's forgivable. And I'm going to put a stop to this right now."

"That would be a felony."

"What?"

"Obstructing a police investigation. I won't be a part of it." It was pretty thin, but Jason could see he had Talmedge thinking for a moment.

There was a soft knock on the door, and the Rotweiler entered. She approached Talmedge very cautiously. He looked like he might strangle her. She went behind his desk and whispered conspiratorially in his ear. How, Jason wondered, could she work for a man like Talmedge? He was like an alligator. There was no possibility that he could evoke any positive emotion.

Talmedge picked up the phone as his secretary slinked out of the room.

"Good morning, Senator." Talmedge became instantly obsequious. The only other words to come out of his mouth were a few "Yes, sirs."

Charles Talmedge gave every appearance of a man receiving his marching orders from a superior who would tolerate no dissent, and the expression on his face left no doubt that Talmedge was a man who did not take orders happily.

As he listened, Talmedge's face darkened to increasingly deeper shades of red, the facial coloring accented by a rim of yellow gray hair that had been ever so carefully combed to cover the balding expanse at the top of his head. Talmedge's eyes were the color of uncooked liver. His teeth were the same color as his hair. Talmedge always wore expensive blue or gray suits with banker's stripes. His ties were invariably yellow or red. His shoes were always black wingtips that looked like they would weigh in at about thirty pounds apiece.

The conversation was suddenly over, and Talmedge was left holding a dead receiver in his hand. He pointed it angrily at Jason.

"Next time, check with me before you agree to any harebrained experiments."

Jason took this as his signal to leave. Under other circumstances he might have been inclined to really leave, to just pack his bags and head back to Boston—after helping the McCalls, of course. But he enjoyed working with Marsden and his work with Psychoden. And there was always his forthcoming seminal work on narcissism. But there was something more. There was something about this place. Something about Talmedge. Something about the omnipresent, heavy-handed security guards. Jason had his nose in the air, doing a little sniffing, and he wasn't about to leave until he'd sorted it all out.

As he headed for the elevator, Jason felt something tickling at his chin. Something vaguely ominous, yet strangely familiar. Deep weeds.

Chapter Four

Lieutenant Briggs was pumped. Jason could see that as he walked back down the hall toward his office. Briggs was standing in the hallway beside Jason's closed office door.

"Dr. Chandler said to tell you that all the papers are signed, and she's taken Mr. Williams to Examining Room Ten.'" Briggs was already headed down the hallway. "Everything's ready."

"How come," Jason wanted to know, "you people don't need me to tell you what happened in Talmedge's office?"

Briggs smiled. "Did you know that her brother is *Senator* Chandler?"

Enough said. Yes, Jason knew that. But it hadn't occurred to him until this moment that it had been Rachel's brother who had twisted Talmedge's arm. Jason would never understand politics. How could a simple phone call have exerted so much pressure on a man like Talmedge?

When they got to Examining Room Ten, Mr. Williams was seated in his wheelchair, still seemingly oblivious to the events taking place around him, but otherwise ready for the Psychoden interview. Rachel Chandler had seated herself on the examining table, legs crossed, waiting. Jason threw her a smile.

"I understand your brother has taken an interest in our work here at the clinic."

"He just wanted to let Talmedge know how pleased he was that the clinic was assisting one of his constituents." Rachel allowed herself a small smile, then back to work. "I think I've got everything ready for you."

Jason permitted himself, almost unconsciously, to continue watching Rachel for a moment after she had turned her attention away from him. There was something intriguing about her, something beyond her striking physical beauty. In someone else he might have called it an aloofness, but in Rachel it was more an inbred aura of dignity. Like an experienced diplomat, she kept any hint of inner turmoil from ever crossing her face. This was all done with no external sign of effort. She never seemed artificial or calculating. Jason had yet to have even the slightest glimpse behind that ever pleasant, patrician exterior.

Jason forced his mind back to his patient. He took a Psychoden patch from the table and made a perfunctory effort to communicate with Mr. Williams. "I'm going to place this patch behind your ear, Mr. Williams. After I've done that, I'll ask you a few questions, then I'll remove the patch. You won't remember anything that happens while you're wearing the patch."

Jason waited, but there was no response. He placed the small adhesive patch on the bare skin behind Mr. Williams' ear, then took a seat in a chair face to face with the patient.

"Can you tell me your name?"

There was no response. Probably the drug had not had time to take effect yet.

"Can you tell me your name?" Jason asked in an even, gentle tone.

At first no response, but then, "Leonard Patrick Williams," in that flat, distracted voice that people had while under the influence of Psychoden. It was as though someone else were speaking through him.

"When were you born, Mr. Williams?"

"September 12, 1927." He appeared much older than that, with his disheveled gray hair and far-off look. "I was born just after midnight on a Monday morning. My mother had hoped I would be born on Sunday. She said it was because it was the Lord's day. Dad said it was because she was hurting and Sunday comes a day before Monday."

This tendency toward long answers was typical of patients on Psychoden. Marsden called it "Psychoden expansiveness." They'd found that the best way to deal with it was simply to ask another question.

"Where were you born?"

"Graves Mill, Virginia." And, as an afterthought, "That's over in Madison County."

Jason continued through the litany of background questions that were always used at the beginning of the Psychoden interview before proceeding to more delicate issues.

Finally, "Mr. Williams, do you have a grandson?"

"Yes, I do. Little Billy. William Patrick McCall. He's just two years old."

"And did you see Billy yesterday?"

"No, not yesterday." In that same monotonous tone.

Briggs' head jerked up, and his gaze shifted from Williams to Jason. What the hell was this?

Jason scratched his head. "When did you last see Billy, Mr. Williams?"

"This morning. I picked him up to take him to the store." Obviously, somewhere along the way Mr. Williams had lost a day. Under the influence of Psychoden people told you what they *thought* was the truth. Sometimes what they thought was the truth was simply not correct.

"His mother said it would be all right." Even through the Psychoden, Leonard Williams sought support.

"Did you go to the store?"

"No. I just drove around."

"Why didn't you go to the store, Mr. Williams?"

No response. Sometimes this happened. Maybe the patient's mind was trying to override the effect of Psychoden; maybe the question just wasn't specific enough.

"Mr. Williams"—Jason took a deep breath—"what happened to Billy?" Everyone in the room felt the tension. Everyone except Leonard Williams.

"Why, he fell out of the car." Very matter-of-fact. "One moment he was safely on the backseat, the next moment he was out the door and run over by a truck."

The room filled with a heavy, oppressive silence. Several moments passed before Jason thought he could trust his voice.

"Where did this happen, Mr. Williams?"

"Old Highway 2, just north of Martin's Ferry."

Martin's Ferry? That was only a few miles from the

clinic. Williams had been found clear over in Charlottesville. Jason felt Briggs' hand on his shoulder.

"Why don't you let us check this out before you say
anything to the parents? News this bad can hold until
we're sure." Jason nodded his agreement to Briggs' back as
the policeman hurriedly left the room.

"Jason." It was Rachel Chandler's voice that brought his
mind back to the examining room. When he looked up
into her face, Rachel nodded toward their patient. Williams' face had become distorted. His tongue was protrud-
ing its full length from his mouth, and his head was
writhing uncontrollably to the right. Mr. Williams made
no sound and gave no sign that he was at all distressed by
what was happening to him.

Jason grabbed the phone and quickly punched in the
number of the clinic pharmacy. "This is Dr. Andrews. I
need fifty milligrams of diphenhydramine for intravenous
injection stat, and I also need a liter of D-5 quarter Normal to hang as a continuous drip. We'll be down to pick
it up in a couple of minutes." The pharmacist repeated
the request, and Jason thanked him for his help.

"Would you mind picking the stuff up from the pharmacy, Rachel? I better stay with Mr. Williams."

"Sure." She started to leave.

"And, Rachel. I know it's asking a lot, but if you would
tell the McCalls there's been a little reaction—nothing
serious—that we have to deal with, it'll buy Lieutenant
Briggs some time." Rachel nodded in agreement as she
left.

Jason took Leonard Williams' hand, more for something
to do than anything else. He could treat the reaction by

simply removing the Psychoden patch, but if he did, Mr. Williams would become aware of his reaction and that could prove stressful. Experience had taught them that it was best to give the intravenous antihistamine first and then remove the patch after the reaction was controlled.

Fortunately, these neurological—so-called extra-pyramidal—reactions to Psychoden were quite rare. And even though the facial contortions appeared grotesque, the reactions caused no damage, did no permanent harm.

When Rachel returned with the materials from the pharmacy, Jason deftly inserted a 19-gauge Teflon catheter into a vein in Mr. Williams' right arm and connected the intravenous solution. He then began the injection of the antihistamine. The response was sudden and dramatic. As the antihistamine entered his system, Mr. Williams' features seemed to melt quickly back into place. Within seconds he returned to normal, and Jason removed the Psychoden patch.

But Jason felt no sense of accomplishment or relief. The easy part of his day was behind him. In a few minutes he would have to tell two loving parents that they had lost their only child.

Chapter Five

They decided it would be best to find a bed in the clinic for Leonard Williams—at least for the next several hours—to make certain no additional, unexpected side effects occurred. Jason and Rachel were more attentive than would ordinarily have been necessary. They both accompanied Mr. Williams to his room, attempting to put off, for as long as possible, the inevitable. Lieutenant Briggs had said it all. News this bad could wait for confirmation. On the other hand, they had waited for Briggs about as long as possible. They couldn't leave the McCalls dangling forever.

"I'll go back down and talk to the family, Rachel. You don't have to put yourself through that."

"I don't mind. Maybe I can provide some additional support."

"For them or for me?"

"Wherever it's needed." She smiled gently. "What are you going to tell them?"

"I don't have the slightest idea." He truly didn't.

Their legs didn't carry them very swiftly back to Jason's office. They looked for Briggs, but he had not returned.

No message. With one last look into each other's eyes for moral support, Jason opened his office door.

The McCalls sprang instantly to their feet. Jason asked them to sit down, gestured for Rachel to take a chair. He himself leaned back against his desk.

"Your father is fine, Mrs. McCall. He had a slight reaction of a type we occasionally see with drugs of the Psychoden class, but it's completely over with now. We found a bed upstairs for him so that he can rest. It's been a terrible day for him."

Mrs. McCall's voice quavered as she asked, "Was he able to tell you anything about Billy?"

Mr. McCall put his arm around his wife, instantly sensing the worst. "It's something awful, isn't it, Doctor? Something more horrible than we ever imagined."

Probably, Jason thought. He himself had assumed a kidnapping, a child snatching of some kind. Jason's mind would never, on its own, have conjured up the image of a tiny two-year-old body being run over by a truck.

"Your father didn't tell us very much. Billy was in the backseat, as you know. He must have somehow gotten out of his infant seat, managed somehow to get the back door open—"

Jason never had to go any further. The office door suddenly flew open, and there was Lieutenant Briggs.

Walter Briggs had seen just about everything in nearly twenty years with the state patrol. He figured he was about as hardened as a man could get. Around the force he was known as one tough cop. And in all his years of driving the interstate, he thought he'd seen it all. Not even close.

Today, this big, tough cop, all six foot three inches and two hundred and twenty-five pounds of him, stood in that doorway with tears in his eyes . . .

. . . and a squirming little boy in his arms.

"Billy!" Both McCalls in unison. They were on their feet and had their son in their arms almost before Briggs knew what had happened.

"We found him sound asleep under a tree," Briggs said to anyone who might be bothering to listen. "That big old truck must have just blown him off the road."

Jason took Briggs' hand and shook it. "Like I said, people under the influence of Psychoden can tell you only what they *think* is the truth. Thank God Mr. Williams was wrong."

They took Billy into an examining room, and Jason did as much examining as the little boy would permit. Billy had apparently gotten quite a lot of sleep during his adventure and was now going to be very active for the next several hours. Jason found a scratch on Billy's knee, but that was about all.

Their last bit of unfinished business was awaiting them upstairs.

Leonard Williams lay flat on his back, eyes wide open, staring at the ceiling tiles. As the group entered the room, Billy was chattering on about something he had seen down the hall, and the sound of his voice seemed to have a subtle effect on his grandfather. Perhaps a slight, purposeful movement of the older man's eyes. Maybe the tiniest contraction of the muscles of his face.

"Grandpa!" Billy screamed as he noticed his grandfather

for the first time. Once again Billy was in motion, squirming against his father's powerful grip.

Again, the changes in Leonard Williams' countenance were so minimal as to defy description. But he seemed to teeter on the brink of awareness.

And then a single tear formed in the corner of his right eye and slowly found its way down his cheek.

Jason and Rachel, standing there together, totally caught up in the emotion of the moment, spontaneously threw their arms around each other and shared a desperately needed hug. It was a perfectly natural thing to do. It was that kind of human moment that cries out for physical as well as emotional sharing.

But as the seconds passed, what had been entirely spontaneous became something else. Jason became intensely aware of the woman nestled in his arms, of Rachel's body pressed against his, of his own desire to prolong the moment. When at last they separated, Jason felt quite self-conscious. Had she felt it too?

Rachel took a couple of steps back from him, her head cocked to the side, one eyebrow arched inquiringly, just the slightest hint of a smile on her lips, and for the briefest of moments she permitted Jason to glimpse behind the patrician facade. Yes, she seemed to be saying, I felt it too.

Chapter Six

Ten o'clock on a Sunday evening in late February, and the President was alone in the Oval Office. Nothing unusual in that. At least he'd been able to spend the weekend at Camp David with his grandchildren. There was a great deal the President liked about his job, and some things he didn't like, and one thing he truly hated. He hated that he was able to spend so little time with his grandchildren.

The President opened his briefcase and pulled out some papers he'd reviewed at Camp David. On top was a letter to the British prime minister. It was covered with tiny chocolate fingerprints. The President smiled and put the page aside. Couldn't send that to London. He'd file it away for now, maybe get it framed after he left office and give it to his daughter. Long after he was gone, his granddaughter could look at the letter and be reminded of snuggling in her grandfather's lap with a candy bar in her hand while he conducted the affairs of the nation and the world.

The phone buzzed to announce the Vice-President's arrival, and moments later he was ushered in. The President rose, smiling, and gestured for the Vice-President to take a seat on the couch.

"Sit down, Herb. Take a load off." The President took a nearby wing chair. "You figure out a way yet to keep that horse's ass Hiram Bates from becoming speaker of the House?"

The Vice-President shook his head. "Too many people either owe him or are scared to death of him—or both. No one's even going to run against him, let alone beat him."

The President nodded in silent agreement. Several quiet seconds passed, penetrated only by the reassuring meter of a nearby grandfather clock. The two old friends had done battle side by side for decades. Fifteen years ago, the big question was which of these two would become president. Now it was a virtual certainty that they both would. Herb's turn was coming up in just four short years. A more seamless transfer of power could not be imagined.

The Vice-President had asked for the meeting, and it was he who broke the silence.

"This is so difficult—" His voice suddenly choked with emotion.

The President felt his own heart sink. He had seen his friend this dejected only once before, when he had learned that his son was missing in action in Vietnam.

"Janet?" the President asked.

The Vice-President shook his head.

"Not Susan?"

Again the head shook. And then, with sudden and unexpected formality, "Mr. President, I am hereby submitting my resignation from the office of vice-president of the United States—effective immediately." He reached into his suit jacket and pulled out an envelope which he offered to the President.

A jumble of emotions cascaded through the President's mind. In the first instant there was grief and empathy for a dear friend in a moment of terrible personal tragedy. But there was anger too. How could the President not feel, however briefly, a sense of betrayal?

The Vice-President's reversion to formality had been a deliberate attempt to dissociate their years of friendship from this moment of anguish. The President understood this immediately and responded in kind.

"Might I know the reason for this decision . . . uh, Mr. Vice-President?"

"I can't . . ." There was great pain in his face and in his voice. He was finally able to force out one more word, ". . . health . . ."

The President left his chair and sat down beside the Vice-President. "Herb, surely there's something we can do. We'll get the best doctors, the best hospitals."

But the Vice-President shook his head. "We'll *say* it's health." His voice was barely audible. "We'll ask everyone to respect my family's privacy. If I resign immediately, they might just let me go. It might work."

"Herb, can it be so terrible?"

"Worse." The word came out of him like the last bit of air escaping from a leaking tire. Then he pulled himself together and rose to his feet. Looking the President straight in the eye, he said, "I'm so sorry."

The President found his friend's hand dangling at his

side and held it warmly. "You know that Mary and I are here for you, anytime, day or night."

The Vice-President nodded, unable to speak.

"Let's keep this between us for now, Herb. Go ahead and cancel all your meetings for the next couple of days. Tell your secretary you're under the weather. Try to get some sleep. We'll talk again first thing in the morning."

The Vice-President turned and left the room. The President watched him go, repressing the urge to run after him, embrace him, tell Herb that they would somehow manage to get through this—whatever it was. But he didn't. And for the rest of his life he would never forgive himself for failing the best friend he would ever have in his moment of desperate need.

The Vice-President died that night. They said it was suicide. And it probably was.

Chapter Seven

More than a week ago, Jason had noticed that Robert Chandler was scheduled to meet with him this morning. It was an appointment that Jason had looked forward to with more than a little interest, not so much on account of the senator's national prominence as for more personal reasons: the ease with which Senator Chandler had been able to control Charles Talmedge had piqued Jason's curiosity; and, of course, Robert Chandler was Rachel Chandler's brother.

So when Jason opened his office door he hardly noticed the white-haired gentleman seated in the waiting room. The man quickly rose to his feet.

"Hello, Doctor. I'm Robert Chandler." He offered a very firm handshake.

"Jason Andrews," Jason said as he shook the hand. Then, realizing that the man could not have helped but notice his confusion, he added, "I'm sorry. For some reason I had assumed that this appointment was with"— understanding came to Jason in mid-sentence—"your son."

"Don't give it a second thought, Doctor. Happens all

the time. I'm proud to have my son follow in my foot-steps."

Something in Robert Chandler's demeanor suggested to the psychiatrist in Jason that Chandler was not nearly as complacent about playing second fiddle to his son as his words suggested. Jason motioned for Chandler to take a seat on the couch while he took his usual chair.

"I'm not supposed to lie down or anything, am I?" Chandler asked with a wink.

"It's your hour, Ambassador. You can do whatever you want." Some patients were actually quite eager to lie down—if for no other reason than that it gave them an ex-cuse to avoid eye contact with the therapist. "As you know, this session is just part of the clinic's complete medical package. I would be happy to discuss any specific issues you have in mind—or we can just chat."

"Actually," Chandler said, stealing a quick glance at his watch, "I'm afraid I won't be able to spend much time with you this morning, Doctor. I've had to make a bit of a change in my schedule."

Chandler was a tall, distinguished appearing man who looked every bit the senior statesman. Despite his age he still sported a full head of hair, its whiteness contributing to a conspicuous aura of nobility. Chandler's movements betrayed not a hint of age. He seemed vigorous, athletic even. But the single most striking physical attribute was the eyes: an intense cobalt blue. Jason imagined that they might with equal ease shine with joy or burn with anger.

"So you're retired now, Ambassador?"

"Well, out of the ambassador business anyway. I still find some odd jobs to do behind the scenes." Chandler had assumed a self-deprecating tone that was meant to suggest that he was a master of understatement.

"How long ago was it that you left the Senate?"

"My son's had the seat now for just over ten years. I went to the State Department for a while after that—sort of an ambassador-at-large for the Middle East—but that was several years ago."

"So you don't have an official government appointment at this time?"

"No, nothing official—unless you want to call me an official mourner. It seems like I spend a lot of time at funerals these days. In fact, that's why I can't stay and talk with you for very long. I've got to head back to Washington for Vice-President Allen's funeral."

It was all spoken in a very offhand way, but experience had taught Jason that patients frequently approached major issues with such oblique references. At Robert Chandler's age, coming to grips with one's own mortality was an important life event.

"Was the vice-president a close friend?"

For some reason the question seemed to amuse the ambassador. "No, I don't guess anyone would have ever called us 'friends.' It's no secret that I opposed his nomination. My worst fear was that he might some day become president." Then he added, almost as an afterthought, "Can't say I was very surprised when I heard he'd committed suicide."

That kind of armchair psychiatry always irritated Jason—this time all the more so because he had recently interviewed Vice-President Allen in the same way he was now interviewing Ambassador Chandler. They had spent a very pleasant hour chatting, and Jason hadn't detected the slightest hint of depression in the vice-president—much less any suicidal tendency.

"What makes you say that, Ambassador?"

"The man was weak. He didn't have the courage of his convictions—or maybe he just didn't have any convictions. Herbert Allen always wanted to know what the polls showed. He never wanted to be out of step with the majority."

"Some might say that's what democracy is all about."

"That may be what *democracy* is all about, but it's not what being in government is all about. You're elected to lead, not to follow. The people, God bless 'em, don't always know what's best for their own good. That's why they need leadership."

"And if the people don't like where you're leading?"

"They can always vote you out of office. The problem with people like Allen is that they spend too much time worrying about holding onto their jobs and not enough time thinking about what's best for the country." It was clearly a topic Chandler had spent a considerable amount of time pondering. "Old Alexander Hamilton saw this problem coming. He proposed to the Constitutional Convention that the president be elected for life. The rest of the founding fathers wouldn't hear of it, though— probably too worried about what the voters might think."

"I guess the next best thing to being elected for life," Jason suggested, "is to be able to pass the reins of power to your son."

"Rob has a lot to learn yet," Chandler said, "but I have no doubt he'll go far—much farther than I've come."

"The presidency?"

Chandler smiled knowingly. "We'll see." Then he looked at his watch and suddenly was on his feet. "I've enjoyed meeting you, Doctor, but I'm afraid I'll have to be going—got a funeral to get to."

Jason rose and the two shook hands.

"You know," Chandler said, "I was eager to come by and have a look for myself, to see all that Talmedge has been able to do for the old place. Arthur Marsden is a brilliant scientist, but he's not much of a businessman. Talmedge is just what this old place needed to get it back on its feet. Marsden didn't think so at first, but I was able to talk some sense into him."

Ambassador Chandler started for the door, then turned one last time. "I hope I didn't seem disrespectful of Herbert Allen. Like I said, we weren't exactly friends. I'm certain I'll be able to rely on your discretion not to repeat anything I've said." Then he added, "I guess I *know* I can count on your being discreet—doctor-patient privilege and all that."

"Of course," Jason said.

"In fact, I could come in here and tell you I'd committed murder, and you'd have to keep it to yourself, right?"

"Some would consider that a gray area."

The ambassador gave Jason one last charming smile as he left, and Jason watched his back as he made his way down the long corridor to the clinic's main entrance. What would it be like, Jason wondered, to have grown up with the burden of being the son of Robert Chandler? And then, almost as an afterthought, he wondered, what would it be like to have been his daughter?

Chapter Eight

Congressman Hiram Bates sucked at his bourbon slowly. He had to make it last tonight, needed to keep his wits about him. He set the glass down on the fine white tablecloth and admired the cut of the crystal. Four ounces of Kentucky's finest floating three translucent cubes of ice. The ice was supposed to be from some glacier up in Alaska. He took another sip.

Why anyone would pay a hundred fifty to two hundred dollars a plate was beyond him. He didn't care how many stars the restaurant had in the tire guide. But it had been a long, long time since Hiram Bates had had to pay for a fancy meal. One of the perks of office. Just call some lobbyist or other, tell him you wanted to discuss this or that bill, you could name whatever restaurant you wanted. They didn't care. It wasn't their money either. Hell, you didn't have to call them. There were always more invitations than days in the week.

Bates closed his eyes and savored the effect of the bourbon. A steady undercurrent of soft music and muffled voices greeted his ears. No distinct conversation could be discerned, one of the most important attributes of the restaurant as far as Hiram Bates was concerned.

Fish. His wife had told him he ought to eat more fish. Supposed to be good for him. He'd even considered ordering the fish tonight—till he spied the scrawny little piece the lady at the next table had on her plate. That put the thought right out of his mind.

Steak was what he felt like tonight. A great big piece of meat. The biggest one they had, not one of those dinky little filet things wrapped in ten cents worth of bacon. Steak and potatoes, that's what a real man had for supper. And bourbon. And you didn't let a good steak waste a lot of time on the grill, lose all that juice. Just pass it over the flame a couple of times real quick and bring it right on out to the table.

Yes, sir, his mind was all made up. He'd have the steak for his second course of the evening. He'd already picked Charles Talmedge to be his first.

Bates had been planning this night for weeks, hell, months. Ever since Talmedge had started contributing to his "campaign fund" again. Now, everybody in Washington knew that Bates didn't have to do any campaigning to hang on to his seat in Congress. It was probably the safest seat in the country. And everybody knew that anything Bates didn't spend campaigning, well, that was money he could take right along with him into retirement. But, all of a sudden like, Talmedge was putting money into Bates' retirement account again. Which was pretty interesting since no more than a couple of years ago Talmedge had been completely out of money.

What Talmedge wanted Bates to do was steer his cronies into this new clinic Talmedge had set up. No problem. Bates would be happy to help him. Next thing Bates knew, everybody in Washington was getting Talmedge money. First off, it was pretty clear, to Bates anyway, that little clinic in Virginia was never going to do enough business to justify that kind of investment. Second, it was obvious that Talmedge had a silent partner stashed away somewhere, a partner with very deep pockets. And it wasn't the Sisters of Mercy. Bates' most highly developed instinct, honed over many years of congressional experience, was to seek out the deepest pocket.

Bates remembered an episode in his life from over fifty years ago, a story his Sunday school teacher had told the class that had served as an object lesson—though, at least for little Hiram Bates, not the one the teacher had intended.

Two little boys were sitting on a curb when a man pulled up in his shiny new convertible. "Hey, mister," one of the boys said, "where'd you get that fancy car?" And the man smiled and looked down at the little boys and said, "Why, my brother gave me that car." And the little boys looked at each other and said, "Wow!" Then one of the little boys said something wistfully, and the Sunday school teacher wanted the kids in the class to guess what the kid said, and of course everybody knew what the kid had said: "I wish I had a brother like that!"

The teacher had smiled patiently and said no, that wasn't it. What the little boy said was: "I wish I could *be* a brother like that." All by way of demonstrating what a good little Christian soul he was. Better to give than receive and all that. End of lesson.

But Hiram Bates, at the tender age of ten years, understood the true meaning of the story. The brother on the receiving end, what's he got? A car. And presumably he didn't even have the bucks to buy the car on his own. But the other brother, not only does he have the bucks to buy the car, he can buy it and then give it away! Hiram Bates would like to be a brother like that, and it wasn't Christian charity that motivated him either. At the age of ten, Bates already knew a thing or two about deep pockets.

As soon Bates sorted out where Talmedge's money was coming from, he had a pretty good idea of what they were up to. Last April he had run Senator Saunders through the clinic as a test, and bingo! The former senator was now teaching civics to hippies at some junior college near San Francisco. Bates still hadn't quite figured out all the details, but he knew enough to run a pretty good bluff, and he counted himself a pretty good poker player. By the end of the evening Talmedge would have revealed most of his cards. Bates would know enough to spoil their party if he wanted to, and it was going to cost them one hell of a lot more money if they expected Hiram Bates just to sit back and let them get away with it.

He caught a glimpse of Talmedge coming through the dining room, working various tables as he made his way toward Bates. Talmedge should have been a politician, then Bates could have stepped on him at will. There weren't many men Hiram Bates hated more than he hated Charles Talmedge, but for now he couldn't play too rough with him, not with Talmedge still laying those golden eggs.

"Charlie, how the hell are you?" Bates shook Talmedge's

hand vigorously and clapped him on the back. Talmedge hated to be called Charlie.

"Pretty fair, Congressman, pretty fair. Sorry I'm running a little late."

"I was just about to order us a bottle of wine. What would you like?" Pretending to forget that Talmedge was a teetotaler. There was no one Bates despised more than a teetotaler. Self-righteous son of a bitch. "I was thinking maybe this Lafite Rothschild," Bates said, indicating a four-hundred-dollar bottle of wine.

"Whatever you'd like. I won't be having any." There was a definite edge to Talmedge's voice that Bates ignored.

"Cutting back, eh? Never saw the need myself."

The waiter appeared and Bates ordered the wine. Talmedge asked for tonic water.

"You want that on the rocks, Charlie?"

Bates decided he'd better ease up on Talmedge for a while, let the man relax a little, get him to let his guard down. He steered the conversation toward neutral subjects for half an hour or so and gave Talmedge a chance to bring up anything that was on his mind. Apparently there wasn't much. Bates ate his steak with gusto while Talmedge picked at a little piece of fish just like the one the lady at the next table had ordered.

When the waiter asked them if there would be anything else, Bates asked for whatever kind of pie they had, à la mode. Talmedge ordered coffee. It was time for Bates to go to work.

"I had a nice little chat with your boss the other day." It was a lie, but Talmedge couldn't know that. "He thought there might be a bigger part for me to play in your clinic operation, thought I might be interested in playing a more active role."

Talmedge didn't say anything. He just eyed the congressman cautiously over his coffee. Bates could see he'd have to play out a little more line.

"I understand, of course, from the point of view of your boss's people this is a pretty good deal. And for you, I guess it kept you out of bankruptcy—not having to pay for all that oil you'd taken delivery of. . . ." Bates was guessing here, but Talmedge's expression told him he was right on the money. "And Marsden, he gets to continue with his research, which I guess is all he cares about. But for me, as a patriotic American citizen, I'm not sure how I can go along with all this. I've got to tell you, it just about broke my heart when Tom Saunders didn't run for reelection." Bates decided he'd said enough for now and turned his attention to his pie and ice cream.

Talmedge watched him eat for a while, then said, simply, "He's not my boss."

Bates shrugged, knowing he'd hit a nerve but not wanting to overplay his hand. "*He* sure thinks he's your boss." Then he quickly moved the conversation on. "Anyway, like I was saying, Tom Saunders was sure a shame."

Talmedge waved his hand dismissively. "Couldn't be helped. Saunders was never going to be an asset—too hard to control. He was a threat to Gerald."

Hiram Bates nodded as though he understood and shoveled in another forkful of pie. Who the hell was Gerald?

"I don't think you need to worry about many more, uh, disruptions like we had with Saunders," Talmedge said.

"We've got just about everything we need—except for choosing Gerald."

"Who are the leading candidates . . . for Gerald?" Bates figured he'd better wade back in and see what he could find out.

"I don't know yet. The list keeps getting shorter and shorter, though. We'll obviously have to decide very soon."

The congressman let his mind play with it for a little while. Gerald . . . obviously have to decide very soon . . . Gerald . . . soon . . . Gerald . . .

Bates felt his hand shaking and wondered if Talmedge had noticed. He quickly put down his fork and put his hand in his lap. He got the waiter's attention and ordered a brandy. His mind was racing ahead, and he needed something to calm his nerves. It was just too much for his mind to take in all at once.

He suddenly understood exactly who "Gerald" was.

Chapter Nine

Jason waited patiently for Dr. Marsden to return to Earth—or, more accurately, for Marsden's mind to come back from wherever in the universe that it had wandered off to. When he first came to the clinic, Jason had suspected that Marsden's absentminded professor pose was simply an affectation. No one could be *that* distracted. But over time Jason had become convinced that Marsden wasn't playacting after all.

Rachel had tried to explain the phenomenon when Jason first arrived at the clinic. You know how when you're at the beach and a girl in a bikini walks by, your eyes automatically follow? Jason said no, he had no idea what she was talking about, which earned him his first Rachel Chandler smile.

Okay, she said, when *I'm* at the beach and *I* see a man in a little Speedo, *my* eyes tend to automatically follow. Would this man, Jason wanted to know, be walking toward you or away from you? No smile this time, just the arched eyebrow. So Jason followed with, Just to help me visualize better, would *you* be wearing a bikini in this example?

Pay attention, Doctor, Rachel had said. I'm trying to

make a point here. For Arthur Marsden, ideas are what girls in bikinis are for most men. When an idea floats across his brain, there's no point in trying to bring him back into the conversation until he's dealt with it.

Jason had considered her observation at some length, allowing his own mind to appear to wander for too long, permitting a lengthy silence before finally coming back to Rachel, his eyes looking through her and focusing somewhere behind her head—all very Marsden-like—and asking, A string bikini?

You are incorrigible, her only response. To which he had replied, Thank you.

So Jason now sat patiently behind his desk and tried to imagine what exotic tangent Marsden's brain was pursuing instead of discussing the patient whose family was due to arrive in less than ten minutes.

Rachel saw Marsden as a combination of brilliant, albeit somewhat distracted, scientist and benevolent grandfather figure—like someone who'd just walked out of a Norman Rockwell painting. And as Jason studied the man seated in his office, he certainly looked the part: Marsden was balding, but the soft white hair that remained was allowed to flow down over his collar. He had sharp blue eyes amid a somewhat florid complexion. He wore a colorful bow tie to offset his white shirt and long white laboratory coat. Marsden was slightly plump but remarkably well-kempt considering his chronically distracted state.

"At any rate"—Marsden suddenly emerged from his thoughts—"I think you'll find it a very interesting case."

He rose to leave.

"You haven't really told me anything about the case, Arthur." Jason was patient. It was typical for Marsden to assume they'd talked about things when they hadn't. "What is the child's problem?"

"Oh, she's a classic obsessive-compulsive, very bizarre behavior. Fascinating. An excellent case for Psychoden."

And with that Arthur Marsden was out the door.

It was a pretty good illustration of why Marsden didn't see many patients himself, and why he was so delighted to have Jason on board at the clinic.

So the Rhinehardts arrived with very little advance explanation.

"I assume Dr. Marsden has explained to you why we are here," Mr. Rhinehardt said, and it was not an entirely unreasonable assumption although it was an entirely incorrect one.

Earl and Emma Rhinehardt sat close together on the couch as though for mutual support. He wore an impeccably cut three-piece suit with a striped tie and shoes shined to such a high gloss that Jason couldn't help but wonder if they were plastic. His hair was closely cropped and his hands neatly manicured. He had penetrating black eyes held in check by a too-earnest manner.

Mr. Rhinehardt was the spokesman for the couple. His wife sat demurely beside him, her eyes taking only occasional furtive glances at Jason, her ankles neatly crossed. Her shoulders were hunched and her head slightly bowed, making her seem quite diminutive next to her husband. This picture contrasted sharply with Jason's initial impression of the woman when she'd entered his office with her husband. With her three-inch heels, Emma was nearly as tall as Earl. She wore a tight skirt that quit well above the knee, and the sweater she had selected did nothing but accentuate what could quite conservatively be described as an already prominent bosom.

As a psychiatrist, Jason found the psychodynamics of couples fascinating. He'd long since learned not even to attempt a guess at what went on behind closed doors.

"I think, Mr. and Mrs. Rhinehardt, that it would be best if we started at the beginning. What is it about your daughter's behavior that worries you?"

Mr. Rhinehardt moved forward to the edge of the couch, elbows on his knees, fingertips together, "She prays all the time."

If Jason had taken a year to list possible descriptions of Earl and Emma Rhinehardt, the term *atheist* would not have made the list. It would not have entered his mind.

"Perhaps you had better explain."

Earl Rhinehardt tried. "She prays *all the time*. Don't get me wrong, Doctor, we're Christian, God-fearing people." Was that a sigh from Mrs. Rhinehardt? "We go to church every week. We pray at home every day. But Abigail is completely out of control. She prays *constantly*. Every night at dinner it's the same thing. She gets up out of her chair and gets down on her knees and starts praying. After a few minutes, or sooner if we say something, she gets back in her chair and tries to eat a bite or two, but in less than a minute she's back down on her knees."

"Does this happen just at dinner?"

"No, like I said, it's *constant*. All day. Her mother has to get her out of bed and keep pushing her, or she'd never be able to get dressed in the morning. Sometimes Emma goes into her room in the morning and finds Abigail praying—naked." He almost choked on the word. Emma nodded in silent confirmation. "She can't go to school because she's such a disruption to the class. It hardly matters: She's not learning anything anyway, not with all that praying."

Rhinehardt's voice displayed a mixture of frustration, embarrassment, and anger. He seemed beyond feeling either sympathy or compassion for his daughter. "We've tried everything. Discipline doesn't seem to help. The doctor tried some drugs that just about put her into a coma. We're at our wit's end. We can't go out in public anymore. Everyone goes, 'They're the ones with the daughter who's the nut case.'"

"Can you tell me when all this started?"

Earl Rhinehardt seized on the question with a vengeance. "I can tell you *exactly* when it started. It started when she began going to that *boys'* school."

For the first time Emma stirred briefly. "It's a coed school." Barely more than a whimper. "She used to go to a girls' school, now she goes to a coed school." Having said her piece, she quickly bowed her head once again.

"And when did she start her new school?"

"At the beginning of the school year. In September. She finished middle school last spring. I thought it would be best if she went away to a girls' boarding school in the fall. She and her mother wanted her to go to the local high school." There was a certain sense of vindication expressed in Earl Rhinehardt's tone.

"So, as far you know"—Jason's gaze included both parents—"she *wanted* to go to the local high school. She didn't seem to be especially afraid of the new school?"

"Not as far as we knew," Earl said. His wife shook her head in agreement. "So far as we knew she was eager to go to the new school. All her girlfriends were going there too. That was the main reason she wanted to go to the local high school."

"And since she's been there, have there been any problems? Any teachers giving her a hard time? Any arguments with old or new friends?"

"Not that we know of—except for this praying thing. It's pretty hard for her friends to be around her now. I can't say that I blame them."

"How about boyfriends?"

It was as though he'd said the magic word. The Rhinehardts both shifted on their cushions. There was a barely perceptible pulling away from each other. As usual, it was Earl who spoke.

"That's my guess. I think some boy's done something to her, and she's afraid to tell us." Now there was anger in his voice. "I think she may have gotten raped or had an abortion or something."

"Mrs. Rhinehardt?"

She hardly looked up. "I don't think so."

Her husband clenched his jaw muscles.

Jason considered all this in silence for a few moments. Nothing wrong here that a few hundred years of family counseling couldn't straighten out. Finally, with carefully chosen words, he spoke:

"It is possible that the use of Psychoden might help us begin the process of understanding Abigail's behavior, and help her to get better. I believe it would be worthwhile to try, but I can't make any promises." Both parents nodded in apparent understanding. "One thing I need to make very clear. *Abigail* is my patient, and I will hold her best interests above all other considerations. My conversations with Abigail—whether under the influence of Psychoden or not—will be held in strict confidence. Even though you are her parents, I will divulge nothing unless I believe it is in Abigail's best interest."

Earl Rhinehardt started to protest, but his wife took his arm as though to hold him back. For the first time her voice had a strong, unfaltering quality. "Whatever you think is best for our daughter, Doctor. We'll do whatever you think is best."

Chapter Ten

Arthur Marsden was behaving strangely—even for Arthur Marsden.

He had asked Jason to come to his office at five o'clock "on the dot." It was a peculiar request from a man who normally had no concept of time; a man who generally gave the impression he didn't know whether it was day or night out—and didn't much care.

When Jason arrived in Marsden's laboratory, he found Rachel Chandler working at her computer.

"Any idea what Marsden has on his mind?" he asked her.

"No," she said, "but he's definitely up to *something*. He asked me to give this to you." She handed Jason a sealed envelope.

Jason tore it open and found a note scrawled in Arthur Marsden's nearly illegible hand:

Jason,
I'm in my office. Come in and shut the door behind you.
                                              Arthur

P.S. Ask me anything you want.

Jason showed the note to Rachel. "Call the pharmacy and ask them to send up three hundred milligrams of Thorazine and a big syringe. I think Arthur has really flipped out this time."

He found Marsden seated at his desk, staring out the window—not a terribly unusual pose for him. You might think he was watching something outside, but if you asked him, he couldn't tell you whether or not it was raining.

"You wanted to see me, Arthur?"

"Yes, I did." If it was possible, Marsden appeared more distracted than usual. He continued to stare off into space.

Jason waited patiently for a few moments, then offered, "I've scheduled a Psychoden interview with the Rhinehardt girl. That should prove interesting." If it was of any interest at all to Arthur Marsden, he didn't say so.

To fill the void, Jason allowed his own thoughts to wander. His mind quickly came to that morning's interview with Robert Chandler, Sr. Almost without thinking he asked, "How long have you known Rachel Chandler's father?"

"More than twenty years." At last it seemed that there was something Marsden wanted to talk about. "The Chandler estate is only a few miles from here."

"I guess," said Jason, "that Chandler and Talmedge are good friends."

"They hate each other's guts." Marsden's voice was flat, completely devoid of emotion as he spoke.

Jason was trying to make sense of all he'd heard today.

"But didn't Senator Chandler introduce you to Talmedge and get Talmedge involved in the clinic?"

"Yes," Marsden answered, "but he said you didn't have to like Talmedge to like his money. Chandler said not to worry, Talmedge could be controlled." His voice trailed off at the end as though he was losing interest in the conversation.

"Where did all of Talmedge's money come from?"

"Oil."

"But didn't he lose all his oil money?"

"I don't know. People said that he did."

The contradiction didn't seem to bother Marsden. His mind drifted off once again.

"Arthur, are you feeling okay?"

"I'm fine."

"Was there something you wanted to talk to me about?"

"No."

Earlier, Jason had kidded Rachel about Marsden's mental condition, but now he was beginning to worry. He'd better have a talk with Rachel.

"I'll be back in a couple of minutes, Arthur." No response.

Jason turned to open the door and saw the sign Marsden had left there for him:

Jason, please remove the Psychoden patch from my neck before you leave.

The patch was behind Marsden's ear, hidden under a shock of white hair. Jason removed it and sat down once again while he waited for Marsden to recover. He didn't know whether to be angry or relieved.

"How do you feel, Arthur?"

"I'm fine." The response was automatic. Marsden still wasn't quite back to the real world. Then, "Oh, Jason!" As though noticing Jason for the first time. A look of excitement came over Marsden's face. "How did it go?"

"You scared me to death, Arthur. I was afraid you'd had a stroke or something."

"I'm sorry." Marsden did his best to appear contrite. "I'm working on a new Psychoden formulation, and I always try them on myself first. This patch is supposed to deliver a lower dose. Did it seem to have much effect?"

Jason couldn't help but smile. "I'd say you were pretty much of a zombie, Arthur. What effect were you going for?"

Marsden ignored his sarcasm. "How long did it take me to recover?"

"I'd say about a minute and a half." Jason felt obligated to add, "You know very well this isn't scientifically useful, Arthur. If you want to evaluate a new formulation, we need to design a controlled study and line up some volunteers."

"I know, I know. I just wanted to see if this would work. We can always do a formal study later. Like I said, I always try everything on myself first."

"That's not a good idea, Arthur." Jason used his sternest tone for effect, but Marsden was already busying himself

67

with his notes and seemed not to hear him. Jason got up to leave.

"Good night, Arthur." Again, Marsden did not appear to hear.

Chapter Eleven

By the time the Rhinehardts were able to arrange to bring their daughter back to the clinic, tensions in the family were at the flash point. Mrs. Rhinehardt seemed more assertive than before.

"Abigail, this is Dr. Andrews."

"I'm pleased to meet you, Dr. Andrews." She reached to shake the hand he had offered, and then continued—in a single, fluid motion—to turn to the far end of the couch, where she knelt in prayer.

"She prayed the whole way over here. It's worse than ever." Her father was beside himself. "Now she never stops. She's losing weight because she won't sit still long enough to eat."

Abigail continued her prayers, seemingly oblivious to the anxiety she was provoking. She was a tiny sparrow of a girl with large, vulnerable black eyes and matching hair. She wore a plain white blouse and a full navy skirt, black patent leather shoes with white anklets. Abigail could have as easily been thirteen years old as sixteen. They regarded her in silence until her father could tolerate it no more.

"Mary, come sit on the couch so Dr. Andrews can talk to you."

This brought a sharp look from Emma Rhinehardt.

Her daughter said simply, "My name is Abigail," and went on with her praying.

"Her full name is Mary Abigail Rhinehardt," Mrs. Rhinehardt explained. "We've always called her Mary. Then, when this all began, she said she wanted to be called Abigail. She has never been able to give us a good reason for the change, but we've tried to go along with her wishes." She sighed softly. "Sometimes we forget." Her tone somehow implied that the forgetting might not always be unintentional on her husband's part.

Earl Rhinehardt clearly took all this personally. "Mary is my mother's name. My wife's mother is named Abigail."

There was a soft knock on the door, and Rachel Chandler entered. Jason had asked her to drop by, thinking that Abigail might be reassured by the presence of another female. The introductions were made and Jason suggested that Mr. and Mrs. Rhinehardt return to the waiting room. Abigail's father balked at the idea.

"I'm not sure I can go along with that, Andrews. I want to know what's happened to my girl. I have the right to know."

On one level, at least, Jason could be sympathetic. "I do understand your feelings, Mr. Rhinehardt, but without the assurance of confidentiality I think it is highly unlikely that Abigail can be helped. I wouldn't be able to proceed without it, and I doubt you'd be able to find a competent psychotherapist anywhere who'd agree to go forward on any other terms."

His wife tugged at his arm. "We've already discussed this, Earl. We're going to do whatever is best for Abigail."

Earl shook his head slowly, but he allowed his wife to pull him through the doorway.

As soon as they were alone with their patient, Rachel coaxed Abigail onto the couch. She sat there for several seconds, appearing entirely normal, then suddenly fell to her knees and began to pray once again.

"Abigail, can you hear me?" Jason used the gentlest voice he could muster.

"Of course I can hear you." How could he think that she couldn't hear him? Her praying, if anything, intensified.

"How old are you, Abigail?"

"Sixteen." She stopped praying and returned to the couch.

"Do you know why you're here?" Jason asked.

"You're going to help me get better."

"Better in what way, Abigail?"

"You're going to help me stop praying." And with that she returned to her knees.

"Would you like that, Abigail? Would you like to stop praying so much?"

"Oh, yes! More than anything!"

"Then why don't you just stop?"

"I can't." She sounded utterly defeated.

"Would you rather I called you Mary or Abigail?"

"Abigail."

"Why is that?"

"I prefer Abigail."

"Why?"

"I just do."

She was a pretty girl. At sixteen her face and figure were just beginning to hint at the beauty she would become, perhaps an Audrey Hepburn look-alike. It was not difficult to imagine her as a victim.

"Do you understand why you're here, Abigail?"

"You're going to try to help me."

"Do you know how we're going to do that?"

"Give me pills." She stopped praying and took a seat on the couch again.

"No. No pills."

"Shots?" There was now fear on her face.

"Oh, no, Abigail. No shots. We'll just put a little patch on your skin—like a Band-Aid. The medicine is on the patch. While you're wearing the patch, I'll talk to you and try to see if I can find a way to help you. Then we'll take the patch off and you won't remember a thing that we've talked about."

"What questions will you ask me?"

"We'll just talk about your life, your family, what's troubling you."

Abigail returned to her knees.

"Is that okay with you, Abigail?"

Her answer touched Rachel and Jason deeply. "If you know what I'm thinking, you'll hate me." And with that, Mary Abigail Rhinehardt went back to praying, harder than ever.

Jason and Rachel eased her back onto the couch and placed a Psychoden patch on her neck. Within seconds she appeared quite tranquil. She looked like she might fall asleep. The poor little girl was probably exhausted.

Jason began to work his way through the introductory questions. "What is your name?"

"Mary Abigail Rhinehardt. But I prefer to be called Abigail." Her voice sounded distant, detached.

"How old are you, Abigail?"

"Sixteen years and three months."

"Where do you live?"

When Jason thought that Abigail was comfortable and relaxed enough to do so, he proceeded to more probing questions. "You used to go by the name Mary, didn't you?"

"Yes, but I prefer Abigail."

"Did the name Mary come from your grandmother?"

"It's from the Bible."

"I thought your grandmother was named Mary."

"She is, but her name comes from the Bible."

"Why don't you like to be called Mary?"

"I don't deserve to be called Mary. She was the mother of Jesus, the most perfect woman who ever lived. I'm a terrible person."

"What makes you such a terrible person, Abigail?"

"I think terrible thoughts."

"Is that why you pray?"

"Yes, to try to drive those terrible thoughts out of my mind. I can't pray and think those thoughts at the same time."

"What are your terrible thoughts about, Abigail?"

"Boys. All I ever think about is boys."

"That sounds perfectly normal to me, Abigail."

"Not the way I think about them. Sometimes I think about boys without any clothes on. Sometimes I think about them touching me. It's terrible."

"Abigail, sometimes Jesus' mother is called the Virgin Mary. Did you know that?"

"Yes." She didn't offer anything more.

"Are you a virgin, Abigail?" The question needed to be asked.

"I don't know what that means."

Jason hesitated for a few moments. He would have to take a slightly different tack. "Has a boy ever touched a part of your body that would normally be covered by a bathing suit?"

"No."

"Has anyone ever done anything to you that is in any way like the thoughts you've been having?"

"No."

"None of your schoolmates?"

"No."

"None of your teachers?"

"No."

"No adult has ever done anything like that to you?"

"No."

"Abigail, has either of your parents ever done anything to you that was anything like the thoughts you've been having?"

There was a hesitation—very unusual for someone on Psychoden. It was almost as if her mind couldn't comprehend the question. Then came the brief, definite answer. "No. Of course not."

Jason was acutely aware of how tense he had become. He leaned back in his chair and allowed himself to relax. He and Rachel exchanged understanding glances. Marsden had been exactly right. Abigail suffered from an extreme form of obsessive-compulsive behavior.

Jason remembered a similar case he'd read about somewhere of a priest who suffered from obsessive thoughts that he considered to be blasphemous. The poor man's mind tried to deal with it by the continuous, compulsive recitation of his rosary, over and over and over.

Abigail's thoughts were perfectly normal for a developing adolescent, but something in her life experience had taught her to be ashamed of those thoughts. Jason had a pretty good idea where she'd gotten that impression.

The road ahead would be difficult for Abigail, but with proper therapy for her *and* her parents, the prognosis was good. Without Psychoden to break down her psychological defenses, many years of psychotherapy might have been required to get to where they were right now. And this was, at best, only the starting point for her recovery.

Within minutes of removing the Psychoden patch, Abigail was once again on her knees, praying. Rachel put her hand on the young girl's shoulder.

"We understand what's troubling you now, Abigail. We're going to be able to help you."

A look of fear came over Abigail's face once again. "Oh, no, Dr. Chandler. I don't deserve to be helped."

Chapter Twelve

March came cold and gray, without the slightest promise of spring. The White House lawn was blanketed by snow, but long afternoon shadows now crept slowly across the landscape, darkening it to match the threatening skies. It was, for all practical purposes, the dead of winter.

But inside, spirits were high. The President had made his decision—with the full support of his closest advisers. Congressman Joseph Lucas of Utah would be his nominee to become the next vice-president of the United States. No one would be terribly excited about his choice, but there would be little opposition. The Lucas nomination could be summed up in a single word—*safe*. The Senate would quickly confirm.

There were only the three of them in the Oval Office: the President himself, his chief of staff, and the attorney general. Joseph Lucas would arrive soon to hear the decision, and the President was looking forward to that moment. Lucas had never aspired to the presidency, but it was well-known that the congressman had long hoped that favorable political winds might one day place him in the number two position. Joe Lucas had served his constituency well through years of hard service. He was liked and trusted. He and the President had not always come down on the same side of every issue, but they had always regarded each other with respect. Rewarding Lucas' many years of public service with this nomination would give the President a great deal of personal pleasure. He was eager to get on with it.

"No skeletons in the Lucas closet, then?" The President asked the question of his attorney general at the close of her summary of the obligatory pre-nomination FBI investigation.

"I don't think there's even an off-color tie in his closet. The man is a Mormon. He's never been sighted sneaking so much as a soft drink. His wife has served as his chief of staff for over twenty years—without salary, I might add—and she's never more than about ten feet away from him. So it doesn't seem likely there's any big sex scandal about to blow up. And the guy's put seven kids through college, all of them now responsible members of their respective communities. My advice is to nominate him for vice-president as quickly as you can—before he gets put up for sainthood."

The President smiled at that. Charlotte Moran had done her usual exhaustively thorough job. Some eyebrows had been raised when he'd appointed her, at the tender age of thirty-nine, to be his attorney general, but time had vindicated him. She was brilliant, aggressive, compulsive. She would go far in this town. And her cover girl beauty wasn't going to hurt her any, either. She had long blond hair and beautiful blue eyes you could get lost in.

"What's your reading of the Senate's mood, Bernie?"

The President turned to his chief of staff, Bernard Conn, who had himself spent two terms in the Senate.

"No change. Joe is generally well liked. He doesn't have any major enemies. There may be some partisan speech making, but no one's going to try to block the nomination. Joe's at the end of his career, so no one has to worry that he'll use the vice-presidency as a platform for a run at the presidency next time around. When it comes time for the vote, there may be a senator or two who'll find it necessary to be out of town, but I doubt *anyone* will actually vote against the nomination."

The President nodded in agreement. For his money, Bernie Conn was the most politically astute man in Washington. If Bernie said it was so, then it was so. The three of them passed a few more minutes in quiet conversation. Then the phone on the President's desk buzzed. Congressman Lucas had arrived.

Everyone stood and shook hands with the congressman, then settled back into their comfortable chairs: the President in his usual wing chair, Charlotte Moran and Bernie Conn on the couch, Congressman Lucas in the other wing chair. It could have been a friendly gathering in any living room in the country. A few pleasantries were exchanged. No one seemed in any hurry.

Joe Lucas had put on a few pounds over the years. He was close to six feet in height and would tip the scales at well over two hundred pounds. He was gray and balding and sixty-six years old. He seemed nervous, almost wary. He kept moving in his chair as though he couldn't quite get comfortable.

The President found Lucas' nervousness strangely reassuring. Congressman Lucas would certainly have guessed why he had been summoned to the White House. This nomination would mark the pinnacle of his career and also carried with it important responsibilities. It was appropriate that Lucas should have some apprehension and anxiety about it. The President realized that he would have been concerned, and perhaps more than a little angry, had Lucas simply taken the nomination for granted.

"This has been a very difficult time for all of us, Joe," the President began. "I doubt any of us will ever be able to make any sense out of Herb's death. I saw him every day and had no idea of the anguish he was going through. To this day, I can't imagine what could have driven him to take his own life."

The mention of Herb's name seemed to unsettle Lucas even more, making the President sorry he'd mentioned him. He knew that Herb and Joe Lucas had been close. It was a strange chain, the way many friendships were. The President had been close to Herb and had known that Joe Lucas and Herb shared a close friendship, yet the President and Lucas had never had more than a professional acquaintance.

"At any rate," the President continued, "we have to put this personal tragedy behind us, hard as that may be to do. The affairs of state must go—"

The President stopped in mid-sentence, completely distracted by Congressman Lucas' obvious distress. Lucas was perspiring profusely. He continued to fidget in his seat and appeared increasingly agitated.

"Are you all right, Joe?" There was real concern in the President's voice.

The congressman nodded repeatedly. "Yes, sure, I'm fine. Just a little hot after coming in from the cold. And it's upsetting, thinking about Herb."

The President was beginning to have second thoughts about his decision, but reminded himself that Joe Lucas had been on the Hill for a very long time. He was a known quantity. He had never been known to crack under pressure.

"At any rate, Joe, we need someone of great skill and experience to replace Herb. Yours was the first name that each of us"—the President made a gesture which encompassed the attorney general and his chief of staff—"considered. With your permission, I'd like to nominate you to be the next vice-president of the United States."

Even before he had the words out, the President knew that the moment of happiness that he had anticipated would never come. Lucas was shaking his head vigorously almost before the offer had been made.

"No, oh, no. I'm not . . . I mean I'm flattered, of course, but I'm not the right man for the job. You need someone younger. I mean, my health isn't what it used to be. I only hope I can last out my current term; then I just want some time with my kids, the grandchildren. Thank you, Mr. President, for the offer, but I'm sure you'll realize, when you think about it, that I'm just not the person for the job. I mean . . ."

It was as though Lucas couldn't stop talking. Who was he trying to convince? His agitation increased until he could no longer stay in his chair.

"I'm sorry, Mr. President. I mean, thank you, Mr. President. I'm *very* flattered, but I must say no. I mean, there are so many who are just so much better qualified than I."

Congressman Lucas continued to talk as he backed slowly out of the room, almost bowing as he spoke. And then he was gone.

The Oval Office was filled with excruciating, stunned silence. It was the President who finally spoke. His voice thundered with anger.

"What the hell is going on in this town? Can anyone tell me that?"

There was no response.

Chapter Thirteen

The faces of attorneys general of the United States of America had undoubtedly graced the covers of countless magazines over the years. But, Jason thought, Charlotte Moran was surely the first attorney general to find her face on the covers of *glamour* magazines. The image, he noted, lost nothing in translation to flesh and blood.

She sat on the couch in Jason's office. There had been the usual awkwardness about the mental health interview, and Jason had provided the usual explanation: it's just part of the complete physical exam package; the hour is yours to do with as you please; etc. For some reason she still seemed uncomfortable.

"You must find your work terribly challenging—and fascinating," Jason said, mostly by way of trying to open up a neutral area for conversation.

"Most of it is remarkably mundane," she said. "Ninety percent of my time is spent on administrative details—and dealing with the federal bureaucracy."

Her gaze wandered about the room as she spoke, as though she were searching for something. Or, Jason decided, she simply wanted to avoid eye contact. Her green eyes settled on him only occasionally and very briefly.

"Are you enjoying your work?" he asked.

"I'm not sure that 'enjoying' is quite the right word. It's important work." This last was said with remarkably little conviction.

Charlotte Moran had dark brown hair accented by dazzling highlights. It had been very precisely cut. Of that Jason was certain: short enough to be taken seriously, yet long enough to convey a carefully calculated amount of softness and femininity. There was nothing accidental about this woman. She wore a suit that at first glance was quite conservative. Most observers would not notice how carefully it was tailored to take full advantage of every feminine curve. The hem was cut fashionably above the knee, the effect aggravated as she sank deeper into the soft couch. Her legs were tightly crossed, the left foot suspended in midair and in constant, fidgety motion. An otherwise successful attempt to present a facade of placidity and self-assurance was betrayed by wayward eyes and an obstinate extremity.

"Are you here for the day or staying overnight?"

For an instant Charlotte Moran's eyes met his and her foot stopped moving. "I had planned to stay several days and relax a little, but unfortunately I need to get back to Washington this afternoon." Something in her tone suggested fear that Jason might not believe her. "I did stay here last night. My suite was as nice as any hotel I've ever stayed in."

Jason smiled. "*Nicer* than any hotel I've ever stayed in."

"Talmedge has certainly spent a fortune on this place," she said.

"Someone has," Jason replied.

It was as though the lawyer switch inside Charlotte Moran had suddenly been thrown. "What do you mean, 'someone has'?"

"Nothing," Jason assured her, "I'm just not very knowledgeable about how the financing works around here." He had never quite understood how, if Talmedge's oil business had gone belly up, he could suddenly turn around and underwrite the Marsden Clinic operation. Jason hadn't lost any sleep over it. It was none of his business, and, besides, what difference did it make who financed the clinic?

"You're originally from Texas?" Jason asked.

"Same as Charles Talmedge?" she countered.

Jason put on his most reassuring smile. "Actually, I was trying to change the subject." But in spite of himself he said, "You seem to have some familiarity with our Mr. Talmedge."

"Everyone in politics is familiar with Charles Talmedge. He makes certain of that."

"Now, officially changing the subject," Jason said, "I think I read somewhere that you come from a very large family."

"Ten children," she answered, suddenly wistful, "but only eight of us survived to become adults."

It was a subject she seemed willing, but not eager, to talk about, as though she found both comfort and pain in reliving those old sorrows. Jason listened attentively as Charlotte Moran told of a baby sister's struggle against leukemia, a twelve-year-old brother's death in a boating accident.

Despite all the sadness of her childhood, the attorney general seemed, for a while, much more at ease discussing it than she had been earlier discussing her successful political career. Some of her previous nervousness had been shed. Then suddenly, without warning, the agitation and uneasiness returned.

Dealing with patient anxiety is an everyday event for any psychiatrist, part and parcel of the profession. But the attorney general was not a patient in the usual sense. These mental health interviews were almost an afterthought. She didn't need to be there if she didn't want to be. There was nothing pressuring her to discuss anything she didn't want to discuss. So what did she have to be nervous about?

Maybe there was some crisis brewing back at the capital. Jason would pick up the newspaper in the morning and instantly understand what had been on the attorney general's mind. Or maybe it was something to do with the clinic. Some physician or other employee had done something to upset Charlotte Moran, and she had simply decided to pack her bags and go back to Washington.

But there was another possibility that Jason had learned from experience to be on the lookout for. Some patients scheduled their annual physicals at the clinic specifically because of the mental health interviews. The interview provided an opportunity to see a psychiatrist without the stigma that might be associated with making a psychiatric appointment per se. Patients sometimes didn't even admit to themselves their true motive for coming to the clinic.

As the end of their hour approached and it appeared to Jason that they hadn't yet broached any substantive issues, he decided to make a direct approach.

"As I said earlier, Ms. Moran, this is absolutely your hour to utilize in any way you see fit. You should feel under no pressure whatsoever to discuss anything you don't want to. At the same time, you should feel equally free to take advantage of my professional services. If there is anything you'd like to talk about, I'm a pretty good listener."

The nervousness returned now with a vengeance, but she shook her head. "No," she said, "I don't think there's anything." Her tone was hardly convincing.

Jason was aware that he might himself be the problem. He was male and just slightly older than the attorney general. She might have come to the clinic with every intention of baring her soul but found herself uncomfortable talking to Jason. The pairing of patient and therapist is a very delicate process.

"You should also feel free, Ms. Moran, to ask for a referral to another therapist. For example, it might be much more convenient for you to see someone in Washington. . . ." This gave the attorney general the opportunity to request a referral without worrying that Jason might feel rejected. "There are many well-qualified therapists in the area: male, female, old and young. If you'd like a name, just ask."

"Thank you, Doctor, but I don't think that will be necessary."

When their hour concluded, the attorney general thanked Jason for the session. She said that she had enjoyed their talk. As she left, **Jason** could not escape the notion that this was not the confident, strong-willed Charlotte Moran he had watched so many times on television. This was a very troubled woman. And he had been able to do nothing to help her.

Chapter Fourteen

Hiram Bates sat in a cocktail lounge next to an indoor mall out in Rockville. He'd parked his car in the high-rise garage adjacent to the mall, then walked over here to kill some time. He'd let the A-rabs cool their heels for a little while, let them know Hiram P. Bates was in charge now.

He'd been ordering bourbon rocks, doubles, and what they did here was hose the so-called bourbon into a glass of ice shavings. If you waited more than thirty seconds to drink it, the stuff tasted like ice water flavored with cigarette ashes. He flicked the top of the glass with a fingernail. It had all the resonance of a Mason jar filled with prune preserves. Oh, well, there weren't too many options available to him on a Sunday morning.

The waitress was all right, though. Little blond college girl. Nice figure. Very attentive. She'd brought him some complimentary potato skins. The girl might have recognized him, or else she was turned on by a rich-looking older guy in a nice suit. Some of these young ones, they got a whiff of Washington power and they went crazy.

Bates wiggled his way out of the booth and put on his overcoat. If he kept the A-rabs waiting too long, they'd think he wasn't coming. That wouldn't do at all. He put down a nice tip for the college girl, grease her skids a little. Bates had in mind that after his business was done, he might want to come back and see just how power hungry she was.

It was cold outside, with a piercing wind. Bates was glad he'd brought a scarf. He wondered how the A-rabs were doing, up there in that open garage. They say it gets plenty cold out in the desert at night. Maybe the A-rabs were used to it. He hoped they weren't. Serve 'em right. Who the hell's country is this anyway?

The man they knew only as Smith fought to control his anger. Anger only got in your way, made you make stupid mistakes. Especially when it wasn't focused. Right now he was mad at the entire world. Like a cornered animal, he'd snap at anything that came within reach.

He was angry at Bates for being late. In a clandestine situation the last thing you wanted was to spend an extra half hour hanging around the meeting site letting half the population of greater Washington get a good look at you.

And he was mad as hell at the ambassador for making him bring the dictator's "nephew" along. Apparently "nephew" was what you called your son if his mother happened to be your first cousin.

"When Bates gets here," Smith told him, "I'll do all the talking. You just watch and learn." He was supposed to call the kid Your Excellency. Since he wasn't about to do that, he didn't call him anything.

"Don't tell me what to do, Smith." The pompous little twit pronounced it Smythe. He'd been packed off to an

English boarding school at an early age, then spent about six weeks at some fancy New England college before they realized he didn't know anything and threw him out. Which was why Smith was baby-sitting him now, giving the kid some real-world experience.

It must have been about a hundred degrees in the car. The kid insisted on keeping the motor running and the heater on. It was a wonder he didn't want to sit on Smith's lap and play with the horn. What Smith would like to do is reach over, palm the back of the kid's head, and bounce it off the dashboard a few times. Give him some real-world experience.

Smith unzipped the top of his running suit to try to cool off a little. He was wearing the navy one today. The running suit hid his bulk and gave him a generic appearance, made it difficult for anyone to give a useful description of him. Who did you see? Just some guy in a running suit. Medium build. Medium height.

The kid, of course, had worn a shiny silk suit, looked like it cost a couple thousand dollars. Smith figured he should probably just be thankful that the kid hadn't shown up in one of those sheik outfits, riding a camel.

Then Bates showed up, looking all over the garage, like he'd lost a child or something.

"Remember," Smith said, grabbing the kid's arm, "just follow my lead and don't say anything."

"I told you, don't try to tell me what to do." The kid always sneered as he spoke. "And don't touch me. Ever."

Bates expected to see the ambassador standing around, or at least a limousine somewhere on the floor. Since the garage was completely open except for a few structural posts scattered about, Bates didn't see how he could miss the ambassador if he was there. The congressman walked over to the perimeter railing and leaned out to look down toward the garage entrance four stories below. No sign of any activity there either. For a brief moment he almost leaned too far. Whether it was the height or the alcohol, he felt a fleeting dizziness, but quickly pulled himself back. That would have been something, take a fall like that on the brink of his big chance. He looked again. There were some bushes down there to break his fall, but he still would have broken some bones.

When Bates turned back around he saw two figures moving toward him. At first it didn't occur to him that they might be coming to meet him: some guy in a jogging suit and a kid all dressed up for his first communion. Then he saw that the kid was an A-rab.

Bates stood his ground as they approached. This wasn't the meeting he'd asked for. Maybe he had miscalculated. Maybe the ambassador wasn't even in the loop. He'd have to think about that a little. That was the problem dealing with these towel heads, you never knew who they were working for.

For now he said, "Where's the ambassador?"

It was the man in blue who answered. "He couldn't make it."

Bates turned to the young man in the suit. "And who are you, sonny boy?"

"You will address me as Your Excellency!" He was totally outraged at Bates' insolence. "I am fully empowered to represent my government in this matter!"

Bates looked back at the man in blue and rolled his eyes. "Next time I meet with the ambassador, or your little game is over."

The kid started to say something, but Smith held up his hand for silence. "We're here. Let's talk."

Bates shrugged. "Just tell the ambassador that I know the entire operation, and I've decided to help." He waited a couple of beats to let it sink in. "I'm going to be Gerald."

"Kill him, Smith." The kid's words had the effect of a small fly buzzing around the men's heads. If they noticed it at all, their only instinct was to swat at it.

"We figured you were going to ask for money," Smith said. "We were prepared to make you an offer—if you were reasonable."

"Don't worry. I expect to be paid. But I figured, why settle for just the money?"

"If you won't kill him, I will." The two older men continued to ignore him.

Then, out of the corner of his eye, Smith saw the kid reach inside his coat and pull out some kind of small-caliber pistol. It looked like a toy.

"Are you crazy?"

Before Bates quite understood what was going on, the man in blue had snatched the gun from the kid's hand. The kid looked like he was going to cry.

Bates stepped back reflexively and felt the retaining wall supporting the back of his thighs. When Smith pivoted back toward Bates, the gun clutched in his left hand swung into Bates' face. The congressman leaned back and felt his balance go. This time he was falling for sure.

But suddenly he felt Smith's strong grip on his left

shoulder. The man in the blue jogging suit had a secure hold on him. He was no longer falling. Bates felt an instant bond to this stranger who had so unexpectedly reached out to save him from certain serious injury.

Bates never fully understood what happened next.

As the man in blue tugged at his left shoulder, Bates' body turned while it was being pulled back into the safety of the garage. For a brief instant Bates felt his back held against Smith's powerful chest. He was safe. And then he heard an ominous snap, and suddenly he was falling headfirst. It all happened so quickly.

Only the man in the blue jogging suit would ever know that Congressman Bates' neck was broken *before* he hit the ground.

Chapter Fifteen

The uproar over Congressman Parker reminded Jason of the brouhaha the day Leonard Williams had been brought to the clinic. But Jason had felt that he understood why Talmedge was so upset about Williams. Jason hadn't agreed with Talmedge, but he understood where Talmedge was coming from. Today, Jason didn't have a clue why Talmedge was so agitated.

"I understand that the man is talking *crazy*," Talmedge was saying. Jason had been placed in the very difficult position of trying to reason with Talmedge on the telephone while the congressman and his wife sat on the couch in Jason's office hearing every word.

"I wouldn't know about that." Jason tried to keep his voice even. "You haven't given me a chance to talk to him." He shrugged at Mrs. Parker, who was following Jason's end of the conversation with intense interest.

Talmedge's tone became almost pleading in quality. "But the man is insane, he needs help."

That was when Jason lost it. "Who the hell do you think I am, Juan Valdez? I'm a psychiatrist, Talmedge. I've been known to help people. Some of them have actually had mental problems." He gave an apologetic half smile to Mrs. Parker. The congressman himself didn't seem too involved in what was going on.

Finally, Mrs. Parker stood and indicated that she'd like to speak to Talmedge. Jason figured what the hell, Talmedge couldn't get any angrier. He handed her the phone with Talmedge still yelling about something. She clearly had to wait for a chance to say something.

"Hello, this is Joan Parker, the congressman's wife. I'm also a trial attorney with the Washington firm Scudder, Landry. What seems to be the problem?"

Jason could only guess what Talmedge was saying. He must have introduced himself and said something like he was only trying to help.

Joan Parker was patient but firm. "Well, I'm his wife, and all *I* want to do is to try to help him, and right now I think the best thing would be for him to talk with Dr. Andrews." This last was said with undeniable finality. And then, "Thank you, Mr. Talmedge." She hung up the phone and gave a long sigh.

Jason smiled at her. "Thank *you*, Mrs. Parker."

"Do you have any idea what that was all about?"

Jason shook his head.

"We brought Frank here for a complete mental and physical check-up. We know he has certain"—she hesitated, trying to find the right word—"a certain obsession right now. That's why we're here."

Jason could do nothing but apologize and say once again that he couldn't for the life of him, understand why Talmedge was so exercised. "Perhaps we'd better just start at the beginning." He turned to Congressman Parker. "What brought you to the clinic today, Congressman?"

"A car," the congressman said. "We came by car." For a fleeting moment a look of utter hopelessness crossed his wife's face.

"Yes, I understand that, Congressman, but *why* did you come to the clinic today?"

"Well, Joan thought it would be a good idea."

Jason decided he'd better try a different tack. "How have you been feeling, Congressman Parker?"

"Fine. Just fine." Parker's voice was flat. His face was devoid of expression. His eyes remained fixed straight ahead even when speaking.

Jason knew *of* Frank Parker. Just about everybody did. A little more than two years ago, Parker had ridden the winds of change out of the Midwest and into his first term in Congress. He had been an outspoken critic of the status quo and been elected as an independent running a grassroots campaign. They said he wouldn't last, but he'd proven his critics wrong, winning handily when he sought reelection.

The man now sitting in Jason's office lacked the exuberance and intensity that people associated with Frank Parker. He was a small man, very fastidious about his appearance. Despite being less than forty years old, he was already beginning to grow bald at the front and crown of his head, a fact that was exaggerated by his close-cropped hairstyle. His glasses were thick with clear plastic frames. They looked like the kind of safety glasses people wore when they worked with heavy machinery.

Joan Parker seemed larger and older than her husband.

Perhaps it was the gray in her hair; maybe she actually was older. Her expression conveyed the genuine concern she felt for her husband. Jason turned his attention to her.

"Mrs. Parker, perhaps if you could tell me about your concerns."

She took a deep breath and spoke, all the time looking at her husband, never at Jason. "It all started several weeks ago. He seemed preoccupied, distracted. His work wasn't getting done. His chief of staff called to see if I had any idea what was going on. I didn't. I suppose, deep in my heart, I'd have to admit that—if you really pressed me—what I thought was going on was . . . another woman. Not that he has ever given me any real reason to believe that." She was almost apologetic, ashamed that she had ever thought such a thing.

"At that time," Jason asked, "did he seem otherwise normal? Was there any confusion or other problem that you can remember?"

"No, he was just so very far away most of the time, but then I could bring him back—once I got his attention. That's harder to do now."

"What did you notice next?"

"Well, that's pretty much it, except"—once again she was searching for the right words—"except for this concern he's had about what's going on in Washington."

"What do you mean?"

Mrs. Parker seemed wary now. She watched her husband closely. "He, uh, he is very concerned that there may be some sort of a conspiracy going on. That's what seems to be occupying his thoughts most of the time."

For the first time there was a visible change in the congressman. His head jerked around to look at his wife, then at Jason. His eyes betrayed both fear and anger. But he remained silent.

Joan Parker spoke very softly. "He thinks someone's trying to overthrow the government."

"Be quiet, Joan." There was a subtle edge of menace in her husband's tone. Joan Parker appeared stunned, then hurt.

Jason made a slight gesture with his hand that for now Mrs. Parker should say no more. They sat in silence. The congressman seemed to ease slowly back into himself and begin to relax.

"Congressman Parker, how is everything going at work?"

"O.K., fine." Staring straight ahead, not looking at Jason or his wife.

"Does it seem that more and more work is beginning to pile up at the office," Jason asked, "that things just aren't getting done?"

"Dave complains a lot about that. I suppose he's right."

Mrs. Parker interjected, "Dave Roberts is his chief of staff. They've been friends for years."

"Do you find, Congressman, that all these worries you have—about what might be going on in Washington— interfere with your being able to concentrate?"

Parker seemed to rouse a little. He turned to face Jason, but his eyes appeared to focus somewhere behind the doctor. Jason felt the urge to turn to see what was behind him.

At last Parker spoke, "If you knew what I know, you'd have trouble concentrating too, Doctor. All of a sudden *your* work wouldn't seem quite so important either." He crossed his arms and legs and sat back on the couch, his head bobbing up and down as though he were silently agreeing with himself. There was just the vaguest hint of a sanctimonious smile on his lips.

Almost immediately it occurred to Jason how useful Psychoden would be in evaluating a patient like Congressman Parker. They could spend hours fencing back and forth as they were doing now, or a few minutes getting to the bottom of things with Psychoden.

"We have a new drug, Congressman and Mrs. Parker, which is very useful in evaluating patients who are under a great deal of stress. It's called Psychoden. We use it in an interview setting just like this. The patient wears a small drug-containing adhesive patch on his neck during the interview." Jason thought carefully about how to convey the mode of action of Psychoden without unduly alarming the patient. He would find a better time to discuss its action in more detail with Mrs. Parker. After a few moments he said, "The drug acts to relieve anxieties and inhibitions that may prevent the patient from fully expressing his problems. I think it could be very helpful."

Mrs. Parker was quite eager to proceed. "Whatever you recommend, Doctor. I'm sure Frank wants to do anything that will help him get back to his old self." Frank Parker said nothing.

"If it's okay with both of you, I'd suggest we do the Psychoden interview as soon as possible—tomorrow if you can manage it?"

Joan Parker was emphatic. "We'll be here."

"Let's schedule you for eight o'clock tomorrow morning, then." Jason made a note of the time, then picked up the congressman's file. "Now, is there anything else you need to do today? Have you had your blood work drawn?"

"Oh, yes," Joan Parker volunteered, "there was *quite* a commotion about that."

Once again the congressman felt compelled to speak. "They suck your mind out with those little tubes."

Jason and Mrs. Parker exchanged glances. Neither commented. There was nothing for Jason to do but shake hands with the Parkers and start them toward the door. The congressman went on ahead, once again in his own private world, giving Jason the opportunity for a brief private conversation with Mrs. Parker.

"Has the congressman given any indication that he might harm himself or others?"

Joan Parker shook her head. "No, he's just been very withdrawn."

"If you should become the least bit afraid, Mrs. Parker, please call me. I can't say for certain what's going on, but it is possible that your husband could become violent. If an emergency should arise, don't hesitate to call the police. I don't think it will happen, but if it does, you should be prepared to act quickly. We'll know a lot more tomorrow. Then we can begin to think about the next step."

"I appreciate your helping, Dr. Andrews. I'm just about at the end of my rope."

"Why don't you give me a call sometime later today when we can talk alone? I need to give you more details about Psychoden and what we'll be doing tomorrow. I don't want to upset your husband any more than we already have."

As he watched Mrs. Parker shepherd her husband

down the clinic hallway, Jason felt a cold shiver work its way down his spine. Something the congressman had said now triggered a grotesque image in Jason's brain. It could have been a painting by Salvador Dali: an unsuspecting patient, sprawled on a couch, having his blood drawn; instead of blood, tiny pieces of the patient's brain were flowing from a vein in his arm.

"They suck your mind out with those little tubes."

Chapter Sixteen

Jason sat by himself at a quiet table in the bar of a country inn not far from the clinic. He had started out actually sitting at the bar itself, but when this particular table became available he grabbed it immediately. He watched the door, trying to look casual. That was the watchword for tonight—casual.

Jason had been captivated by the little inn from the first time he saw it. It was solid and old and breathed generations of character—classy without being stuffy. There was a huge fireplace in the lobby and smaller ones in the main dining room and in the bar. Roaring fires were blazing in each, adding coziness against the unseasonable March cold. On another night Jason would have preferred the excellent dining room, but the bar was charming in its own right and had an ambience which was—in keeping with the theme of the evening—decidedly more casual.

He had left the clinic early, with the thought that he really should go home and freshen up a bit before dinner. One thing had led to another. Now here he was, freshly showered and shaven, wearing his best sports coat and favorite tie. There had been a brief moment of panic in front of the mirror that he had dealt with in a very mature manner: Jason, this is the best you can do. If it's not good enough, then it's just not good enough.

Despite all the effort, Jason thought the overall effect was quite casual.

His invitation had been a study in offhandedness. They had been reviewing some Psychoden studies together up in Marsden's lab when Jason broached the subject. Why didn't they get together for an early dinner after work? Rachel had said yes, she would like that. She sounded very casual. Marsden, who was working at a bench just out of sight, said, "I wondered when you two were finally going to get together."

They had decided to take separate cars and meet at the inn. It would make everything seem more—*quel est le mot?*—casual.

Jason was lost in his thoughts and did not see Rachel Chandler enter the bar. She might have taken him entirely by surprise had he not been alerted by the gravitational effect of every male head in the room turning at the same time. Jason stood and waved her over. He noticed with a certain amount of satisfaction that she was wearing a different dress from the one she had worn at the clinic earlier in the day.

"You look fetching," he told her. It was a carefully chosen word, not overly intimate. She brushed against him as he pulled back her chair.

"I'm sorry I'm late," she apologized, "I spilled creosol on my dress, and I had to run home and change. It was a terrible mess."

Jason's heart made a slight sucking sound.

"Is that a new tie you're wearing, Jason? I liked the one you had on this afternoon, but I guess it wouldn't go with that new jacket."

She took a sip from her water glass, clearly oblivious to the slow and agonizing death Jason was suffering. Then, suddenly she smiled.

"I'm only kidding. I left the lab at three this afternoon to go home and get ready."

Jason felt a great deal of tension leave his body. "As long as we're telling the truth," he said, "you might as well know that I had a little plastic surgery done this afternoon."

"Really?" she said, playing along.

"Just had the nose shortened a little bit, and the chin strengthened."

"You shouldn't have. I liked the old ones."

They held each other's gaze for a moment, a mutual acknowledgment of the evolution of their relationship from a cordial but collegial friendship to the promise of something more.

She was probably the most beautiful woman he had ever seen. Certainly the most beautiful he had ever had dinner with. She had hair of the deepest auburn that would have been shoulder length had it not been pulled back in a French braid. Her dark brown eyes could fill with humor or turn unabashedly sensual.

She was beautiful, brilliant, witty—totally charming and altogether flawless as far as Jason could ascertain. Surely Rachel Chandler must have some subtle defect somewhere. Perhaps that left hand she kept in her lap had a slightly chipped fingernail. Or possibly a tiny character flaw, a lifelong struggle against a slight homicidal tendency, for example—something Jason was pretty certain he could get into perspective and not let interfere with their budding relationship.

Conversation flowed effortlessly throughout dinner, staying mainly away from work-related issues. They shared their life stories.

"I've basically lived in Massachusetts all my life," Jason told her. "I grew up on a farm in the western part of the state. My parents still live there. Then I went off to Boston for college and medical school and never left."

"Until now."

"Until now."

"Why now?"

Jason tried to think how best to explain such a complicated process. "Lots of reasons. I needed a change of venue. I'd been too long in one place. And when my marriage ended, I just decided it was time to take advantage of some of my sabbatical time."

"You were married?" Rachel's voice was even. There was no hint of either disapproval or surprise. Maybe she just wanted details.

"For five years. No children. After about four years I realized I just didn't love her anymore—which was about two years after she'd decided she didn't love me."

"Another man?"

"Not so far as I know. I think it was mostly her work—advertising. She really wanted to be in New York. In the end, that was what she cared about most."

Jason gave Rachel a few moments to sip her wine before turning the tables. "Now, what about you?"

She smiled. "All pretty boring." There was just the slightest hint of a Southern drawl in her voice. Very sexy. "Like you, I've never really lived outside the state where I was born. Got all my education at the university in Charlottesville. My father has always had close ties to the University of Virginia. He met my mother there. He was a member of the Board of Regents for many years after he left the Senate. There was never much doubt where I would go. Then I did a little postdoctoral work in Charlottesville before I started working with Marsden."

"You've probably never had any time for a personal life. . . ." Jason just let that hang right there between them.

Rachel's smile saddened. "I've had only one long-term relationship. It lasted almost the entire time I was in Charlottesville. He was a brilliant biochemist." She hesitated briefly, then added, "He was killed in a car accident."

"I'm sorry."

Rachel tilted her head slightly and stared into her wineglass. "It's funny how things work out. Mark was a biochemist, but his primary research interest was neuropharmacology. He and Arthur Marsden were competitors—and not very friendly ones at that.

"They competed directly against each other for government grant money, and once Mark even accused Arthur of staging a sham demonstration of Psychoden for a grant review committee. It was all pretty ugly."

"How was Marsden supposed to have staged the demonstration?"

"Mark said that the 'patient' was nothing more than an

actor, that Arthur didn't even have a formulation of Psychoden yet that was suitable for human trials."

"What did the committee think?"

"Arthur got the funding. Mark didn't. That was just a few weeks before Mark was killed."

"How did you end up at the Marsden Clinic?"

"Mostly because of my father. He had known Marsden for many years and assured me that Arthur would not do anything unethical. Arthur had sent me a note after Mark's death expressing sympathy and saying how very sorry he was that there had been any rancor. After I finished my Ph.D., he wrote again to offer me a job.

"Charlottesville was filled with memories of Mark and our plans together. I had no desire to stay there. Like I said, my dad convinced me that Marsden was an honorable man and that his dispute with Mark was purely professional jealousy."

"What do you think of Marsden now?"

That seemed to bring some of the light back into Rachel's eyes. "I like him. I always think of him as kind of grandfatherly. And I like to think he needs me to keep him pointed in the right direction."

"That's for sure. I wonder how he ever got along without you."

"Actually, he had a wife who worked with him in the lab for years. I think she must have done a lot of the things I do now. She died just before I came to the clinic."

Jason knew that would have made for a pretty strong bond between Rachel and Marsden, the two of them grieving together, providing for each other's needs at a time of wrenching mutual sadness.

Throughout the rest of their dinner, Jason and Rachel were able to steer the conversation clear of the minefield of ancient sorrows. It had been a very long time since Jason had experienced such a pleasant evening. More than two hours into their dinner, any flaw that might be part of Rachel Chandler remained undiscovered.

After prolonging dessert as long as humanly possible, Jason finally helped Rachel on with her coat, then walked with her out into the night. She slid in behind the wheel of her car and looked up at him.

"Thank you for this evening, Jason. I enjoyed it very much."

"Me, too, Rachel. Let's do it again soon." And then he offered, "I'd be happy to follow you home, make sure you get in all right."

There was a moment's hesitation as Rachel seemed to consider his offer, or perhaps its possible implications. "Thank you," she said, "but I'll be fine."

He watched her drive off, knowing that—for better or worse—their relationship had changed forever. Jason wondered what the future might hold for the two of them.

In his wildest imagination he could not have guessed.

Chapter Seventeen

Congressman Joseph Lucas hadn't slept a wink all night. He'd been breaking out in cold sweats ever since yesterday afternoon when Michael Cordova had scheduled today's appointment. In one sense, Lucas knew who Cordova was. He was the director of the FBI, had been for nearly three years.

But the question was, was Cordova one of *them*?—whoever *they* were. Whose side was Cordova on? One thing was certain. He wasn't on Joe Lucas' side. No one was. Not anymore. Not since he'd turned the President down.

Lucas had never been one of Cordova's admirers. Put quite simply, he had never trusted the man. Cordova was a fanatic, one of those self-made, driven men who always saw Truth very clearly and let nothing stand in their way. Cordova had made his reputation as a no-nonsense prosecutor when he headed the U.S. attorney's office in Manhattan. His success against organized crime was the stuff of legends and had made him the object of political overtures from both parties. When the President offered him the top spot at the FBI, Cordova grabbed it.

But some said that Cordova had never let the law stand in the way of his prosecutions, that in his zeal he had bent a lot of rules and twisted more than a few arms. Cordova was the kind of man Lucas trusted least—and feared most—a man for whom the end justified any means.

Outside his window, the snow showed no sign of relenting. Everywhere he looked, the same blinding whiteness. Winter in Antarctica. When would this season finally end and allow Washington to return to its old self?

His phone buzzed. The director had arrived. Lucas tensed the muscles of his arms and legs, then let them relax—a trick he'd learned from public speaking. He wiped a sweaty palm on his trouser leg, then told his secretary to show the man in immediately. No point in angering him. Don't tease the animal. He might bite.

"Director Cordova"—Lucas forced a smile as he offered his hand—"how nice to see you."

"I appreciate your taking time out of your busy schedule to meet with me, Congressman."

Cordova's handshake was hard, like the man. He was a small man with dark hair and intense black eyes. Lucas motioned him to a chair and then took refuge behind his desk.

"How can I be of help to you, Mr. Cordova?" Lucas tried to fix a neutral smile on his face.

"This is merely a routine inquiry, Congressman, into a very unusual event. For a vice-president to die in office—of other than natural causes—is certainly cause for concern."

Instantly more anxious than ever, Lucas struggled to keep his agitation from showing. He had thought that he himself, of all people—with his special insight born of shared experience—had understood the nature and conditions of the vice-president's death. But what was Cordova suggesting now? Had they actually *murdered* Herb Allen?

Lucas' entire being was now focused on the effort to keep his voice even. "Is there some reason to believe that the vice-president's death was other than suicide?"

Cordova fixed his gaze very pointedly at Lucas. "Do you have any reason to think that his death might have been other than by his own hand?"

"Of course not. I only know what has been reported in the papers." What game was Cordova playing? Was this official FBI business, Lucas wondered, or was the director on a fishing expedition of his own, trying to find out if Lucas had any suspicions that he might be tempted to divulge? Which team was the FBI director playing for?

"You and Vice-President Allen had been close friends for many years?" the director wanted to know.

"Yes." That was common knowledge.

"Do you know any reason why he might have wanted to take his own life?"

Lucas hesitated a moment, then decided to provide Cordova with the truth. "Herb had seemed somewhat depressed to me of late. Of course, I had no idea he was contemplating suicide."

"What was he depressed about?"

"He talked about a lot of things, especially about Herb Jr., his son who was lost in Vietnam. Herb had never really gotten over that. Lately, he seemed preoccupied with Herb Jr." Lucas watched the director's eyes as he spoke, like a student searching for some small sign of the teacher's approval.

Cordova let Lucas dangle in silence, long experience having taught him that, given the opportunity, people would often say too much for their own good. When the congressman failed to fill the void, Cordova prodded him.

"I understand that the President offered to nominate you to be the next vice-president."

Lucas could feel sweat accumulating under his suit. He picked a paper clip up off his desk and began to untangle it. "I was flattered," he said. "I mean, who wouldn't be? But I'm much too old a dog . . ." Lucas shrugged his shoulders as the words trailed off.

Cordova pressed a little harder. "Some said you practically *campaigned* for the nomination."

"People say lots of things. If I had wanted the job, I would have accepted the President's offer." Lucas didn't look up as he spoke. The paper clip was now consuming nearly all of his concentration. His heart pounded and he was beginning to feel the first twinges of chest pain. But there was no way he would give Cordova the satisfaction of watching him take a nitroglycerin.

An eternity of silence followed. Then, suddenly, Cordova was on his feet.

"Thank you, Congressman. I know I've taken too much of your time. I appreciate your cooperation." He extended his hand.

For an instant Lucas didn't know what to do. Like a fish that suddenly finds itself released from a hook, he was momentarily motionless. Then, with a burst, he sprang back to life. He was on his feet, pumping Cordova's hand.

"Sorry I couldn't be of more help, Mr. Cordova. Just let me know if there's anything more I can do for you."

As soon as Cordova was gone, Lucas sank back into his chair. He felt limp and exhausted. He opened his bottle of nitroglycerin and put a tablet under his tongue.

What was Cordova up to? Was this really just a routine inquiry, or was he one of them? And who the hell were they?

Chapter Eighteen

Jason blamed himself for the deaths of Congressman Parker and his wife.

The death of a patient is something every physician must somehow come to grips with. It is unavoidable. The sun will set; taxes will be collected; patients will die. But good physicians constantly second-guess themselves, and for them, the most devastating situation that can occur happens when a medication they prescribe or an operation they perform results directly in the death of a patient. Physicians know full well—in the abstract—that every medication prescribed, every operation performed, is potentially lethal. But when the inevitable adverse reaction occurs, the weight of perceived personal guilt can be extremely difficult for the doctor to bear.

Of course, the reverse is equally true. The failure to diagnose accurately and prescribe appropriate therapy can also prove fatal. Nowhere is this more true than in the practice of psychiatry. And in the psychiatric population there is a unique additional risk: fatal consequences may extend beyond the patient. Someone mentally unbalanced can endanger not only himself but also his friends, family, business associates—even the general public.

Jason had warned Mrs. Parker that her husband could become violent, but why had he failed to recommend hospitalizing the congressman for a period of observation? Had he really believed that Parker was sane, that he had actually uncovered some vast conspiracy to overthrow the government? No, of course not. The man was obviously paranoid.

Jason heard the breaking story on the radio as he drove to the clinic for his 8:00 A.M. appointment with the Parkers. Apparently someone had anonymously called 911 to warn that the congressman had said that he intended to kill himself and take his wife with him. Before the police could check out the story, there had been an enormous explosion at the Parkers' house. The authorities were just beginning the process of sifting through the rubble to search for bodies.

The clock on the wall said 7:45 as Jason made the long walk down the hallway to his office. He hadn't felt this down in a long time, and he figured he'd need the suddenly vacant first hour of his schedule just to put his own emotional house in order.

Jason's pangs of self-doubt had begun after Vice-President Allen's suicide. The vice-president had been at the clinic only a couple of weeks before. Jason had detected nothing, not the slightest suggestion that the vice-president was suffering from depression. Next, there was Congressman Bates. The police were officially calling his death an accident, but some of the newspaper accounts hinted strongly at suicide. It hadn't entered Jason's mind that Bates might be suicidal.

Jason found the door to his outer office open, but his secretary wasn't at her desk. He had his head down, still reeling from the news he'd just heard on the radio. His hand was on the door to his private office before he abruptly became aware that he wasn't alone in the room.

Seated in chairs across from his secretary's desk, waiting patiently for their appointment, were Congressman and Mrs. Parker.

"I know we're early, Doctor," Mrs. Parker said brightly. "But we spent the night at an inn very close to the clinic and decided we might as well just scoot on over. We're ready when you are."

"So you didn't go home last night?"

"We decided there was no point," Mrs. Parker said, "in driving all that way just to be back here first thing this morning. We've stayed at the inn before. It's one of Frank's favorites." Frank didn't seem to have anything to add. He just stared off into space.

Jason took a moment to consider the best way to deal with the situation. "I guess we might as well get started, then," he said. "Congressman, if you'll come on into my office." The congressman moved very slowly, as though each step he took required a separate decision. "Just have a seat, Congressman. I need to get some supplies. I'll be back in a few minutes." Jason shut the door, leaving Congressman Parker alone with his thoughts.

He turned to Mrs. Parker. "I guess you haven't heard the news this morning?"

She shook her head.

"I thought it best not to mention this in front of the congressman," Jason said. "I don't want to do anything that might upset him, not until I understand his psychiatric condition a little better." He sat down next to Mrs. Parker.

"A few minutes ago, on the radio, I heard that there had been an explosion at your home. I was afraid that you and your husband had been killed."

Joan Parker gasped. "Did they say what it was? The gas, I suppose . . ." And then she said, "So lucky no one was in the house."

"Were you and your husband together all night last night?"

"Of course. We had dinner, then went to bed. They don't even have televisions at the inn, so there wasn't much to do. Frank isn't such great company right now. Why do you ask?"

"According to the news report, someone called 911 and said that the congressman was going to kill himself—and take you with him. Just a few minutes later there was a big explosion."

The attorney in Joan Parker seemed to take over. "I'd better go deal with this. I need to call Frank's office, the police, my office. The news media is going to want to talk to Frank." And then, almost as an afterthought, "My God, Dr. Andrews, do you suppose someone could really be after Frank?"

Jason shook his head. "I have no idea. I would recommend that we go ahead with the Psychoden interview, then see where we are."

Mrs. Parker headed off down the hall to begin to deal

with the mass of problems she and her husband would now have to face. Jason went back into his office to begin the interview with her husband. It was, in the end, a sad but fascinating experience.

Jason allowed a few minutes for the Psychoden to begin to take effect, then he began with the usual questions.

"What is your name?"

"Franklin Thomas Parker."

"How old are you?"

"I'm forty. My birthday was January eleventh." Parker hesitated as though listening to another question, then said, "Don't worry, I won't tell him about that."

The congressman's voice was flat, his features expressionless. The first part of his answer was typical of Psychoden expansiveness, but what was that at the end?

"What do you do for a living, Mr. Parker?"

"I'm a United States congressman serving my second term—" He quit speaking quite suddenly, as though he had been interrupted, the way people on Psychoden did when you asked them a follow-up question.

Jason watched him intently, pretty certain now what was going on. "Who are you talking to, Congressman?"

"You, Dr. Jason Andrews."

"Who else?"

"The Vent People."

"What do they say?"

"They say I shouldn't talk to you. You may be part of the conspiracy."

"Who are the Vent People?"

"They live in the heating ducts. Wherever you go, they're there."

"Can you see them?"

"Sometimes."

"What do they look like?"

"Wisps of smoke. All different colors."

"Do they tell you to hurt people?"

"No, just to be careful. People are after me."

"Who is after you?"

"The bloodsuckers, and others. They're after everybody in Washington."

Psychoden had stripped away the last vestiges of control from the congressman's mind. Jason now had direct access to Parker's delusional system, but it was all too jumbled to make heads or tails of.

When Mrs. Parker returned, Jason allowed her to sit in on the remainder of the interview so that she could get a feeling for what was going on. They could discuss the congressman's problem freely in his presence. After the Psychoden patch was removed, he would remember nothing of the interview.

"He's suffering from both auditory and visual hallucinations, Mrs. Parker. He appears to have a severe thought disorder."

"What does that mean, in layman's terms?"

"Essentially that his thoughts are scrambled. He's seeing things that aren't there. He hears voices. Over time these hallucinations may completely take over his life, or they may simply go away—for a short time or forever. If his symptoms persist, and we don't find some underlying cause such as drug abuse—and we have no evidence for that—then we're probably headed toward a diagnosis of schizophrenia."

"A split personality?"

"That's a popular term that doesn't really have much application to the actual disease. Schizophrenia is a severe type of thought disorder that can be very disabling. Sometimes it improves on its own, sometimes it responds to drug therapy."

Mrs. Parker didn't seem terribly surprised to hear that her husband had a serious mental illness, but the weight of the day's events was beginning to tell. She looked haggard. She was in desperate need of a solution.

"What do you recommend, Doctor?"

"For now, hospitalization. The congressman clearly can't go back to work, and knowledge of what happened today at your home would only add further stress and feed his paranoia. He needs to be in a place where he can feel safe and where he can be observed until a firm diagnosis can be made and appropriate therapy can be instituted."

They talked briefly about the explosion. Mrs. Parker really knew nothing more except that there were apparently no injuries. Fortunately, they didn't have as much as a pet in their house, and most of the mementos of their lives were safely stored in their "real" home back in Wisconsin.

They talked about various options for the congressman's hospitalization and decided that Bethesda was the best place for now. Then Jason took the Psychoden patch from Congressman Parker's neck. Unlike most patients, the congressman looked about the same whether or not he was under the influence of Psychoden: the same flat features and droning speech.

Then, unexpectedly, the congressman spoke. "I think I'll like Bethesda."

"What made you say that?" Jason was astounded. People weren't supposed to remember anything that occurred during a Psychoden session.

Congressman Parker answered calmly, "The Vent People told me I'd be going to Bethesda."

Chapter Nineteen

The President sat behind his desk in the Oval Office. He held the telephone receiver to his ear even though the line had long since gone dead. It was a trick he had used for years. His schedule of appointment after appointment left no time for reflection. With the dead phone to his ear, he was allowed time to think. He could even close his eyes and relax for a moment. He only had to remember to speak an occasional word into the receiver and give the impression he was listening intently to something very important.

Also, being "on the phone" gave the President a chance to do a little surreptitious people watching. He learned a lot by observing how the people who came to the Oval Office interacted among themselves. They were always less on guard when they thought his attention was elsewhere.

As the President watched, Michael Cordova slipped into the room, totally unnoticed by the others. Cordova remained off to the side, making no effort to involve himself in the conversation. Was he aloof or only shy? Or was he, like the President, a watcher?

His country could not have asked for a more intelligent, more hardworking FBI director. The man appeared to have no life whatsoever outside his work. But the President had also noted Cordova's evolving disillusionment with Washington political life. Cordova was far too rigid. He hadn't adapted to the give and take of politics. The director's single-mindedness prevented flexibility. In order to survive in Washington, one lesson must be learned above all others: you will never be able to get anything unless you're willing to give up something in return. That's politics. That's Washington.

The problem with Cordova, the President had decided, was that he liked government *in theory.* The practice of government was not for those with delicate stomachs. It was one thing, he had told Cordova, to savor a plate of sausages. It was quite another to watch sausage being made.

Then Bernie Conn, the President's chief of staff, noticed Cordova and rose to greet him. The two shook hands like old friends, belying their underlying mistrust of each other. The reason for the antipathy was simple: Bernie Conn was the most purely political animal the President had ever known. If they ever made a statue of Conn, the President had said more than once, it would have one moistened finger in the air and be able to swivel one hundred and eighty degrees without making a sound.

As he took a seat, Cordova nodded to his boss, Attorney General Charlotte Moran. The pair were another case of oil and water, as different in personality as they were in physical appearance. But the President felt they counterbalanced each other well. Moran had good political instincts as well as brains. Above everything else, she was ambitious.

The President made a show of ending his phone conversation, then abandoned his desk to join the others.

"I guess we'd better get started," he said as he took a seat in his favorite chair. "So, Michael, what have you got for us? Were you able to find out what the hell Lucas is so afraid of?"

Cordova looked, as always, very serious. "In a word, no. I approached the congressman very gently. Still, he seemed quite nervous."

"Maybe," Bernie Conn suggested, "*gentle* is not what he needs. Maybe he needs to have a little pressure applied. My guess is he'd break pretty quickly if you leaned on him a little."

The President held up a hand. "I don't think Joe Lucas needs any *more* pressure placed on his head. When he was in here the other night, he looked like he was already about to explode. We all remember what happened to Herb Allen."

"You're not suggesting there's any connection between the two?" Charlotte Moran's tone was incredulous.

"Obviously I don't have any proof of anything, but I'm naturally suspicious of coincidences. There've been a lot of strange events surrounding the vice-presidency over the last few weeks." The President hesitated, then added, "If there's something really big going on, we need to get on top of it before any more innocent people are hurt."

"Something *big*?" Charlotte Moran asked. "Some sort of conspiracy or something?" She wasn't smiling, but her tone suggested that she thought the idea ludicrous.

"For crying out loud," Conn chimed in, "don't anyone use the word conspiracy outside this room. We'd be the laughingstock of Washington."

The President was known for his tolerance of diverse opinions. He encouraged his advisers to challenge him. Only the ever taciturn Cordova remained silent.

"Well, Mr. Director," the President asked, "what do you suggest?"

"I can continue a very quiet, behind-the-scenes investigation. I'll personally take charge and involve others at the Bureau only on a need-to-know basis."

"Do it," the President said, ending the discussion. "Now, what's the latest on the Parker explosion?"

"It was definitely a bomb. We know that much for sure. Plastic explosive, the kind of stuff the old Czech regimes used to supply."

"That crazy Frank Parker," Conn interrupted, "he would use *commie* explosives!"

Cordova adopted a patient tone. "We have no evidence that Parker was involved in any way. In fact, I believe it's highly unlikely that he was involved. His wife can account for his whereabouts, and we have nothing to contradict her."

"Oh, I think it was just an accident," Conn said. "I bet old Frank was just storing the stuff for some of his commie friends."

The expression that crossed Cordova's face was as close as he ever came to a smile. "I seriously doubt that the congressman was involved in any way. We've got a voice on the 911 tapes claiming that Parker is about to kill himself and his wife. The voice isn't Parker's, so I think we can rule out that the bombing was an accident. And another thing, and this is very confidential, apparently Congressman Parker has had a serious mental breakdown of some sort. They're admitting him to Bethesda for evaluation."

The room grew quiet as everyone considered this latest revelation. It was the President who finally broke the silence.

"Michael, I want you to enlarge the scope of your investigation. My wife says I'm getting paranoid in my old age, but I'm worried about something even bigger than any of you has imagined. In all my years in politics, I've never seen anything like the last year or so.

"It all seemed to start with people deciding not to run for reelection—in *droves*. Hell, we had two senators from the same state just decide they didn't feel like running again. Who's ever heard of anything like that happening? And now we've got Herb committing suicide—at least you tell me it was a suicide—and somebody bombing Parker's house and then whatever the hell happened to Hiram Bates. I tell you, I've never seen anything like it.

"What I would like the FBI to do is just start collecting information. Look at all the retirements, deaths, mental breakdowns, what have you, and see if there's a common denominator."

Conn was on his feet. "Mr. President, if you send the FBI on some fishing expedition that involves investigating members of the other party, there's gonna be hell to pay. They'll call it dirty tricks."

"I'm willing to take my chances, Bernie. Hell, I'm a lame duck now anyway."

"But, Mr. President, we've got all these new faces in Congress. Who knows how they'll react? They might even try to impeach you!"

"That's enough, Bernie." The President's tone ended discussion on the matter. "I value your counsel, as always, but I've made up my mind. The FBI will go forward with the investigation, and I'll take the heat if it comes. It's my decision."

Bernie Conn started to say just one more thing, but thought better of it.

"Now, Michael," the President continued, "where are we with the background check on Senator Chandler?"

"Just beginning, Mr. President. Nothing to report. Once again, we're taking a very cautious approach."

"So, we have Senator Chandler and just one more name on the list of potential nominees for vice-president," the President said.

Charlotte Moran turned in her seat. "I thought we were down to just Senator Chandler."

"It'd be a mighty short list, Charlotte, if we had just one name on it. Besides, Chandler's bound to have made some enemies in the Senate. The John Tower debacle proved that the Senate can no longer be counted on just to rubber stamp a nomination simply because the nominee is one of its own.

"I wanted another name on the list, a person with equal but somewhat different credentials. I need someone that I feel confident the Senate would approve, and someone I know I can work with." The President paused for effect. "I thought we needed a woman's name on the list.

I've added the name of our distinguished attorney general, Charlotte Moran."

Moran was obviously taken entirely by surprise.

"Now, Charlotte," the President said, "you're not going to start talking gibberish and backing out the door as fast as you can, are you?"

The attorney general drew herself up in her chair. "No, sir," she said without a hint of a smile, "I'm not. What I *am* going to do is convince you that I would make a far better choice for vice-president than Senator Chandler."

Chapter Twenty

Jason leaned forward and adjusted his tie, briefly believing that he was actually going to make it out the door this time. For a few seconds he teetered on the brink of overcoming the inertia that had kept him pinned in his chair for the last half hour, but in the end he fell back once more, sinking deeper than ever into the soothing cushions.

The last thing in the world he wanted to do tonight was go to a party. If it hadn't been for Rachel Chandler, he wouldn't have even considered it. As it was, he was committed. No way to get out of it. Sooner or later he would have to force himself out that door.

Jason's mind was awash in conflicting tides of suspicion and guilt, and he worried that the wild imaginings he was able to conjure up were simply a primitive psychological mechanism that his mind had devised as a smoke screen to prevent his having to take responsibility for his actions.

He recognized that all this self-doubt had been triggered by Congressman Parker's brush with disaster. The man was so obviously paranoid that a medical student would have recognized it. So why had Jason questioned the diagnosis? The answer was obvious.

Subconsciously, Jason *wanted* to believe much of what Parker was saying. If he was right, if there really was a conspiracy afoot, then maybe some of Jason's psychiatric instincts were not so deficient after all.

The vice-president's suicide still weighed heavily on Jason's conscience. They had talked only briefly when Allen had come to the clinic for his executive physical. It had been a very routine interview. Jason had not detected the slightest hint of depression or even serious stress. The vice-president had been pleasant, even jovial. Two weeks later, he was dead. Had Jason overlooked some major psychiatric pathology in Herbert Allen, or did some disastrous event occur in the intervening days to precipitate the suicide?

And what of Hiram Bates? In a vacuum, the entire Bates affair would have been merely a curiosity, not a stimulus for rigorous self-examination—but placed beside the others . . . Still, Bates' death was probably nothing more than a drunken fall. It was hard to imagine anything that would drive a man like Bates to suicide.

But if Jason was correct, and neither the vice-president nor Congressman Bates had any significant psychiatric dysfunction, then one had to look to other explanations for their deaths.

In the case of Congressman Parker, there was little doubt that he was suffering from an acute—or possibly chronic—psychosis, but, paradoxically, he was the only one of the three for whom there was clear evidence of some external malevolent force. *Someone* destroyed the

Parkers' house with a bomb, and it wasn't the congressman.

Jason rose again, this time determined to make it out the door. The image of Rachel Chandler dangled before him, coaxing him forward. In an acknowledgment that his thoughts about Rachel were not always completely pure, Jason wondered to himself if once again some primitive area at the base of his brain hadn't risen to dominate his more highly evolved upper brain, so that certain basic urges tended to push aside more calculated behavior.

Put more succinctly, Jason followed that image of Rachel right out the door, not at all unlike a donkey pursuing the proverbial carrot.

Chapter Twenty-one

The Chandler estate was classic Old Virginia. From the road bordering the property Jason could see nothing but acres and acres of rolling pastureland surrounded by white board fence. Even at the gated entrance the view was of a long, meandering drive ending in a clump of trees. But as he drove forward, the massive brick colonial that was the Chandler family home came into view. If the architect's intention had been to inspire awe, he had certainly achieved his goal.

On the circular brick driveway in front of the house, where Jason would have expected to see dozens of parked cars, stood a single valet. The young man verified Jason's invitation, then whisked his car away. Jason was left standing alone in front of the magnificent mansion, bereft of any easy means of retreat. But inertia is a two-sided coin. It is not only the tendency of an object at rest to remain at rest, but also of an object in motion to remain in motion. It was inertia that had earlier kept Jason firmly planted in his chair, and it was inertia which now propelled him up the steps toward the muffled party noise.

As Jason's foot reached the top step, the front door swung suddenly open.

"Welcome, Doctor. I'm Rob Chandler."

"Jason Andrews, Senator." He shook Chandler's hand. How could the senator have possibly known who he was?

"I know that my sister has been looking for you. Here, let Richard have your coat and we'll go find Rachel."

Jason let the butler help him with his coat and then followed Senator Chandler from the main hallway into a vast drawing room filled with Washington's most prominent movers and shakers. Most of the faces were quite familiar, giving Jason the illusion of being among friends. Senator Chandler greeted many of his guests as he worked his way through the crowd, and Jason kept a half smile on his face as he followed. Some of the guests nodded at Jason, covering for their inability to place him.

Senator Chandler was every bit as much a classic as was the family home. If you called central casting and asked them to send over a Kennedy, they'd send you Rob Chandler. He was several years older than Rachel, but still had a full head of blond hair and sparkling teeth that couldn't possibly be his—but undoubtedly were. He was over six feet tall and had a physique that suggested he could as easily have rowed a scull down from Washington as driven his car.

"*There* you are!" Rachel suddenly appeared from out of the crowd, looking absolutely stunning in a black cocktail dress and a single strand of pearls. "I was beginning to think you weren't going to make it." She gave him a chaste kiss on the cheek.

"Had to get my earlobes reset," Jason explained. Then,

in response to the senator's confused expression, "Kind of an inside joke."

The senator looked somewhat relieved. He took Jason's hand once again. "A pleasure meeting you, Doctor. I'll leave you to Rachel's care." After one last smile worthy of an actor in a toothpaste commercial, the senator turned and moved on toward other guests.

"Okay, Rachel, how did your brother know who I was?"

"You're the only one of his guests who looks like a psychiatrist."

Jason gave her his "give me a break" look.

"You can't tell anyone about this," she said. Jason crossed his heart. "The valet gets the names off the invitations, then radios them in to Richard, the butler. Richard tells Rob who's about to come up the steps."

Jason shook his head. "Politicians."

Rachel shrugged. "Let's get you something to drink."

They each grabbed a glass of champagne, then slipped out a side door so that she could give him the grand tour. The house was enormous, but there were personal touches everywhere that kept it from feeling cold and formal.

"The house belongs to my folks," Rachel explained, "but they go to their place in Rancho Santa Fe after the holidays each year, and Rob keeps an eye on the house for them. He has a townhouse in Georgetown, but he comes here on weekends or to get away, and he uses the family home for large parties like tonight."

"Does he do this often?"

"A couple of times a year. My dad did the same thing

when he was in the Senate. It's just part of their political thing."

Rachel opened a door and led the way into a large, paneled library. It was very quiet and gave the illusion of being far removed from the rest of the house. The room seemed familiar to Jason. He couldn't place it at first, but then realized that some of the rooms on the top floor of the clinic were done in a very similar fashion.

"This was my favorite room when I was a little girl. I would come in here and read during the week when my father was in Washington. On the weekends it was his room. That's probably why I loved it so much." She walked over to a darkened window. "In the spring there's such a beautiful view from here. There are dogwood trees and apple blossoms, and then, beyond, the pastures. When I was young, there were always new foals each spring."

She seemed almost wistful as she stared out into her past, and Jason wondered about the relationship between this woman and her iron-willed, politically motivated father. Jason felt a strong desire to walk up behind Rachel and slip his arms around her, to comfort her—but he didn't, and the moment passed.

Rachel turned from the window. "We'd better be getting back to the party. I always have to act as hostess for my bachelor brother. Let's see if we can find Marsden, so you'll have someone you know to talk to. Then I'll have to abandon you for a little while."

Again there was a fleeting moment, as she spoke to him, looking directly up into his face, when Jason thought he might take Rachel in his arms. He wondered if she felt it too. Again, he let the moment pass.

They found Arthur Marsden in the center of the main drawing room, regaling a large group of Washington elite with tales of his internship. Jason had never seen Marsden so animated and gregarious. He looked at Rachel with questioning eyes. She responded by making a drinking motion with her hand.

"He gets like this about twice a year," she said. "I've decided it's good for him."

Marsden was telling about some old nurse he had known years ago who seemed to hate patients—and everybody else, for that matter. "Meanest woman I ever saw," Marsden said. "Mean and lazy. Patients hated her. Then one day she's leaning over yelling at some poor patient for not taking his pills, and the crazy guy in the next bed sneaks up behind and takes a big bite out of her keister. She went berserk. We had to call Security to pull her off the guy. Then she yelled and screamed that she was going to catch some horrible disease from the bite. She would sue the patient, sue the hospital. We had to do all kinds of blood tests to see what the patient had, had to draw them on the nurse, too, just to prove she'd actually gotten whatever the horrible disease was from the patient.

"In the end, I got the honor of reporting the results. Nurse Norborg, I said, I've got some good news and some bad news. The good news is that the patient came through his tests as clean as a whistle. . . ."

Jason never quite got the rest—something about Nurse Norborg and syphilis and a spinal tap and penicillin—

because at just that moment a hand clapped him on the back.

"Dr. Andrews, I was hoping I'd get a chance to talk to you tonight." It was none other than Charles Talmedge, who was greeting him like a long-lost brother. Rachel took the opportunity to disappear into the crowd.

"Enjoying yourself?" Talmedge asked.

"Sure." It was all Jason could think to say and about as verbose as he cared to be.

Talmedge didn't appear to notice Jason's reticence. "Wanted to ask you to do something for the clinic, Andrews. You know we're having the dedication ceremony for the new research wing coming up—lots of important Washington people will be there. I'd like to have you sit up front. You wouldn't have to say anything. I'd just introduce you as the kind of talent we're attracting to the clinic. Harvard professor and all that."

Jason couldn't think of a ready excuse for not going along with Talmedge. "I suppose, if it doesn't conflict with any appointments."

"Good!" Talmedge gave Jason's shoulder another squeeze, and then he was gone.

Jason was suddenly alone in the middle of the crowded room. Marsden was continuing his monologue, but Jason wasn't in the mood for any more stories. If it wasn't for Rachel, he would leave. Hell, if it wasn't for Rachel, he would never have come in the first place.

He wandered around the room, picked up another glass of champagne, and finally sidled out of the same door Rachel had led him through a half hour earlier. Several minutes later, he found himself once again in Rachel's favorite room, the library. He closed the door, took a seat in a comfortable leather chair, and nursed his champagne in refreshing solitude. For about three minutes.

The man who entered the room was small and dark and neatly dressed, perhaps not quite as fashionably as most of the guests. As he came into the library, the man's eyes were drawn immediately to the walls of books. When he finally noticed Jason, he appeared to be taken completely by surprise.

"I didn't realize anyone was in here," he said. He transferred his drink, then offered his right hand. "Michael Cordova."

"Jason Andrews." He started to rise, but Cordova motioned for him not to. "I was just escaping to a little peace and quiet," Jason said. "This isn't my usual crowd."

"Mine either." Cordova sipped his drink thoughtfully. "You were Congressman Parker's psychiatrist?"

Jason sidestepped the question. "I work at the Marsden Clinic."

"I'm with the FBI." Was Cordova trying to be reassuring, or had he meant to apply pressure?

"I know." The director's face was familiar from the evening news.

"You also saw the vice-president professionally, I believe. And Hiram Bates." Cordova recited the names as though this were all a matter of public record.

Jason was beginning to believe that maybe it wasn't an accident that Cordova had ended up in the library. "Look, Mr. Cordova, I don't mean to be difficult, but surely you know that I can't discuss my patients with you. If you get permission from their families, I'd be happy to cooperate with you. I'll tell you everything I know. Until then I'm afraid that I can't be of much help."

Cordova considered this for several seconds, then said, "Have you ever noticed, Doctor, how people go to the Marsden Clinic and then a short time later they die or resign from office or their house blows up?"

Jason took a sip of champagne, then looked directly into the eyes of the director of the FBI and said simply, "Yes."

Chapter Twenty-two

After Cordova left the library, Jason got up and started walking around the perimeter of the party once again. It was like an inaugural ball or something, all these important political figures all dressed up and milling around. It wasn't anything that Jason felt a part of—or could ever feel a part of—but it was certainly an entertaining spectacle.

And there, glad-handing in the middle of it all, was Charles Talmedge. Cordova had wanted to know if Jason thought Talmedge could be up to something. Jason allowed that if there was money to be made stealing blankets from orphans, he was pretty confident that Talmedge would be more than happy to provide seed capital for the venture. That was what he thought of Talmedge. Still, it was very difficult to imagine exactly *what* Talmedge could be up to at the clinic, and even more difficult to figure out what possible motive Talmedge might have. From the look on Cordova's face, Jason figured the FBI director had reached similar conclusions.

Cordova had given Jason his card. Call that number if you think of anything. They can get me anytime, day or night. It all seemed a little too weird to Jason, other people sharing his delusions. It made him worry that maybe Cordova had some hidden motive of his own. But Jason couldn't make any more sense of that than he could of what Charles Talmedge might be up to.

Just then a voice startled Jason back into the present.

"He's really something, isn't he?" It was Senator Chandler, who had obviously been observing Jason as Jason watched Talmedge.

Jason nodded in agreement. "Any idea what his political leanings are?" As near as Jason could tell, Talmedge was a political chameleon.

"Sure, everybody knows what Talmedge is. He's a knee-jerk asshole." They both laughed. "By the way, Rachel says you and I will get to have a little chat next week when I come to the clinic for my annual physical. My dad has been telling me for years that I ought to take advantage of the clinic's facilities—what with the clinic being so close and all. I'm finally getting around to doing it."

Jason felt an acute sinking sensation that he tried his best to hide. "I imagine you'll be impressed. I think, overall, the clinic does a very good job. The little mental health interview at the end is kind of a freebie—a throwback to when psychiatric work was all the clinic did."

"So you mean I don't have to bare my soul?"

Jason laughed. "Not if you don't want to."

As they watched, a man came up beside Talmedge and touched him on the elbow. Talmedge excused himself and quickly followed the other man out of the room and up the central staircase to the second floor.

Without thinking, Jason asked, "What's upstairs?"

Chandler smiled. "My dad. He's up there holding court—just flew in from California this afternoon. He didn't want to have to deal with all the people at the party, but said there were one or two he needed to talk to."

Jason had noticed that the room was beginning to thin out. Apparently Senator Chandler had made the same observation.

"I'd better go say some good-byes," the senator said. "It was a pleasure meeting you, Dr. Andrews."

"The same, Senator. Thank you for inviting me." They shook hands, and Jason decided it was time to find Rachel and make his own good-byes. She was helping to organize the guest departures, and Jason had to wait for an opportunity to speak to her privately.

"I guess I'd better be getting along, too, Rachel. Thank you for the evening."

Rachel put a very disappointed look on her face, then took a long stage look at her watch. "It's awfully late. I was hoping you'd be able to follow me home and make sure I get in safely."

. . . which was how Jason came to be sitting on the couch in Rachel's living room drinking coffee at 12:15 A.M.

He had had a rough idea where Rachel lived, but hadn't put together that her house was actually on a corner of the grounds of her parents' estate. It was a small brick colonial consistent in architecture with the main house. Inside, the feeling was also remarkably like the main house, only cozier. Cozy was the operative word here. Jason was beginning to feel very cozy.

They were drinking coffee, discussing some of the characters who'd attended her brother's party. Jason was unable to shake off the concerns that had dogged him all evening.

"What do you think of Talmedge?" he asked her.

"I really don't have much interaction with him. He saved the clinic; that's for sure. If he hadn't come along, Marsden would have gone bankrupt. I don't know what would have happened to Psychoden."

"What did you think about his interference when we were trying to help find Billy McCall?"

"I didn't agree with him, of course, but I understood where he was coming from. He was just trying to protect his investment. He's put a lot of money into the Marsden Clinic."

"So you think it's all just a question of money to him?"

"If it is, Jason, I don't have a problem with that. Marsden never gave a thought to finances, and it almost ended his research career. Someone has to keep an eye on funding." There was a note of impatience in her voice. "What's the matter, Jason?"

"I don't know. I guess I'm just naturally suspicious."

"Tilting at windmills again?" She gave him a hint of a smile.

"Again?"

"I heard a little about what happened at Harvard. Actually, I overheard Marsden talking to someone about it on the phone before you came."

"Frankly," Jason said, "when that graduate student first came to me, I thought she was either lying or deluding herself. Then I decided that the professor probably just didn't realize that he had appropriated her work. In the end, it was evident that he had deliberately stolen her ideas and published them as his own. When he refused to acknowledge her contribution, I thought he should have been fired."

"He wasn't?"

"Did I mention that he was chairman of the department? Anyway, most of the faculty seemed to believe that the work of graduate students was pretty much the property of their mentors. To make a long story short, the graduate student in question went on to take a faculty position on the West Coast, and I was suddenly alone in the hornets' nest. I had alienated most of the department, and I no longer had a cause to defend."

"My Don Quixote," Rachel said softly.

Jason was suddenly very aware of their closeness on the couch, the soft, intimate lighting of the living room, the subtle fragrance of Rachel's perfume. He leaned forward, ever so slightly. Did her head tilt just a little in anticipation? They kissed, briefly. They kissed again.

Rachel made the tiniest backward movement of her head. He could feel her warm breath as she spoke, feel the slight friction of her lips just brushing his as they moved.

"Do you think you have time for another cup of coffee?" Rachel asked.

He kissed her once more, deeply, before replying.

"I don't think so," he said.

Chapter Twenty-three

Marsden's laboratory looked a lot like every other chemistry laboratory Jason had ever seen in his life. There were beakers and open flames and workbenches and strange odors and lots of expensive-looking machines. Marsden was hunched over his desk, scrawling something in a notebook. Rachel was nowhere to be found.

"She's up in Talmedge's office," Marsden volunteered.

"I didn't think they had much interaction with each other." Jason let the inflection rise at the end, making it more of a question than a statement, inviting Marsden to provide information. But Marsden didn't. He was once again completely involved with his notebook.

Jason decided he'd just leave a note on Rachel's desk, then saw her tape recorder and had a better idea. The recorder was one of those little micro-cassette jobs, smaller than a package of cigarettes. Rachel often carried the recorder with her in the pocket of her lab coat. Jason flipped it on and left a simple message: "Does this mean we're going steady?"

Back in his office, Jason tried to sort out the jumble of emotions his life had become. His involvement with Rachel was just one more unsettling variable, but mostly he was preoccupied with his concerns about what was going on at the clinic—and what was happening to its patients. There was very much a déjà vu quality to all of this. Jason could feel himself once again sliding very far out on a limb, and, as though the risk of the branch breaking on its own wasn't enough, he thought he was beginning to hear the old familiar sound of sawing.

Written on the piece of paper that lay on his desk were two telephone numbers. When he tried the one marked "home," there was no answer. The other number was marked "daughter" and appeared—from the area code and prefix—to be very close to the clinic. Jason drummed his fingers on his desk; then he looked out the window for a little while; then he picked up the phone and punched in the numbers.

"Hello." The voice was that of a young woman. She sounded tentative.

"Hello. This is Dr. Jason Andrews calling—from the Marsden Clinic. I'm sorry to bother you, but I've been trying to call Mrs. Herbert Allen at her home and I get no answer. We have your number here at the clinic, so I thought I'd try to see if you could help me reach her."

There was a pause on the other end of the line, and Jason worried that he might not have the right number. "Is this Mrs. Susan Johnson"—he read from the piece of paper—"Mrs. Allen's daughter?"

"Yes, this is Mrs. Johnson. Could you give me your name again, Doctor, and your phone number there at the clinic? I'll have to call you back in a few minutes."

Jason gave her the information, hung up the phone,

and waited. Several minutes passed before the phone rang.

"I'm sorry, Dr. Andrews, but frankly I wanted to call back through the clinic switchboard so I could be certain who I was talking to. Mother gets a lot of strange calls these days, and the press will say just about anything to get her on the line. That's one reason why she's come down here to stay with me—to get away from all of that."

"I'm sure," Jason said, "that this is a very difficult time for your mother, and I don't wish to trouble her. . . . It's just that I interviewed the vice-president when he was at the clinic—I'm a psychiatrist—and he impressed me as a very happy, very well-adjusted man. When I heard the terrible news of his death, I was stunned. I thought that perhaps I could gain some insight from Mrs. Allen that would help me to understand what happened. It might someday benefit another patient."

The reasoning sounded a little weak, even to Jason's ears. He wondered if Susan Johnson thought he was some kind of kook.

"Actually, Dr. Andrews, I think that it might be a good idea for you to talk to my mother. She's resting now, but I'm sure I can convince her. Would you want to see her in person?"

They agreed that Jason would come by after work that evening. It was only a fifteen-mile drive from the clinic.

Jason hung up the phone and was left to face alone once again the turbulent stream of his emotions. He

sensed that he had edged slightly further out on that proverbial limb.

What worried Jason most about the limb metaphor was
the nagging suspicion that the hand that held the saw was
his own.

Chapter Twenty-four

Mrs. Michaels had asked to speak with Jason before her husband's appointment. There were a few things, she said, that the doctor needed to know.

"We're working people, Dr. Andrews. It's all we've ever known. My parents were working people, so were Ben's." She had more to say, but her voice had begun to waver. Her eyes welled up with tears. "That's why this has all been so hard for us—for me, I mean. It doesn't seem to bother Ben all that much." Mrs. Michaels' shoulders began to shake. She began to sob openly. Jason passed her a box of Kleenex.

"I'm sorry, Doctor. I'll be all right in a minute. It's just that sometimes I don't know how I'm going to get through this." Then she corrected herself, instantly ashamed of what she had just said. "I shouldn't talk like that. God will grant me whatever strength I need."

Jason said nothing, waiting for Mrs. Michaels to regain control. Her husband had been referred to Arthur Marsden from the university in Charlottesville by Dr. Klein, the same man who had sent Leonard Williams to the clinic. Klein and Marsden had both thought there might be a role for Psychoden to play in the evaluation of Ben Michaels.

Mrs. Michaels was probably in her late forties. She had quite a bit of gray in her hair, and it occurred to Jason that the judicious application of a little hair dye would probably take ten years off her appearance. But Jason guessed that Mrs. Michaels would not have time for such foolishness as hair dye. She appeared to be a woman of solid build and equally solid constitution. It was difficult to imagine the amount of stress that would be required to bring her to her present state of despair.

"Perhaps, Mrs. Michaels," Jason said when it appeared she could continue, "if you would just start at the beginning."

She took a couple of stuttering deep breaths and began the story. "Well, I know I'm not a doctor, and it's not my place to say, but I lay it all on to when the factory closed down. Somebody bought the whole thing up and moved the entire operation to North Carolina. That's when our lives changed, and Ben hasn't been the same since. He wasn't as bad then as he is now, I don't mean that, but he was changed all the same.

"What you have to understand, Doctor, Ben is a master craftsman. He's a woodworker, a furniture maker—the best they ever had at that old factory—at least since his daddy retired. He was a respected man. He earned a good paycheck. When the factory shut down, suddenly that was gone—like that." She snapped her fingers to show just how quickly it had all evaporated.

"Sure, they told Ben if he would pick up and go to Carolina there'd be a job there for him. They'd make him a foreman. But Ben said there were two things he'd rather die than do. One was leave Virginia; the other was make his living telling other people what to do. He didn't want some fancy job like that. And that was the end of it." When Mrs. Michaels spoke of her husband, there was pride in her voice.

"I guess Ben thought they might change their minds and leave the factory in Virginia if they had trouble hiring enough experienced men. Or else he thought, good riddance, and he'd just hire on at another factory, a man with his work record. I don't know for certain. He doesn't like to worry me with all the details. Anyway, whatever he planned, it didn't work out. He was out of a job, and that was that. By the by, don't even mention government unemployment insurance to Ben. He can't abide welfare.

"We had a little savings, down at the bank. That kept us for a while, but it wasn't much. When it began to look like we were going to starve, well, then I—don't you dare tell Ben I did this, Doctor—well, I didn't see much choice—I asked my brother if maybe he had something for Ben to do at his garage. Jim—that's my brother—Jim said sure, a hard worker like Ben, he could get to be a mechanic, pretty soon make nearly as much as down at the factory. Sounded like a pretty fair offer to me. Ben wasn't so sure. I could have hit him on the head with my iron skillet. I said, Ben, you either take that job or say good-bye to me and Brenda. Brenda, she's my youngest—the only one still at home. Well, Ben said he'd give it a try, which was all anyone had a right to ask. For a couple of weeks there I thought it was all going to work out.

"Ben didn't say much, but I asked Jim, on the sly like, and Jim said Ben was a hard worker and a quick learner. He'd have to watch him or pretty soon Ben would open up his own garage right across the street, run Jim plum out of business. Then came the accident.

"I was doing my wash when the phone rang. It was Jim, said Ben had been working up under a car and it had come down on him somehow. Jim said Ben didn't look busted up, but he couldn't move his legs, and the ambulance had come and carried him down to the hospital.

"That's when all the doctorin' started. Don't tell Ben I said this, but he never did believe in doctors. Well, the long and the short of it is, they tested everything, then said there was not a thing in the world wrong with Ben's legs. It was all in his head. They claimed it was psycho something or other."

"Psychosomatic," Jason offered.

"That's it—meanin', of course, that it's in his head. So they called in the psychiatrists to see if they could talk some sense into him, but old Ben wouldn't budge. So there we were. I just put Ben in a wheelchair and took him home."

"What has happened since then?"

"Nothing. Ben just sits in that wheelchair and watches TV. Oh, he tries to help around the house a little, but there's not much he can do."

"How are you making ends meet?"

"We're not." The tears were beginning to build up once again.

"What about workmen's compensation or unemployment benefits?"

"It's welfare. Ben won't take it."

"Does Ben seem to blame anyone? Does he blame your brother, or has he ever mentioned taking any legal action?"

Mrs. Michaels looked at Jason as though she didn't quite understand. "If there's nothing wrong with him, how could he blame anybody? Except himself, of course."

Jason considered this in silence for a few moments. It seemed as though Mrs. Michaels had said everything she'd come to say. Then, with a final burst of tears, she spoke again.

"What I don't understand, Doctor, is why Ben would pretend he can't use his legs if there's nothing wrong with them. He's never been a slacker. I always felt like he'd rather be working down at the factory with his buddies than home with me.

"And here's another thing—I've never told anyone before." She suddenly stopped, uncertain whether to go on. And then, "At night, when Ben's asleep, and sometimes when he's watching TV, I see him move those legs."

Jason didn't know which was more difficult for Mrs. Michaels, seeing with her own eyes that her husband could use his legs or having to report her proof to a stranger.

"If you're ready, Mrs. Michaels," Jason said, "I think it's time for me to meet your husband."

Ben Michaels was in the outer office, waiting patiently in his wheelchair. He refused to allow anyone to push his chair, insisting on wheeling himself through the door and into the inner office.

"Hi, Doc," was Ben Michaels' greeting to Jason. He was dressed in overalls and work shoes, as though he were headed for a day at the factory. There was a wide grin on his face that suggested complete indifference both to his own condition and his wife's distress. If you look up the word *inappropriate* in the dictionary, you will find it illustrated with a picture of Ben Michaels' smiling face.

"How are you today, Mr. Michaels?"

"Fine, Doc. Couldn't be better."

"Well," Jason said, "I imagine you *could* be better."

"I don't see how."

"What about your legs?"

"Oh, that's just a matter of time. The legs are getting better every day."

"Do you mean you're starting to be able to use them again?"

Ben Michaels looked down at his legs. A look of concentration came over his face. The legs did not move.

"Not yet, Doc. But any day now I'm gonna get right up out of this wheelchair."

"How do you mean your legs are getting better? Do you have any feeling in them?"

Michaels slapped each leg. "Not yet, but any day now. I just know I'm getting better."

Mrs. Michaels' eyes searched Jason's. See what I have to deal with?

Jason carefully explained the use of Psychoden and what he planned to do. Ben Michaels was eager to get on with it. If Jason had suggested cutting up Michaels' legs

154

for shark bait, Ben would have enthusiastically agreed without the slightest change in his ear-to-ear grin.

The Psychoden interview was scheduled for the following day. Ben Michaels said he would be looking forward to it.

Chapter Twenty-five

The vice-president's widow made no effort whatsoever to conceal her hostility toward Jason.

"My daughter is not my appointment secretary, Doctor. She had no business telling you that you could come here."

"This is *my* house, Mother. *I* will decide who comes here and who doesn't. If you don't want to talk to Dr. Andrews, you don't have to. I'll help him as best I can."

"You have no right, Susan!" Tears were beginning to form in Mrs. Allen's eyes.

"I have every right, Mother. He was my father, and I for one want to try to understand what happened."

"What's done is done, Susan. Nothing is going to bring your father back. *Please,* let it be."

They were in the living room of Susan Johnson's modest home. Looking through to the next room, Jason could see that it had been redone as an artist's studio. Its northern wall was mostly glass to catch the light that Susan's work required. She had apologized for her appearance when she opened the door for Jason. There were smudges of paint on her blouse and cheek. She wiped her hands on a rag before offering to shake with Jason.

Susan Johnson was a small, wiry woman. She might have been a gymnast or a ballerina instead of a painter. Her mother was similar in size, but otherwise they were total opposites. Whereas Susan was relaxed and casual about her appearance, her mother did not have a gray hair out of place. And despite her anger at Jason's presence, Mrs. Allen had nonetheless dressed herself very meticulously. She looked as though she were going to a luncheon at the White House. Her body language, though, told an entirely different story. She had scrunched herself up at one end of the couch, her shoulders hunched and her arms folded in front of her, a posture that signaled unequivocally her desire to be left alone.

"She's been like this since my father's funeral." Susan Johnson said this, almost under her breath, to keep her mother from hearing.

But her mother did hear. "How dare you stand there and talk about me as though I'm not right here in the room! *She!* The very idea!"

"I'm sorry, Mother." There was genuine apology in her voice. "I'm only trying to help."

It had all started so badly that Jason was uncertain whether it wouldn't be best for everyone if he simply made his own apologies and left before the family rift became irreparable. No, he decided, there were still far too many unanswered questions.

"I do understand, Mrs. Allen, what a terribly difficult time this is for you—"

But she didn't let him finish. "Do you, Doctor? Do you really think you have any idea what I've been through?"

"Mother, you're not being fair."

"Why am I the one who always has to be fair?" Mrs. Allen asked her daughter. "When is life going to be fair to me?" She crossed her legs and huddled her shoulders in closer, incredibly making herself appear even smaller on the couch.

Jason decided to try a very direct approach. "Mrs. Allen, when I interviewed your husband at the clinic, there was nothing to suggest that he was suicidal. There were no signs of depression. It didn't even appear that he was experiencing any significant job-related stress. He seemed completely relaxed. Frankly, I've worried that I might have missed something, and what I'd like to know, Mrs. Allen, is whether you had noticed anything—prior to that time— that suggested to you that your husband was terribly unhappy about something."

There was silence. Susan Johnson gave her mother a look that said she'd better make a civil response. Mrs. Allen glared back at her daughter momentarily before relenting.

Mrs. Allen shook her head. "Not then. He was fine before he went to the clinic. A week or so later is when it hit him . . . whatever it was." This last, the *whatever it was,* was spoken with attempted nonchalance and accompanied by a furtive glance at Jason out of the corner of her eye.

The net effect was to convince Jason, beyond the shadow of a doubt, that she was hiding something. But was this *whatever it was* any of Jason's business?

Mrs. Allen had confirmed for him—from her untrained but far more intimate perspective—that her husband had indeed been in good mental health when he visited the clinic. It appeared certain that the vice-president's suicide had been precipitated by some acute event that had occurred after his interview with Jason.

"Did he become depressed, Mrs. Allen?"

"Oh, yes, he was depressed—at the end. But it would come and go. He could suddenly be filled with purpose and plans for the future, and then, just as suddenly, he would turn sad. You couldn't even talk to him. I think I saw that side more than anyone else did. He would come home and just deflate, like the air going out of a balloon. There was nothing I could do to cheer him up. Then he'd improve, and for a while he would be better."

There were other questions Jason might have asked, but he worried that he had intruded too far already.

"I want you to know, Mrs. Allen, how very much I appreciate your speaking with me today. I always admired your husband, and it was a great personal honor for me to have had the opportunity to meet him." There were very few politicians Jason had met about whom he could make such a statement. "I'm sorry to have disturbed you."

Mrs. Allen simply nodded. More than anything, she appeared relieved that Jason's visit had been so brief. Susan Johnson led Jason to the door, then stepped outside so that she could have a private word.

"That woman you met in there is not the same woman I've known for the last thirty years. I don't know where she came from." She was both embarrassed and concerned.

Jason put his hand on her shoulder. "Your mother's re-action to your father's death is not at all unusual. She feels abandoned, and that makes her angry. There may be an element of guilt involved as well. After a suicide every-one asks themselves what they could have done to prevent it. That's certainly the question I've been asking myself."

"I don't know, Doctor. I just have the feeling there's something she's holding back."

"You could be right, but it may be something more imagined than real. I expect she'll begin to get back to normal soon. Your mother's not quite ready yet, but in a couple of weeks it might be helpful for her to see some-one, to give her the opportunity to talk this through. Also, there are several support groups that might be of help to her. Just give me a call. I'll be happy to provide names."

Susan Johnson thanked him for coming, and shook his hand once again. Then she turned and went back into the house. Jason had walked all the way to his car when he decided that he should return to the house and give Mrs. Allen's daughter the name of a psychologist he thought might be especially helpful. Jason reached for the door-bell, but was stopped by the sound of Mrs. Allen's plead-ing voice coming from the living room.

"He did it for *us*, Susan. Why can't you understand that?"

"No, Mother, Father didn't kill himself for me."

Jason turned and walked back to his car.

Chapter Twenty-six

As expected, Ben Michaels was right on time for his Psychoden interview and eager to get started.

"Let's have at it, Doc. Anything to get me up and going again."

The man *is* an intriguing study in contradictions, Jason thought as he placed the patch on Mr. Michaels' neck. But the riddle of Ben Michaels might be difficult to solve even with the help of Psychoden.

Jason began the usual litany of general, unthreatening questions. "What is your full name?"

"Benjamin Robert E. Lee Michaels."

This was new information to Jason. "Who were you named after?"

"Benjamin Franklin."

Sometimes in psychiatric practice, events occur that can only be described as humorous. The experienced clinician can almost always disguise his amusement. Not this time. Jason lost it completely. *Ben Franklin!* The beauty of Psychoden was that only Jason would remember.

"How old are you?" Jason fought to regain control. Tears were beginning to form in the corners of his eyes.

"Forty-six." In that far-off Psychoden drone. Ben Michaels was oblivious.

After a few more routine questions, Jason moved on to more delicate areas. "What kind of work do you do, Mr. Michaels?"

"I'm a furniture maker, a master craftsman."

"Do you enjoy your work?"

Ben Michaels hesitated. Somehow his circuits weren't quite integrating in response to the question. So Jason changed it slightly. "You take a great deal of pride in your work, don't you?"

No hesitation this time. "We make only the finest furniture, none of that bargain-basement stuff. It's very satisfying to know you've turned out a fine piece of furniture and know that some family is going to treasure it—maybe for generations. It *is* something a man can take pride in."

"Your father worked in the same factory?"

"Nearly fifty years—the only place he ever worked."

"How long were you at the factory?"

"Twenty-eight years."

"But the factory is closed now. What kind of work are you doing now?"

Ben Michaels opened his mouth but didn't say anything. Once again the circuits weren't quite integrated.

"I understand that you worked at your brother-in-law's garage for a while after you left the factory."

"For a while."

"How did you like working there?"

"I didn't. Jim meant well, but I knew it was just charity. I might as well have been collecting on unemployment."

"Would you like to do that kind of work, though, if someone else offered you a job?"

"I don't see how there'd be much to take pride in. I mean, it'd just be going to work, putting in your hours, waiting till you could afford to retire. Not much satisfaction in setting a carburetor or changing a tire. I don't mean to criticize Jim. He's a good man. It's just not a kind of work I'd like to do."

"You must have hated working there."

"I was ashamed. Everyone knew it was charity. Jim only hired me on 'cause I'm married to his sister. A man can't find any self-respect in a deal like that."

"But you don't work at the garage anymore?"

"No."

"Why not?"

"My legs give out."

"What happened?"

"I was fixin' a car and it fell on me."

"What did the doctors tell you was wrong with your legs?"

"They said it was all in my head."

"What do you think?"

"I think I can't move my legs."

"Mr. Michaels, I'd like to see if you can move your legs now. Don't try to stand, just move your right leg forward."

Michaels did as he was told, seemingly without difficulty.

"Now, move your left leg." Again, Ben Michaels followed Jason's instruction. There was no change in his expression. "It looks like your legs are working just fine right now, Mr. Michaels."

"Yes," Ben Michaels agreed, "they seem to be okay now." He said this with the same flat voice, the same flat expression.

Jason thought he had learned about as much as he needed to know. He had a pretty good idea now what was going on in Ben Michaels' mind. "I'm going to ask your wife to join us, Mr. Michaels." Michaels nodded.

Mrs. Michaels had been waiting patiently in the outer office. When she entered Jason's private office, the first thing she noticed was that her husband's feet were planted firmly on the floor, beyond the footrests of his wheelchair.

Jason saw immediately what was going through her mind. "You can put your feet back on the footrests, Mr. Michaels." Instantly, the feet were returned to their customary position.

Mrs. Michaels smiled broadly and took her husband's hand. "I knew you could do it, Ben. I knew you could lick this thing."

Jason spoke very gently. "I wanted you to see what is possible, Mrs. Michaels. As we suspected, there appears to be no significant physical problem with your husband's legs, but he's still under the influence of the Psychoden. When the patch is removed, he won't remember any of this, and I'm afraid he'll return to the same condition he was in before."

The tears of the day before came back to Mrs. Michaels' eyes. "I just can't understand him, Doctor. If there's nothing wrong with his legs, why would he fake all this? That's not the way Ben is."

"He's not really 'faking' anything, Mrs. Michaels. There is no doubt that Mr. Michaels believes that his legs are useless. That much is clear from the Psychoden interview. Mr. Michaels has suffered what we call a conversion reaction. By understanding what has caused this psychological reaction, we may be able to help him overcome it."

"Does that mean you know what's gotten into Ben, Doctor?"

"I think I can make a pretty good guess as to what has happened psychologically to Mr. Michaels. You were right, of course, about how important his work at the factory was to him. A lot of his personal identity—and dignity— were tied up in that work. When the factory closed, it was a terrible blow. Then he had to take the job at your brother's garage, which wasn't nearly as personally satisfying to him as making furniture. Worst of all, he regarded your brother's offer as charity. That was the final blow to his self-respect."

She nodded, "I was afraid he took it that way. Ben didn't say anything, but I could tell. I just thought he would eventually get over it."

"I think that, in the end, it was all simply too much for him to bear," Jason said. "Then, when the accident occurred at the garage, there probably was a brief moment of pain in his back or legs. Maybe his legs were pinned or something. Anyway, his mind latched on to that as a solution to his humiliation. If he couldn't use his legs, then he had a reason not to be working—not to continue the humiliating job at the garage. Please remember, this wasn't a conscious decision on his part—no more than you can decide what to dream about. This was simply the only solution his mind could work out to deal with the situation."

Mrs. Michaels seemed to understand. "But will he get better, Doctor?"

"I expect him to, with time. He'll need lots of support at home. Everyone has to recognize that this is an illness, just like if he'd caught the flu. Shaming him won't help. In fact, it would probably decrease his chance of recovery. It's his sense of shame and humiliation that has brought him to where he is now."

"I understand, Doctor."

"He'll also need psychiatric support and physical rehabilitation—exercises and so forth—but it seems to me that the best thing for him would be some prospect of returning to a line of work that would give him his self-respect back."

Mrs. Michaels may not have been highly educated, but she was a very bright lady. "Ben's friend Clyde went down to Carolina to work. He said Ben could have a job there in a minute if he got his legs back." She thought about this for a few seconds, then added, smiling, "But Clyde said there wouldn't be any chance of them making him a foreman now."

Chapter Twenty-seven

After his experience with Janet Allen and her daughter, Jason approached the Widow Bates with more than a little apprehension. But he was, after all, a psychiatrist. Who better equipped to deal with the vestiges of bereavement? On the phone Mrs. Bates had seemed, on the one hand, perplexed that Jason wanted to speak with her, while on the other perfectly willing to see him.

The Bates home was in Maryland, just north of Washington. It was a white clapboard colonial of rather modest dimensions. Its green shutters especially could have used a fresh coat of paint. Jason had to pick his way through the minefield of boxes and odd pieces of furniture that littered the front walk and steps. The front door stood open. He could see through to what was apparently an office on one side of the house, where a woman was picking items off a bookshelf and tossing them rather carelessly into yet another cardboard box.

"Hello." Jason spoke softly so as not to startle her.

The woman turned her body sideways without moving her feet and saw Jason at the door. "Are you Dr. Andrews?" Jason nodded. "Come on in. I'll be with you in a second."

Jason stepped into the front hallway. There was hardly a place to stand among the boxes. He took off his coat and put it across a chair. The woman he took to be Mrs. Bates chucked a couple more momentos into the box, then turned and walked into the hallway to greet Jason.

"Barbara Bates," she said, extending her hand. She was a pleasant-appearing, rather heavyset woman who looked to be in her mid sixties. She was wearing a pale blue pants suit and very little makeup—and a broad smile.

"I appreciate your taking time to see me, Mrs. Bates." Jason glanced around once again. "Are you moving?"

"Oh, no." Her expression more serious now. "I'm just throwing out a lot of painful reminders. By this time tomorrow there won't be any evidence left that the son of a bitch ever lived here."

"Your husband?" Jason could hardly keep the incredulity out of his voice.

"My *former* husband," she replied. "Why don't we see if we can find a place to sit down in the living room, Doctor, so you can ask your questions." She led the way. "Would you like a cup of coffee? I've got a pot on."

It took Barbara Bates a few minutes to get things organized. When she finally sat down, it was only for a brief moment. Then she was up again to close the front door.

"I'm trying to air the house out," she explained. "My husband was a cigar smoker, and he wore this obnoxious cologne—I guess he thought it drove all the young girls wild up on the Hill. Did you notice it when you came in?"

Jason shook his head. "Good. Would you like sugar or cream?"

There was only a little more small talk before Mrs. Bates asked, "Okay, Doctor, what was it you wanted to know?"

"As you know, Mrs. Bates, I met the congressman when he was at the clinic for his annual physical."

"I only know that because you told me on the phone the other day. My husband didn't spend much time at home, and on the rare occasions when he was home he didn't waste a lot of his valuable time talking to his wife. But frankly, I would have said he wouldn't have gone to see a psychiatrist if you put a gun to his head."

"He didn't really come to see *me,* Mrs. Bates. The mental health interview is just part of the annual physical package. We never really talked about anything that was the least bit personal. But still, as a psychiatrist, I couldn't help but have some professional impressions. What bothers me is this: your husband just didn't seem to me to be the kind of man who would commit suicide."

"He wasn't." That case was closed as far as Barbara Bates was concerned.

"Then there was nothing that happened, nothing after I talked with your husband, which might have caused him to take his own life?"

"Of course not. You're the psychiatrist, but it always seemed to me that people who kill themselves must be either very sad or very crazy. The only emotion my husband ever felt was greed. The only person he ever thought about was himself. And he wasn't crazy; he was just plain mean." Mrs. Bates displayed no emotion whatsoever as she spoke. There was no anger, no sadness. She was merely reciting historical facts. None of which, incidentally, contradicted any of Jason's impressions.

"So you think he may have just fallen?" Without thinking, Jason lowered his voice. "Perhaps he was drinking and simply had an accident."

"My husband was a drunk, Dr. Andrews. Everybody knows that. And anyone who knows anything at all about drunks knows that it's the family that bears the brunt of the damage that drunks cause. So there's no need for you to bring it up like it's some secret I might not have heard."

Jason felt appropriately embarrassed. This was Barbara "No Nonsense" Bates. He wondered if she had always been this forthright or whether this was a result of forty years of marriage to Hiram Bates.

And Barbara Bates wasn't finished yet. "Another thing you probably know, drunks have nine lives. My husband was in more accidents than you could shake a stick at. He demolished two of our cars and came out of it both times without a scratch."

"Maybe he'd just used up his nine lives."

Mrs. Bates shook her head. "I went up to that parking garage just to have a look for myself. That wall he 'fell' over came up nearly to my waist. How could anyone possibly fall over a wall that high?"

"So what do you think happened?"

"He was pushed, of course. Or picked up and thrown over the edge." Again, there was no emotion. She might have been describing what happened to a teacup—one that was old and cracked and soon to be discarded anyway. *I just bumped it with my elbow and over it went. Must have broken into a million pieces.*

"But who would do a thing like that? Who would want to murder your husband?"

"Me. Any one of my kids. The thing is, he would have never let himself get close to the edge with one of us around. My husband made enemies like Carter makes little liver pills, and he did it the old-fashioned way—he *earned* them." She suddenly stopped speaking. Her mind seemed to go far away. Her eyes became watery. "There was a time when I loved him, but that was many, many years ago."

They sat in silence, taking sips of their coffee. Then Jason asked, "Did you tell the police about your suspicions?"

She shook her head. "I didn't have my thoughts as well organized then. I hadn't been to see the parking garage. They mostly just told me what *they* thought happened. They asked me if my husband had any enemies. I said, does Carter have liver pills? That was about it.

"Another thing, while I was down identifying the body and making arrangements, someone was in the house ransacking the place, looking for something. Nothing was missing as near as I could tell, so I didn't report it. I'd had enough of the police for one day."

"You *never* mentioned it to the police?"

"No, not to the police. I did mention it to the FBI. The director himself was here to talk to me. He didn't seem too surprised about the break-in—made me think maybe the FBI or CIA or somebody had been involved."

Jason stored the information away. Michael Cordova

didn't seem to be the kind of guy that would be involved in anything like that, but you never knew.

Jason figured he'd probably learned about as much as he was going to for now. He could think of lots of questions he might ask, but they would be more appropriate coming from a policeman than a psychiatrist. He was about to thank Mrs. Bates and take his leave when she spontaneously volunteered the answer to one of his questions.

"One thing, at least my husband left me well fixed. He always refused to spend any money, and now I've got more than I know what to do with. First thing, I'm going to fix up this old house. Then I've got an idea I'm going to take a cruise. Hiram never took me anywhere. I've got four children, all married, and what I'm going to do, I'm going to book an around-the-world cruise on the *QE-2*, and I'm going to divide it into fourths and have each of my kids— and their spouses—accompany me on one fourth of the cruise."

She had a very dreamy-eyed look as she spoke. Jason had the distinct impression that her real pleasure was not in taking the cruise for herself but in giving the trips to her children.

Chapter Twenty-eight

It was well after midnight and Jason had abandoned, for the time being at least, any hope of sleep. He was sitting up in bed, his back propped up against a stack of pillows, listening to the soft sounds of Rachel's whispered breathing. For some reason she preferred not to use a pillow. She lay on her stomach, her hands pressed against the mattress just above her head, her face turned, for now, away from him. A thin sheet was pulled halfway up her back, exposing little more than her shoulders. Who would have thought shoulders could be so sexy?

The room had been dark during their lovemaking but now was filled with moonlight. Coincident with the moonlight, perhaps because of it, Rachel's sleep had grown gradually more fitful. She became restless and fidgety, and with every movement she made, the sheet covering her body was working its way slowly, sensuously southward.

Jason had been distracted throughout the evening, even during its most intimate moments—an occurrence which, as a teenager, he would not have dreamed possible. Had Rachel noticed his preoccupation? Jason hoped not. It wasn't the kind of thing a woman was likely to find very flattering.

His meetings with the two widows had provided Jason with more questions than answers. Their statements had reassured him with regard to his own performance as a psychiatrist. He had not, it now appeared, overlooked some lurking psychiatric pathology in either Vice-President Allen or Congressman Bates. On the other hand, Jason was more convinced than ever that *something* sinister was going on, and he was increasingly suspicious that the Marsden Clinic was somehow in the middle of it all. Today's events had done nothing to assuage his fears.

Jason had started the day by asking himself a very simple question. If Vice-President Allen had been in good mental health at the time he visited the clinic and *subsequently* became depressed, was there a straightforward, nonconspiratorial explanation that was still directly related to his clinic visit? For example, after the vice-president left the clinic, was he told of a test result that suggested some life-threatening disease? It would be, Jason figured, very simple to review Herbert Allen's clinic chart and look for any ominous laboratory reports. A chest X ray showing a possible tumor would help to explain a subsequent suicide. It was a long shot, but easy enough to check—or so he had thought.

Jason had made the journey from his office up to the top floor, where they kept the medical records, maybe a hundred times over the past few months. Every time he saw a patient, he dictated a report. When the report had been typed, the medical records sent him a note asking him to come up and sign it. At least a hundred times he'd done it and never given it a second thought. So why, this time, did he feel so guilty? Why, this time, was he convinced that he *looked* guilty?

"May I help you, Dr. Andrews?" It was the same polite gray-haired lady who had retrieved records for him so many times in the past. Why, all of a sudden, was she so suspicious? Jason felt like the diamond smuggler who was the only one of the three hundred passengers on an airplane who was stopped going through Customs. Why did you stop me? Because you looked so suspicious. How did you know the diamonds were hidden in the heel of my right shoe? Because you were limping, stupid.

Jason put on his most innocent smile. "I need to sign my consultation reports on Herbert Allen and Hiram Bates."

"Just one moment." Was that a frown which crossed her brow? "I'll see if I can find the charts." She disappeared into the recesses of the medical records department for what seemed like an hour. When she returned, she wore the incredulous look of the head librarian who isn't buying your claim that you put the book in the night-depository slot.

"I don't understand, Dr. Andrews. The data from those charts have already been entered into computer files. The original charts have been sent to the warehouse. You must have already signed them. You've just forgotten." She was making a definitive statement. The charts had been signed.

"Maybe I could just pull the charts up on the computer, then," Jason suggested. "That way I could review my reports and make certain everything is in order."

"You still wouldn't know if you'd signed them, Doctor. The consultation report goes from the word processor to the computer file. The only signed copy is in the warehouse."

Jason tried to keep the frustration out of his voice. "I'd still like to review what I dictated."

"I'm sorry, Dr. Andrews. Once it's in the computer, you must have administration approval to review the chart." The woman was a stone wall.

What kind of a hospital hid patient charts from its doctors? Jason started to argue, then decided it wouldn't do anything but attract attention to his request. "Thank you for your trouble. I'm sure you're right. I probably signed the charts and just forgot."

The minute Jason arrived back at his office, he got the message that Mr. Talmedge would like to have a word, when Jason could find a moment. *Uh-oh.* Jason didn't see any point in putting it off, so he just turned himself around and trekked right back up to the top floor.

Talmedge seemed calm. He wasn't frothing at the mouth or anything. "Hello, Jason." Big smile. First-name basis. But he didn't bother to get up from behind his desk. "I appreciate your stopping by. Just wanted to let you have a look at the program for next week's dedication of the new research center." He pushed a piece of paper across the desk.

Jason looked at it. He saw Talmedge's name, Marsden's name, a couple of senators. So? "Certainly looks like a fine program," he said.

"Half of Washington's going to be here, Jason. Remember, I'd like for you and a couple of our other staff members to sit on the dais. I'll introduce you myself."

Jason couldn't think of any response. He'd already told Talmedge he would be there. Jason wasn't going to pretend it was some great honor to be invited.

When the silence threatened to become awkward, Talmedge spoke once again. "I understand that you're seeing Rachel Chandler socially." He looked at Jason for confirmation. Jason kept his expression blank. "She's a fine girl, has a good head on her shoulders. She understands the special needs of our clinic."

Jason didn't have a clue what Talmedge's point was. He only knew that he didn't need any dating pointers from Charles Talmedge.

"Someone mentioned that you were in medical records, asking to see some old patient charts." Talmedge said this casually, as though it were almost an afterthought.

"Just some consultation notes that required my signature."

"Whatever." Talmedge's tone was dismissive. "I'm sure you understand that we have a special obligation at the Marsden Clinic to safeguard the privacy of our patients. When I first came here, there was an episode where information from a chart was leaked to the press. That's not going to happen again. If there's something you need that's not available to you, come to see me. I'll see that you get whatever you need."

On the way back to his office, Jason decided that Talmedge's stance was not unreasonable, given the nature of the clinic's clientele. At the same time, Talmedge seemed suspiciously sensitive . . .

An increased stirring at his side jerked Jason's mind back to the present. With one final twist of her body, Rachel had managed to lose the last of her covers. Half awake, she was trying to recover the sheet from around her ankles. Jason quietly snaked a leg out over the sheet so that it wouldn't move. Rachel fussed with the sheet for a few more seconds before she wakened enough to understand what Jason was doing.

"I'm cold," she complained—with a smile. She crossed her arms in front of her in mock modesty. Then, with sudden, quick determination, she made one last lunge for the sheet. Jason let her have it, but took advantage of her brief moment of vulnerability to give her a gentle pinch on the bottom.

"I bet you do that to all the girls."

"No. *All* the girls won't let me."

Then, noticing for the first time that Jason was sitting up, wide awake, she gave him a concerned frown. "Can't sleep?"

"I guess I've just got too much on my mind."

"Anything you want to talk about? I'm all ears."

"It's not really anything important." He didn't want to bother her with all his concerns about the clinic. Then one thought did occur to him. "Can you access the clinic's main computer from your lab?"

"Sure. We use it to transfer Psychoden data back and forth. Why?"

"I was just trying to retrieve some old charts up in medical records today. It takes an act of Congress to get anything done up there. Maybe I could access the data from your lab, save some time and effort."

Rachel seemed to hesitate. "Well, I mean, ordinarily you could, but we've got some virus in the system now that keeps eating our data. If you logged onto the mainframe, the virus would probably gobble up everything in the clinic's data banks."

"When did all this happen?"

"Yesterday."

Jason tried to remember: hadn't he seen Rachel working at her computer today? Of course, it was now after midnight. Today had already become yesterday.

"Oh, well," Jason said, "I guess I'll just have to keep on dealing with the bureaucracy up in medical records." He began taking the pillows out from behind his back, thinking he'd give sleep another try. Then he had one last thought.

"Rachel?"

"Yes."

"Just how awake are you?"

Chapter Twenty-nine

The diminutive couple who now occupied the couch in Jason's office had been a fixture in Washington life for decades. The man, Senator Hollis Albright, was renowned for his fiery oratory. He was a classic southern gentleman, the foremost student of the Senate's history and traditions, and, many believed, the last vestige of a passing era. There was widespread conviction that this was not such a bad thing.

It was said that even now no bill made it to the floor without Hollis Albright's approval. There had been a famous episode early in the senator's career when it appeared that the filibuster he was leading would surely fail for lack of votes. Albright had walked into the well of the Senate, Bible in hand, and begun to read. What member of this body, he challenged, will dare to raise his voice to end the reading of the word of God? The answer to the question was "none," and Hollis Albright read for thirty-eight uninterrupted hours. The legend was born.

Jason knew that Senator Albright was referred to as a giant, and he also knew that this was done with deliberate irony. Still, Jason had difficulty believing that the tiny body crumpled onto his couch belonged to the famous senator.

"He used to be taller than me," his wife said. "Now look at him." There was not a trace of kindness or sympathy in her voice. This was something he had done to her, and she made no secret of her resentment.

Lillian Albright, the famous Washington hostess, could not have been much more than five feet tall herself, but she sat ramrod straight, making the most of every inch. She had the bright, alert eyes of a bird of prey and did not have a feather out of place. At the age of eighty, she was six years younger than her husband.

"He's been in a funk for weeks," she said of her husband. "I understand you have a drug that can cure him. That's why we're here."

At first Jason didn't have a clue what she was talking about. Then he realized she was referring to Psychoden. "We have a new drug which may help us understand why a person is depressed," he explained, "but it isn't a form of therapy. It's only a diagnostic tool."

Mrs. Albright's disappointment was vast and immediate. She began to gather herself as though to leave.

"But," Jason hastened to interject, "that doesn't mean we can't help your husband, Mrs. Albright."

Lillian Albright entered a brief period of suspended animation as she appeared to consider this. Then she settled back onto the couch and consulted her watch. She was willing to spare a minute or two.

Jason turned to her husband. "Perhaps, Senator, if you could tell me a little bit about what's troubling you."

Senator Albright did not seem inclined to respond, so

his wife prodded him. It seemed a role to which she was accustomed. "Go ahead, Hollis. Tell Dr. Andrews what's wrong with you."

The senator stirred slightly. His eyes seemed unfocused behind his thick glasses. "Andrews. I knew a man named Andrews once. Secretary of the Interior. The man was a complete horse's ass."

Jason smiled. "No relation to me as far as I know, Senator."

"That's the way he is," Lillian Albright said. "You can't get a straight answer out of him anymore. All he wants to talk about is the good old days."

"Don't pay any attention to the wife, Doctor. You get used to her. After a while you'll learn to ignore her. That's the best thing to do with Lillian, just ignore her."

"That's what you do with everything now, Hollis, you ignore it. You ignore me, you ignore your work." Her voice grew louder as she became more angry. She turned to Jason. "He wouldn't go to the Hill if I didn't get him out of bed and get him dressed. His staff say that half the time they can't get him to pay attention to his work. My God, Doctor, he hasn't even spoken on the Senate floor in more than six weeks!"

The senator seemed unmoved by his wife's complaints. Like so many of Jason's patients, he seemed totally involuted, completely preoccupied by a constant struggle against some internal demon unknown to the outside world. At a glance, Senator Albright looked like his body had shrunk after he put on his clothes. His oversize eyeglass frames made his head look small. There was so much room between his neck and the collar of his shirt, it looked like you could put a fist in the space. His tie was tied in a too-large knot, and his expensive wool suit looked like it belonged on someone five sizes larger. On his feet the senator wore brogues so heavy you had to wonder how he ever managed to get them off the ground. Jason glanced down at the senator's chart and reconfirmed his age. Eighty-six. Hard to believe the man was that young.

"How has your husband's appetite been, Mrs. Albright?"

"He eats like a bird. Hollis used to come home every night with a huge appetite. We'd have cocktails and a big dinner, maybe some wine with dinner. Now all he wants is the cocktails and the wine."

"What was the first change you noticed, Mrs. Albright, when this all started with your husband?"

She thought for a moment. "I guess it would be several months ago, I would find him sitting around at home, just looking off into space. I'd ask him what was wrong. He'd say there wasn't anything wrong. Then he'd go back to staring. That's just not Hollis. Then we'd go somewhere, and he'd just sit there, never join in the conversation. Next thing, he didn't want to go anywhere, just stay home at night. And now he doesn't even want to go to work."

"How about his emotional behavior? Any change you've noticed?"

"He gets angry, doesn't have any patience with anyone or anything. And once I found him crying—"

"That's a lie!" The senator had been quiet, seemingly unaware of their conversation, but his eyes now flashed angrily at his wife.

"See what I mean?" Her tone was triumphant. Her husband had just proved her point. "Hollis never used to talk to me that way."

"I wonder, Mrs. Albright, if I might have a few minutes alone with your husband?" Jason wasn't certain what was going on, but it was pretty clear that the family psychodynamics weren't contributing much to the discussion at this point. When she had left, he said, "Senator Albright, what is all this your wife is so worried about?"

The senator's brow furrowed in concentration. "Lillian can be a pain in the ass. She's been that way for the sixty years I've known her. Why, on the day of our wedding she got all upset about the flower arrangements, wanted to call the whole thing off until they got the flowers right. Can you imagine that? That's Lillian. She gets all upset, but then she settles down. Like the weather. Just wait a little while, it'll change." It sounded like a canned speech.

"Let me ask you a couple of routine questions, Senator. They're just part of the examination we give all our patients. Can you tell me what day it is today?"

Senator Hollis gave Jason a blank look, then narrowed his eyes. "This is a lot of silliness. I'm not going to answer insulting questions like that."

"I'm sorry, Senator. It's just routine. Let me ask you a couple of other things. Can you tell me what this is?" Jason held up a pencil.

"It's a pencil, of course." The senator sounded bored.

"And how about this?"

"A watch."

"Of course," Jason said. "Now what I'd like for you to do, I'm going to name three objects, and I'd like for you to repeat them back to me. An umbrella, a hat, and a banana. Could you repeat that back for me?"

The senator put on a bored look and shrugged his shoulders. "An umbrella, a hat . . ." Then he stopped. His eyes narrowed once again. "I'm not going to play a bunch of stupid games. Where's my wife?"

Jason tried to ask a few more questions, but didn't seem to be making much headway. He had begun to feel that he had a pretty good idea what was going on in the senator's mind, but thought that a Psychoden interview might still be useful, especially since Senator Albright was being uncooperative. Psychoden could help alleviate any uncertainty in the diagnosis.

He called Mrs. Albright back into the room and made the necessary arrangements. Jason watched as she helped her husband stand and shuffle out the door. As they left, a remarkable fact occurred to Jason. Less than six months ago, Hollis Albright had been elected to yet another six-year term in the United States Senate.

Thirty

All day long anger had welled up inside Charles Talmedge. The same thing happened every time he met with them. Just thinking about it made his blood boil. But now he fought to control the anger. Any show of emotion would be viewed as weakness, a vulnerability to be exploited. Above all, they must not think that he was afraid of them. These people were his inferiors in every conceivable way. For the time being, he would kowtow to their wishes, but eventually the natural order would be restored.

He checked the address they'd given him and shook his head, anger building once again. The address turned out to be a bar in a rundown section of the city, and the bar looked no more prosperous than the rest of the neighborhood. Talmedge steered his Lincoln Town Car into the parking lot and found a space he could squeeze into. He guessed there was about a fifty percent chance the car would be there when he returned.

When he walked into the bar, he was surprised to find that the interior was less modest than the exterior, the clientele more upscale than he had anticipated. But the increase in his comfort level was transient. Everywhere he looked in the smoke-filled room, men were holding hands or dancing together. And at the far end, standing beside the piano, was a rather oversized chanteuse in a pink sequined dress who had almost certainly been, at birth, a bouncing baby boy.

Talmedge could just imagine the Arabs falling all over themselves with laughter as they pictured him in the bar. Let them have their fun. The tables would soon be turned. Then see who was laughing.

He worked his way to the back of the bar, keeping his gaze downward as much as possible, avoiding eye contact at all costs, cringing at every touch of another male body against his. At last he was in the back hallway in front of the rest rooms; then the back door was just ahead. It had one of those red handles and a sign that said an alarm would sound if the door was opened. Talmedge pushed the handle. No alarm sounded. As soon as he was outside, he took a deep breath of fresh air. Then, with a screech of tires, an elderly Toyota sedan stopped directly in front of him, narrowly missing his feet. Talmedge pulled the back door open and climbed in. The car was instantly in motion once again, and he nearly lost his balance as he struggled to close the door.

"Get down!" The familiar voice was heavily accented.

The floor in front of the seat was filthy, as usual. Talmedge assumed that this was done on purpose—like the bar—to humiliate him. A blanket was hurriedly tossed over his body, and Talmedge wondered if he'd get flea bites once again. The ride to the embassy took twenty minutes. It was a journey Talmedge always made with great trepidation.

The embassy was, for all practical purposes, foreign soil, and arriving there Talmedge always experienced the same sinking feeling he felt when he traveled to their country. He was friendless and defenseless. He lived or died at the whim of the dictator, which is merely to say that while there, Talmedge shared the uncertain fate of the country's own citizens. And death in that land was unlikely to be either swift or pretty.

The old Toyota finally creaked to a halt, and the engine was turned off. Talmedge heard the heavy metal door of the embassy's garage clank shut like the iron gate of an ancient dungeon. Still he crouched on the floor, waiting for permission before rising. It was a game they played every time. He was not to get up until told to do so. If he did, the driver became threatening and abusive. Sometimes he was forced to remain under the blanket for an additional ten or twenty minutes after they were safely in the garage. Talmedge understood that it was their way of establishing control. He would let them get away with it—for now.

"Get out!" The familiar voice belonging to the familiar driver. He was almost certainly a member of their secret police, but was listed as the embassy's cultural attaché.

Talmedge climbed out and attempted to dust himself off, making a show of taking all the time he wanted to make himself presentable. Then he was led through a door and up a stairway into the embassy proper. He always entered the ambassador's private office through a side door, so there was no chance that his arrival would be witnessed by any unintended eyes. The ambassador's greeting was always effusive.

"Mr. Talmedge, my good friend, so nice that you could come to visit us. I hope that all this cloak-and-dagger business hasn't caused you any discomfort." The ambassador elaborately dusted the shoulders of Talmedge's suit and then straightened the lapels. He stepped back to examine the rest of him, then shook his head and said, "I certainly hope your suit isn't ruined. It's a shame we must take such elaborate security precautions."

"Thank you, Mr. Ambassador, I'm certain the suit will be fine."

"Enough!" The word came from a leather chair where the dictator's "nephew" had been slouched, observing the scene in sullen silence. "I have important affairs to attend to." Despite his clumsy attempt to imply otherwise, everyone knew that the young man could not be trusted with affairs of state. His only quasi-official responsibility was to spy on the embassy staff for the dictator. In that capacity he could prove lethal. But any affairs on his evening schedule were of the social variety. It was widely known that the youth was attracted to very, very young girls— who were procured for him by the embassy's cultural attaché.

As soon as the young man spoke, the ambassador's features hardened. His face was pockmarked, by acne or smallpox—or both. It was said that his body bore other scars, of knife and bullet wounds. He was a cruel man, and looked it. If it wasn't for the dictator, the nephew would not survive five minutes in his presence. But for now the ambassador could not risk a confrontation.

"Perhaps we should begin, then," he said, motioning Talmedge to a chair.

Talmedge nodded to the young man. "Your Excellency, so good to see you again."

The dictator's nephew gave no sign of acknowledgment. Instead, he studied his manicured nails, his hands as soft as his cheeks, his cheeks as delicate as those of the little girls he desired. He was attempting to grow a mustache, but the feeble result served only to emphasize his youth.

The ambassador took his seat behind his desk, then, with deliberate slowness, began arranging some papers as though he was going to take notes. When enough time had elapsed to salve his self-respect, he began. "So, Mr. Talmedge, how are things proceeding with Gerald?"

"Making good progress, Mr. Ambassador. The field grows smaller every day."

"Perhaps you would like to share with us some of the names on your list?"

Talmedge smiled genially. "There wouldn't be much point in that. The list is meaningless. All that matters is the final name."

An ominous silence filled the room. Talmedge kept a pleasant expression on his face and let his gaze wander as he pretended not to notice the ambassador's baleful stare. The room itself, the ambassador's office, provided no comfort. The decor was, to Talmedge, distressingly Middle Eastern. There were potted palms and tapestries and at least three portraits of His Excellency the dictator.

"Do not play games with us, Mr. Talmedge!" It was His

Excellency the nephew, as usual too strident to be taken seriously by grown men.

"I assure you, Your Excellency, I am only being practical. At this point I could provide you with a long list of potential names, one of whom might in the end become Gerald. You could just as easily generate such a list yourself." In fact, the list was much shorter, but Talmedge had no desire to be more cooperative. Eventually he would give them a single name. There was no way to avoid that.

"Then, Mr. Talmedge, why don't you just give us some potential names and tell us why you believe you might have—how should we express this?—*influence* over these persons should one of them become Gerald?"

That Talmedge would never do. Once Gerald was in place, anyone with access to the critical information could control him. If Talmedge allowed the Arabs access to that information, he himself would become expendable. Talmedge's subsequent lifespan would be measured in minutes.

Talmedge cleared his throat and smiled. He adopted the gently chiding tone of a disappointed but patient parent. "Now, Mr. Ambassador, you know that's not how it works. I control the data, and I will control Gerald. When Gerald is in place, I will tell you immediately."

"Ah, yes, Mr. Talmedge, but I control the funds. Surely you wouldn't like to see any slackening in the flow of funds to your account in Grand Cayman."

"Of course not." Talmedge smiled broadly. "You see, we need each other. We depend on each other. We're a team, and a team needs all its members. If one of the members drops off the team, there's no chance of winning. The whole team loses."

His Excellency the nephew had had enough. He made a show of pulling himself to full height and walking purposefully to the door. As he opened it, he turned. "Do not toy with us, Talmedge. We will flood the desert with your blood."

After the door had closed, the ambassador gave an embarrassed shrug, but he said nothing, as though he expected that someone was listening.

When their business was completed, Talmedge was led once again to the garage, where the same Toyota awaited. He had already decided that if his own car had been stolen from the bar's parking lot he would not report it. Charles Talmedge would never admit to having parked his car there.

As he opened the back door of the Toyota and climbed in, a harsh, familiar voice screamed at him.

"Get down!"

Chapter Thirty-one

Weekends with Rachel had fallen into a sort of routine. Routine not in the sense that they were in some sort of rut, but rather a routine which acknowledged that they were a couple, that they now shared a level of intimacy which was not casual. They had expectations of each other, expectations which hinted at commitment. Yet neither of them had ever mentioned the word "love" out loud.

This phase in a relationship, Jason knew, was inherently unstable. He and Rachel were teetering on an outcrop of rock partway up the mountain. They could go up or down, but they couldn't remain where they were for long and expect to survive. It was a very natural point in a relationship to begin to ask important questions, to decide whether it was time to pull back or to begin to move forward. For Jason the decision was obvious, but not for any of the usual, obvious reasons.

Friday night he told Rachel that he needed to work late, that he had some paperwork he needed to catch up on. On Saturday he made the same excuse. Both nights Jason had in mind sneaking up to the medical records area and somehow breaking into the patient computer files. Over the many months he had been at the clinic, back when it hadn't mattered, it had always seemed to Jason that there were neglected computer terminals all over the top floor, sitting around with no more security attention than so many drinking fountains. But on Friday and Saturday nights there seemed to be fewer terminals than he remembered, and the blue-blazered security men were everywhere.

And with each failed attempt to gain access to a computer terminal, Jason was reminded of the computer in Rachel's laboratory, which could provide such easy access to the clinic's mainframe computer and all its secrets. A virus, Rachel claimed, continued to infect her computer. If they used her laboratory computer to log on to the mainframe, they risked transmitting the virus and wiping out the clinic's entire data base.

Part of Jason, *most* of Jason, wanted to believe her story, but the simple fact was that he didn't, and if Rachel was lying, that meant she was part of whatever was going on at the clinic. And if he couldn't trust Rachel, he certainly couldn't love her. For now he needed to slow down the natural evolution of their relationship. When Sunday rolled around, he suggested an alternative to their usual cozy day at Rachel's house.

"I thought me might drive into Washington and spend the afternoon at the National Gallery," he said.

"Is there some special exhibit or something?" Rachel's voice betrayed a certain lack of enthusiasm.

"There's a traveling exhibition from Japan, Ancient Textiles, that could be interesting." What could be more fascinating than Japanese textiles?

"O.K." The K came out with heavy emphasis and about two octaves higher than the O, so Rachel was either expressing skepticism or she had just been goosed by a very cold hand.

They drove to Washington through a freezing, gray rain—which did nothing to elevate their collective mood. Much of the drive was made in tense silence, broken only by the monotonous back and forth slapping of the windshield wipers. Jason decided it was as good a time as any to say what he had to say.

"Please don't mention this to anyone, Rachel, not until I've had a chance to make definite plans, but I'll be leaving the clinic soon. I just can't work there anymore."

Rachel turned in her seat so that she could study Jason's face. "Is it because of me?"

"Of course not. Why would you think that?"

"It's been pretty obvious that something was wrong. I just assumed that I must have done something. . . ."

The sadness and pain in her voice took Jason entirely by surprise. Without thinking, he took her hand. "It's the whole atmosphere at the clinic—Talmedge, the fact that I can't even review my patients' files. It's not an environment I could ever be happy in."

"Are you still worried about Congressman Parker and the vice-president and all that?"

Jason hesitated for a few moments, knowing that this was potentially dangerous territory and worrying once again about Rachel's motives. Was she his best friend in the world or his worst enemy? "I guess I'd have to admit that those two—and Bates—have contributed to my lack of confidence."

"Confidence in the clinic, or in yourself?"

"Both, I suppose."

They considered this in silence for several minutes. Then Rachel said, "Arthur will be very disappointed."

Jason supposed that was true. He couldn't imagine that Marsden was involved in any wrongdoing. "Marsden will do fine. He'll still have you," Jason said, giving Rachel a weak smile.

"*I'll* miss you, Jason."

He squeezed her hand. What could he say?

"Will you go back to Boston?"

"Maybe, probably not. I've been thinking about the National Institutes of Health."

"Well, if you need any political help, my family is not without influence."

"Thanks." He didn't want to appear unappreciative, but that wasn't an offer he would be able to accept under any circumstances.

Probably because of the weather, they were able to find a parking space within reasonable distance of the National Gallery. Before they got out of the car, Jason emphasized one last time: "Please don't mention to anyone that I might be leaving the clinic. I wouldn't want Talmedge to get wind of it before my plans are set."

They made a dash for the museum and managed to make it to the front door without getting completely drenched, but no sooner were they inside than Jason missed his car keys. Had he locked them in the car? He made an apology to Rachel and started back to the door, searching his pockets as he walked, and discovered the missing keys just as he was about to step back out into the rain.

It was coming down in sheets now. Looking through the museum's glass front door, Jason noticed a large man in a suit making his way up the walk, his head bent down against the wind. Poor sucker. It was difficult for Jason to imagine why anyone else would fight through this kind of weather to see an exhibition of decaying Japanese textiles.

In the end, neither Jason nor Rachel was able to feign much interest in the exhibit.

"I understand," Jason said with a quite serious expression on his face, "that next month the museum will have an absolutely definitive presentation of Colonial wall coverings."

Rachel arched an eyebrow. "Just exactly why did we come here, Jason?"

He shrugged. "It's neutral territory. I wanted to let you know my plans and thought it might be awkward at your house."

They decided it would probably be more worthwhile to spend some time viewing the permanent collection. As they moved back through the main lobby Jason saw once again the man he'd seen struggling through the rain. He was bigger than Jason had thought, could have been a football player. The man was nearly dry now. Jason smiled in his direction, feeling a sort of kinship of shared experience. The man didn't seem to notice him.

On any other day the permanent collection of the National Gallery would have provided a very stimulating afternoon, but Rachel and Jason were unable to generate much enthusiasm. They started to leave, but it was pouring outside, so they decided to have a cup of coffee and wait for the rain to let up. As they turned away from the doors to head back into the lobby, Jason noticed the same man he had seen twice before, now entering the gift shop.

It was still raining cats and dogs when they finished their coffee, but Rachel and Jason decided to make a dash for the car anyway. They were both soaked by the time they got inside. Jason took his time letting the engine warm up and waiting for the fog to clear from the inside of the windows. When he finally pulled away from the curb, he looked back over his shoulder toward the front door of the museum. He saw a now familiar dark figure running from the building through the rain.

Chapter Thirty-two

"My brother has had some kind of a seizure."

It was Rachel on the phone. Her tone conveyed a sense of urgency, but there was no panic in her voice.

"Where is he?" Jason asked. He knew that Senator Chandler was supposed to be at the clinic today. He was scheduled for a mental health interview with Jason that afternoon.

"Talmedge said he's up in the blood-drawing room. I'm headed up there now."

"Talmedge?"

"That's who just called me. He sounded pretty upset."

"I'll meet you upstairs." Jason was already on his feet and just starting to put the phone down when he heard Rachel's voice again.

"Jason?"

"Yes?"

"Thank you."

Jason headed for the elevator thinking how unpredictable life really is. When he left Rachel the evening before, after their day at the National Gallery, their parting had been, to say the least, awkward. He had wondered how they would handle their next conversation. Now all that was by the board. The only thing that mattered was Rachel's brother, and she was obviously grateful for Jason's help.

What Jason saw when he stepped off the elevator on the top floor was a sea of blue. Every security man Talmedge had ever hired was standing in the hallway—with nothing to do. As soon as the elevator door opened, they seized on Jason's arrival as their *raison d'être*.

"Where do you think you're going?"

"To see Senator Chandler. I'm his doctor." Jason tried to be patient. Presumably the security men thought they were protecting the senator. He worked his way down the gauntlet of blue blazers until he was at the closed door to the blood-drawing salon. There, nearly bursting with self-importance, stood the final two security men. If you wanted to hear a loud bang, just stick a pin in one of these guys.

"Where do you think you're going?" one of them asked.

They must have learned the line at school in Security 101. Their teacher probably stood in front of the class and waved his arms: "Altogether now, class." And then he would mouth the words with the class as they recited in sing-songy unison, "Where do you think you're going?" When they finally had that down, they'd move on. "O.K., class, now try this: I'd like to do a body-cavity search."

"I'm here to see Senator Chandler. I'm his doctor."

"He already has a doctor with him."

This information took Jason entirely by surprise. "Who?"

"His sister."

Jason was quickly losing patience. "Dr. Chandler is a Ph.D. neuropharmacologist. She is not a medical doctor. In fact, it was Dr. Chandler who called me to see the senator." He started to brush by the security men, but they blocked his way.

"No one gets in without Mr. Talmedge's permission."

"Where's Talmedge?"

"Inside." The guard nodded his head to indicate the blood-drawing room.

"O.K., so tell him I'm here."

The two guards exchanged looks, uncertain what to do now.

So Jason gave them an incentive. "I'm sure you two know more about the law than I do. If the senator dies while you're preventing me from saving his life, do you think you'd be charged with murder or just manslaughter?"

The guards looked at each other one last time, then the bigger one said, "I'll check with Talmedge." When he opened the door, Jason walked through behind him. For a brief moment it appeared as though the security guard was going to try to physically remove Jason. In the end, he merely shrugged at Talmedge and left, closing the door behind him. *Sic transit gloria.*

As always, Jason's first impression of the blood-drawing salon was of its soundlessness. The thick carpet and overstuffed furniture, its paneled walls, all acted to absorb any noise whether it emanated from inside the room or from outside.

When Jason entered, the room's occupants were posed in a sort of *tableau vivant* around a couch at the center of

the room. Senator Chandler lay on the couch, coat off
and tie loosened, his right shirt sleeve rolled up. His eyes
were open, staring, without much conviction, at the ceiling. Jason assumed that the senator was in the postictal
state, the period of decreased consciousness and altered
awareness that follows a grand mal seizure.

Rachel sat on the couch beside her brother. Talmedge,
looking very worried, stood near the senator's head. The
only other person in the room was Helen, the lady who
did all the blood drawing on VIP's. Timid and self-effacing
as ever, she stood nervously to one side.

"Thank you for coming, Jason." Rachel's voice bore the
same concern evident on her face.

As Jason approached the couch, Rachel rose to her feet
to make room. Jason checked the senator's pulse. It was
strong and regular with a rate of approximately one hundred beats per minute.

"Could you get me a blood-pressure cuff, please?" Jason
asked Helen. She nodded and left the room. Jason turned
again to Senator Chandler. "How do you feel, Senator?"

"I'm fine." The senator's voice was weak. He continued
to look upward toward the ceiling.

"Do you know where you are, Senator Chandler?"

"I'm at the Marsden Clinic, in the blood-drawing
room."

"Can you tell me what day it is, Senator?"

"It's Monday, March the twenty-third."

Senator Chandler was surprisingly well oriented for
someone who'd just had a seizure, but his mind seemed
focused elsewhere. Just then Helen reappeared with the
blood-pressure cuff. The senator's blood pressure was 160

over 90, slightly on the high side but certainly not acutely dangerous. Jason performed a cursory neurologic exam that revealed no abnormalities.

"Can anyone tell me what happened?"

It was Talmedge who answered. "The senator had just rolled up his sleeve to have his blood drawn when the seizure started. Helen hadn't started to take any blood—hadn't even put the tourniquet on—before it happened."

"Did you witness the entire seizure?" Jason asked Helen. She gave Talmedge a frightened, questioning look before answering.

"I guess so. The senator just started turning his head, and his tongue sort of stuck out."

"Is that all? Was there any movement of his arms or legs?"

Again Helen looked at Talmedge. "I'm not sure. His arms and legs may have been kind of shaking."

It didn't appear that Helen was going to be of much help. Jason turned his attention back to the senator. "How are you feeling now?"

Senator Chandler looked at Jason as though for the first time. His eyes now seemed quite alert. "Oh, hello, Dr. Andrews. I'm fine. What's all the ruckus about?"

"You seem to have had some kind of seizure, Senator." The senator's cobwebs were obviously clearing quickly now. "Are you experiencing any headache? Any weakness?"

"No. Like I said, I'm just fine. Can I sit up?"

The senator swung his feet onto the floor, sitting up without difficulty, then seemed to notice his sister for the first time. "Hi. Did they think I was going to die or something?"

Rachel only smiled and shook her head.

"Don't try to stand yet," Jason cautioned. "I think we should put you in a wheelchair and get you downstairs into an examining room where I can do a more complete examination, and we can do an EKG and perhaps some other tests."

"Do you think all that is necessary?" Talmedge wanted to know.

"Yes, I do," Jason said, feeling that was all the explanation Talmedge needed.

By the time he examined him downstairs, the senator was, as nearly as Jason could tell, back to normal. The neurological examination revealed no deficits. Senator Chandler's memory was now entirely normal, except that he could remember nothing about what had happened in the blood-drawing salon—which was exactly what you expected in someone who had experienced a seizure. The senator's history revealed no drugs, prescription or otherwise, that might have caused a seizure. There was no history of head trauma. There was no history of anything that sounded like diabetes, and a stat blood sugar which Jason drew himself was entirely normal.

In fact, the only unexpected finding was a tiny mark on the inside of Senator Chandler's elbow that looked for all the world like a recent venipuncture. But Talmedge had been very clear that no blood had been drawn upstairs. Why in the world would he lie about such a thing? Remembering how frightened Helen had appeared and how medically unsophisticated Talmedge was, Jason supposed it was possible that the seizure had occurred *while* Helen was drawing blood, and that Talmedge had lied out of fear that the clinic might in some way be held liable. Unfortunately, the hole in the Senator's memory meant that he would be of no help in explaining the mark on his arm.

"What I would like to do, Senator, is refer you to Dr. Klein at the university in Charlottesville. He can do some additional tests, like a CT or an MRI, and do his own neurological examination."

"Could I just make an appointment to see him next week? I have appointments in Washington later this afternoon and a very important meeting of the Appropriations Committee tomorrow morning."

Jason put the sternest tone he could muster into his voice. "I would strongly recommend that you see Dr. Klein or one of his colleagues *today*. I would like to call the university right now and set it up. A first seizure in a man your age could be a symptom of a very serious underlying disease."

The senator yielded, and Jason was able to make an appointment with Klein. The neurologist was as mystified as Jason had been by the history.

"I also drew a prolactin level," Jason told Klein, "but we won't have the result until tomorrow."

"Do you think that Senator Chandler might have been malingering?" Dr. Klein wanted to know. The serum-prolactin level was almost always elevated after a true seizure. If a patient claimed to have had a seizure and the prolactin level was normal, there was a very strong possibility that the patient was faking.

"No, Dr. Klein, it's really not that so much. I'm pretty certain that the senator experienced some kind of neurologic event. I'm just not convinced it was a seizure."

Chapter Thirty-three

The meeting with Talmedge had come late in the afternoon of a busy day. No explanation offered. Just the usual summons, Talmedge wanted to see him. Jason's mind had been so focused on his patients that he hadn't even stopped to think about what Talmedge might be up to now. He asked his secretary to let Talmedge know that he would stop by Talmedge's office after he was finished with his patients—if Talmedge was still in the building.

When Jason arrived in his office, Talmedge played a little game of pretending to be so involved with the paperwork on his desk that he didn't even notice that Jason had entered the room. In protest, Jason grabbed what looked like the most comfortable chair in the room and dragged it noisily across the floor right up to Talmedge's desk. Then he sat down heavily and made himself comfortable. When Jason looked up, he noted that he now had Talmedge's complete attention.

"You wanted to see me?" Jason asked.

Talmedge, red-faced, was clearly struggling to control his anger. "I understand you're planning to leave us."

Jason felt like his stomach had been hit with a sledgehammer. Only Rachel had been told that he might leave the clinic, and she had been sworn to secrecy. But she clearly hadn't wasted any time before running to Talmedge with the news of Jason's plans.

Suddenly it was Jason's turn to struggle with a rising tide of anger. Above all, he didn't want to give Talmedge the satisfaction of knowing he'd scored a direct hit.

"What makes you say that?" Jason's voice dripped with indifference.

"Then it's not true?" Talmedge was clearly thrown off balance.

"Of course not. I mean, I'm planning to leave at the end of my sabbatical year, at the end of June, but I have no plans to leave before then. Who told you I was leaving?"

"Well, no one in particular. Just one of the administrative people had heard a rumor . . ."

"Was there anything else?" Jason rose to his feet in a show of impatience.

"You're still coming to the dedication, then?" It wasn't clear if Talmedge had some reason to care about this or was just backing and filling.

"Of course."

"Well, then I'll see that my secretary sends an invitation to your office. . . ." Talmedge's voice trailed off. The meeting was over.

Jason left his comfortable chair right where it was and walked silently out of Talmedge's office. He took the elevator down to the first floor, walked out the front door, and got in his car. Then he started driving.

He drove west and then he drove south. He had in

mind to get off by himself, to get some kind of handle on the sandstorm of emotions that clouded his brain. But mostly he just drove, and an hour later he found himself somewhere in the middle of nowhere, enveloped in darkness and in the midst of a driving, blinding rainstorm. He slowed his car to a crawl, the practical necessity of dealing with the weather forcing his mind back to the present and bringing into sharp focus the inevitable decision that his mind had been struggling to avoid. He had to deal with Rachel. There was no point in putting it off. All the evidence was in, and it was too conclusive to ignore.

Rachel had betrayed his confidence, that much was certain. And her betrayal had far-reaching implications. It exposed Rachel's involvement with Talmedge and whatever else was going on at the clinic. Rachel's claim that her computer was contaminated by a virus had raised Jason's suspicions; her betrayal of his confidence had confirmed them.

Jason began to search for a safe spot to turn the car around. He found himself on a winding rural road cut through a broadleaf forest. The only light his eyes could find emanated from his own car, and the swath of light which his headlights would otherwise have cut through the darkness was sharply truncated by walls of rain.

Finally he found a narrow dirt road that ran away from the highway to the east. As he turned his car, Jason's full attention was fixed on the tiny dirt path, taking care above all else not to get his tires mired in the mud out here in the middle of nowhere. As he shifted into reverse to back onto the highway, Jason did look each way, but he saw nothing except the imprisoning darkness. But it wouldn't have made any difference. No matter how hard he looked, he would never have seen the other car.

Jason backed the car out blindly, his back-up lights hopelessly inadequate against the encroaching darkness and sheets of driving rain. By the time he had his front wheels back on pavement, the rest of his car was almost totally blocking the narrow two-lane highway. Then suddenly, as though God had thrown a switch, Jason's entire world was bathed in painful, glaring brightness. Stunned and helpless, Jason squinted into the oncoming light and tried to force his mind to understand what was going on, tried to will his hands to do something.

He sat there, paralyzed, for perhaps no more than some small fraction of a second, and then came a pounding surge of adrenaline and Jason was in motion. He rammed the car into gear and crushed the accelerator with his foot. At the same instant he turned the steering wheel hard to the left. The car fishtailed wildly, uncontrollably, on the rain-slickened pavement, and as the rear end swung around, Jason jerked the wheel back to the right in an effort to control the slide. For a fraction of a second the two cars were parallel, headed in opposite directions, each in its own lane. Jason could clearly see the other driver, and for the briefest of instants their eyes locked. It was a moment that would remain forever fixed in Jason's memory—as firmly fixed as any photograph.

The overwhelming impression Jason had of the other driver during that instant was one of complete composure, as though this kind of terror were for him an everyday event. It was only much later that Jason would remember that face as vaguely familiar.

And then the moment was over. Despite his efforts Jason's car continued its spin. The back end swung around and pushed the front into the other lane. Jason felt a violent shock followed by the high-pitched scream of tearing steel as the front end of his car struck the rear end of the passing car. He now had his foot off the accelerator and his front wheels pointing straight ahead. Jason could do nothing but hang on while the car continued to slide. It finally came to rest at the completion of a 360-degree circle. When he looked back over his shoulder, the other car had disappeared.

Chapter Thirty-four

Jason shook off the urge to pursue the other car. If the man didn't want to stop, that was pretty much his business. A court of law would likely decide that the accident was Jason's fault. After all, he'd backed out clear across the road. But *why* hadn't the other man stopped? *That* was difficult to explain.

The rain was beginning to slacken as Jason headed northward. Finally he found a brightly lighted farmyard where he could pull over and survey the damage to his car, which was not as severe as he had imagined. Perhaps he had overdramatized the entire episode. The left front bumper was dented and the left front quarter panel had been accordioned back. The tire looked okay, but Jason would not be surprised to hear that the wheel was out of alignment. The hood was slightly sprung. The headlights seemed still to be pointed in roughly the right direction. All in all, not as bad as it might have been.

It was not, in the end, a conscious decision, but Jason soon found himself back behind the wheel, headed toward Rachel's house. No matter how he cut it, today had not been one of his better days. A few more like it and Jason figured he'd be ready to join some of his more dysfunctional patients—in a quiet room with no sharp edges. So he couldn't hurt himself. If he went ahead and dealt with Rachel now, got that difficult part out of the way, tomorrow could only be better. It wasn't until he knocked on Rachel's door that Jason fully realized that he didn't have a clue how he was going to approach her.

"Jason." It was after nine o'clock, but Rachel was still wearing the same dress she'd worn at the clinic that day. "This is a surprise." Her tone was pleasant. In a less cynical mood Jason would have said she sounded pleased.

In that first brief moment Jason felt the familiar flood of warm feelings. This was a woman he had, at the very least, *almost* loved. But she had turned out to be someone he could not love, someone he could not risk loving. Her loyalty to Talmedge was greater than her loyalty to him, and the implications of that statement were, to say the least, unsettling.

"Rachel, we have to talk."

Her expression immediately changed, her anxiety evident. As she led the way to the living room she said, "It's Rob, isn't it? Dr. Klein called from the university."

"No, Rachel. Your brother's fine, as near as we can tell. All the tests are negative." Including the prolactin level— which meant that whatever Senator Chandler had experienced, it wasn't a grand mal seizure. But that was a worry for another day.

Jason hesitated. Rachel filled the vacuum: "What?"

"It's about us."

"I've had a feeling this was coming." Spoken with equal measures of accusation and resignation.

Part of Jason wanted to go for the jugular, tell her what he knew and what he thought of her. But a bigger part of him still wanted to deny the evidence, wanted to be gentle with her, wanted very badly not to burn any bridges. "I guess I'm just not sure about us—where we are, where we're going."

Rachel smiled weakly. "Is this the *Commitment Talk?*"

"No." Jason shook his head. "This is the *Jason doesn't know what he's doing or where he's going talk.*" It was a lie. He wondered if Rachel knew it was a lie.

"Then it doesn't sound like there's really very much to talk about." There was now an angry edge to her voice that Jason hadn't heard before. He could only shrug in response.

"I thought I should probably pick up my stuff, get it out of your way."

"You know where it is."

There didn't seem to be much more to say. Jason turned and left the living room, then headed up the stairs. He went into the bedroom and opened the closet, pulled out a couple of shirts and collected an old pair of boots that he wore when they went for walks around the property. He opened a drawer, "his" drawer, and collected a sweater and some socks. There was some stuff in the bathroom, but he decided not to bother with it. He hadn't really come to pick up his personal effects. That was merely the excuse he'd used.

Jason started to leave the room, but stopped and turned to look one last time. A lot of memories. It was his favorite room in the house, for more than just the obvious reason. Rachel had done a good job of making the room warm and comfortable and had avoided making it over-poweringly feminine. There was a large Colonial fireplace and a big pine bed and soft carpeting on the floor. The room had character and class and looked as though it would endure through the years. Not a bad metaphor for a relationship, or a marriage.

Jason turned to find Rachel standing at the top of the stairs, watching him. He hadn't heard her come up. Her eyes seemed slightly moist. He couldn't be sure.

"Do you want to tell me what this is really all about, Jason?"

"I told you."

She shook her head to express her disbelief. "Have I done something wrong? Are you angry with me about something?"

"It's not you, Rachel. Like I told you, it's just me." As he said it, he almost believed it.

"Then why do I feel so guilty, Jason?"

Maybe you should answer that one, Jason thought. Still, as he stood there at her bedroom door, not three feet away from her, he was nearly overwhelmed by the desire to take her in his arms once again and ignore all the warnings his brain had been sending.

But instead he said, "I guess I'd better be going," and brushed past Rachel on his way down the stairs.

Jason didn't look back until he was at the front door, the handle in his grasp. Then he turned to Rachel, wanting to say *I'm sorry.* Instead he said simply, "Good-bye."

Rachel's only response was to very slowly shake her head.

Jason opened the front door and found himself standing face to face with Charles Talmedge.

"Dr. Andrews." If Talmedge was surprised, his voice did not reveal it.

"Charles." It was Rachel's voice, now just behind Jason. Her inflection was identical to that she'd used when he'd arrived and she'd said, "Jason."

For the second time that day Jason felt as though he'd been kicked in the stomach. He gave Rachel one last inquiring look, then walked out into the night.

Chapter Thirty-five

When Jason arrived home, the first thing he did was throw a couple of ice cubes into a glass and pour some bourbon on top of them. He figured he'd earned it. The next thing he did was sit himself down and try to figure out what the hell was going on in his life. Hell, what did he even *think* was going on? Some kind of conspiracy? Involving the clinic, and Talmedge, and now Rachel? Conspiracy to do what?

What he needed to do, as calmly and unemotionally as possible, was to attempt to separate in his mind those things that he knew to be fact from those which he only feared or suspected. Go back to the beginning. Be analytical. Be objective.

Barbara, his ex-wife, had always hated his analytical bent, calling it cold and calculating. When she wanted to fight, he wanted to analyze. And the more he tried to analyze, the angrier she became. Communication became impossible. Just one of their many problems.

But now, alone, this natural inclination asserted itself once again, and he tried to free himself, if only for a little while, from the emotional impact of the breakup with Rachel. Go back to the beginning. Be analytical, unemotional.

At the very beginning, when he first arrived at the clinic, Jason had felt uncomfortable. Too many security guards all over the place. Medical records protected as though they were plans for the D-Day invasion. It had all been explained to him as necessary, unavoidable even, in view of the very special requirements of the clinic's clientele. He tried to be objective. Did he have any evidence whatsoever that security at the clinic was related to anything nefarious? He did not. And there was no doubt in Jason's mind that it was his apprehension over clinic security which laid the foundation for his other suspicions. If you've decided a house is haunted and you begin to hear chains rattling, you're bound to think of ghosts.

Then there'd been the deaths of the vice-president and Hiram Bates. There didn't seem to be much doubt that Herbert Allen had committed suicide. His wife confirmed that the vice-president had undergone a dramatic personality change *after* he visited the clinic, but there was nothing to link that to the clinic itself. Congressman Bates' widow seemed convinced that her husband had been murdered—not that the idea upset her very much. Again, no clear link to the clinic.

Congressman Parker. Now, there was a lobotomy looking for a place to happen. If Jason worried that he himself might be getting just a little bit paranoid, all he had to do was think about Parker. The man showed all the classic signs of paranoid schizophrenia. So why had somebody bothered to blow up his house? The congressman comes into the clinic raving about some conspiracy to overthrow the government, and that night somebody detonates enough plastic explosive in his house to level the Pentagon. Why? Did someone take him seriously, think he was on to something? Not much point in attempting to talk to the congressman about it. Even with the help of Psychoden, Parker didn't have the mental agility of a tossed salad.

Still in all, it was pretty difficult to discount the Parker episode. It was only sheer luck that both of the Parkers hadn't been home at the time of the explosion. Ironically, Congressman Parker, despite his obvious psychosis, had provided Jason with his strongest evidence that *something* was going on, and that that something was somehow linked to the clinic.

And if there was something going on at the clinic, Talmedge was certain to be at the center of it. Which brought Jason back, full circle, to Rachel . . .

The doorbell rang. Jason made an effort to answer it, but he could hardly move. It was as though he were trying to walk under ten feet of water. Then he realized he wasn't moving. He was sitting down. More ringing. The phone. It could be the phone. One more ring and Jason was almost certain it was the phone.

He picked up the receiver. He heard a voice, a woman's voice. Rachel? No, it was Barbara. Why would Barbara be calling?

"Are you awake, Dr. Andrews?"

Jason made some garbled response.

"I've been trying to call you all evening," the caller continued. "I assumed you were out—didn't think you'd had time to get home and get to sleep."

The cobwebs were slowly clearing. Jason eyed his glass of bourbon suspiciously, but he'd had only a couple of sips. He must have been in deep REM sleep when the phone rang. He still had no idea who was on the phone. It wasn't Barbara, his ex-wife. He wasn't sure why he'd thought it was Barbara.

"I'm terribly sorry," Jason's sense of place and time was slowly returning. "I'm afraid I was sound asleep. Who did you say was calling?"

"Barbara Bates, Congressman Bates' widow. You came by to ask me some questions after my husband's death."

"Of course, Mrs. Bates." Jason stood up and blinked his eyes a few times to assure himself that he really was awake now and that he really was talking to Congressman Bates' widow on the phone. "I'm very sorry. I was just sitting here on the couch thinking, and I must have dozed off. I'm wide awake now. What can I do for you?"

"I found something I thought might interest you." Her voice sounded rather matter-of-fact. "Actually, I called the FBI this afternoon. I believe I told you that the director had paid me a visit. Anyway, they said he was out of town, and he would just call me back tomorrow if it wasn't an emergency. I told them I didn't think it was an emergency; then I got to thinking that maybe you're the one I should have called in the first place, since it involves the clinic. So I called the clinic late this afternoon, and they said you were gone for the day, so I left a message for you. Then I decided maybe it would be all right to give you a call at home and let you know what I found, see if you could make heads or tails out of it."

"I'd be happy to help you in any way I can, Mrs. Bates. Just what is it you've found?"

"Well, Doctor, you know I thought I'd long since thrown out everything in the house that had anything at all to do with my husband. I'd cleared out his papers, given all his clothes to the Salvation Army. There's still a desk and some other things in the room he used as an office—that I'm thinking will make a very nice sewing room someday.

"Anyway, I was cleaning up in there, dusting and what not, when I found this envelope. It had gotten shoved up under the blotter on his desk, I guess, and never got thrown away. Well, I was just about to do that, throw it away—just an old empty envelope with a return address of some insurance company—when I happened to notice there was some writing on the back.

"Now, my husband was a doodler." Mrs. Bates paused, then said, "Are you there, Dr. Andrews? You haven't fallen asleep on me, have you?"

"I'm right here, Mrs. Bates, and I'm all ears."

"Let's see, where was I? Oh, yes, Hiram was a doodler. Nonstop. Did it all the time. You'd see him on C-span, chairing his committee, and you'd think he was taking notes for all he was worth, but he wasn't. Just doodling. He told me there was nothing more boring than his damn committee meetings. He had to do something to stay awake. So anyway, the back of this envelope is filled up with his doodling, which I was going to throw away anyway, but then I noticed that right at the top it said 'Marsden Clinic.' He'd gone over and over the letters with his ballpoint pen. I'm surprised he didn't wear a hole in the paper.

"Anyway, that's what caught my attention, the 'Marsden Clinic,' because you had come to see me and said you were from the clinic. I was still about to throw it away when I noticed some of the other writing. It just all seemed a little more deliberate than Hiram's usual doodling.

"Right below where he'd written Marsden Clinic, Hiram had written GERALD, in big capital letters. Then under that there's a list of sort of who's who in Washington. The first name—you can hardly make it out, it's crossed out so many times—is Herb Allen. Then there's a bunch of other names, written and crossed out, starting with Senator Saunders. Then there's a whole lot of names not crossed out, ending with Senator Chandler. Right below that, with a big circle drawn around it, Hiram's written his own name real big, Hiram P. Bates." Barbara Bates stopped once again, maybe to let it all sink in, maybe just to catch her breath. "Can you make anything of that, Doctor?"

"Not off the top of my head, Mrs. Bates, but that doesn't mean I don't think it's important. I'd like very much to see the envelope, maybe even make a copy of it, if that would be all right with you."

"You can have it as far as I'm concerned, Doctor. If the FBI wants it, they can get it from you."

A thought occurred to Jason. "What's the date on the postmark?"

"I should have mentioned that," Mrs. Bates admonished

herself. "The letter is dated six days before Hiram's death."

"Which means he must have made those notes within two to three days of his death," Jason said, thinking out loud. "When could I see the envelope, Mrs. Bates?"

"That's why I wanted to talk to you tonight, Doctor. I'm down here in Virginia visiting my sister. Brought the envelope with me. I'm planning to drive back north yet tonight, so I'd be happy to meet you somewhere and let you have it."

They arranged a convenient place to meet, and as Jason hung up the phone, he actually believed that he was finally going to gain some insight into whatever it was that the Marsden Clinic was trying to hide. It did not occur to him that neither he nor, for that matter, the FBI would ever lay eyes on Hiram Bates' doodling.

Chapter Thirty-six

The rain was beginning once again in earnest as Jason walked to his car. It was nearly eleven o'clock and the sky was starless. A darker night was not possible. He had worried to Mrs. Bates that she shouldn't be out driving at this time of night, in this weather. She said, nonsense, she'd become quite a night owl since her husband's death. Besides, she'd be driving back to Maryland tonight anyway. Might as well meet Jason and let him have the envelope.

Jason hurried in behind the wheel and slammed the door. He gave the ignition key a turn. Nothing. He tried again. Again, nothing. He turned on the headlights. They seemed to work fine, so the battery probably wasn't the problem. Something must have gotten damaged in the collision.

With some effort Jason was able to pry open the sprung hood. He was no mechanic, and he was working in almost total darkness. About all he could do was try to make certain there were no loose connections, try to wiggle a few of the wires and hope he got lucky. After a few trips between the driver's seat and the engine, he was successful, but he was certainly going to be late for his rendezvous with Mrs. Bates. Since she was already en route, he didn't have any way to get hold of her. There was nothing for him to do but get in the car and drive.

The going was slow, because of the rain, and thirty minutes later Jason found himself caught in a developing traffic jam only a few miles from where he was to meet Mrs. Bates. He was on a two-way section of highway in a semi-rural area. The speed limit was forty-five miles per hour, but cars typically moved along this stretch of highway a lot faster than that. Now traffic had slowed to a crawl. Up ahead he could see congestion, probably an accident. No police lights yet, but Jason thought he could hear a siren in the distance.

Jason looked at his watch. He was already ten minutes late for his meeting with Mrs. Bates, but it was very likely that there would be no one else with medical training at the scene. There was no question but that he would stop and offer whatever help he could. About fifty yards from the scene of the accident, he pulled his car over behind a couple of other cars that had stopped to offer assistance. Ahead of him he could see what appeared to be a single-car accident. The car had run head-on into a concrete buttress that formed the side of a narrow bridge. A crowd had gathered around the car. A police car was inching its way through traffic from the opposite direction.

"Does anyone here have any medical expertise?" Jason asked the group around the car. He didn't want to intrude if someone already had the situation in hand. But there was a general shaking of heads. Someone said something about having had some first-aid training in high school.

"I'm a doctor," Jason said, and the group made way for him.

The car had only one occupant, a woman whose head was pressed against the steering wheel and turned toward the right, as though she'd been looking in that direction prior to impact. Jason could hear loud airway noises associated with deep respiration, so it appeared that she was breathing adequately. He felt her neck for a carotid pulse. It was strong and regular. Then Jason very gently examined her skull with his fingertips. There was a significant dent in the upper forehead where her head had struck the steering wheel, an obvious skull fracture.

"Are you a doctor?"

Jason turned to see a very large state trooper standing over him. "Yes, I am. I'm Jason Andrews from the Marsden Clinic."

"Is she alive?"

"Yes. She seems to have a depressed skull fracture and she's unconscious, but as near as I can tell she's moving air okay and her heart so far seems to be strong. Obviously, it's awfully hard to know about neck injuries. I'd suggest leaving her right where she is for now since she seems stable. When the ambulance arrives, we can immobilize her neck with a brace before we move her."

"I'll go call it in." And with that the trooper was off to his car.

While he was gone, Jason continued to monitor his patient, making certain her condition didn't change for the worse, requiring him to intervene. The trooper was back in a couple of minutes.

"She still okay?" he asked Jason.

"She still seems stable."

The trooper walked over to the bridge railing. "Anybody look to see if there's another car down there?" It was obvious no one had thought of it. The trooper had one of those big flashlights that looked like you could put ten batteries in the handle. He flashed it into the deep ravine beyond the bridge. "Actually, she's probably lucky she hit the bridge, instead of ending up down there," he said. "Anybody see what happened?"

At first no one commented; then a young man in his twenties said, "I guess I was the first to stop. I didn't see it happen, just saw that the car had hit the bridge." The kid thought a second and then added, "Actually, I wasn't the first to stop. When I pulled over, there was a man leaning in the car door. He took off when I pulled up. I don't know if he was a passenger or someone who had just stopped to see if he could help."

The trooper frowned. "Or to see if he could help himself to anything in the car. We get people stealing from accident scenes all the time," he said. "It's a wonderful world."

"He didn't seem like that kind of a guy," the kid said. "I mean, he was well dressed. Didn't look like he had to steal for a living."

"What'd he look like?"

"Well, I didn't get a very good look, it being so dark and all. He was big, though. Had on a dark suit. He was white."

"Stay here," the trooper told the young man. "I'll need to get a complete statement from you later." And with that he went back to his cruiser to use the radio once more.

When he returned, he began to inspect the accident scene. Then the ambulance arrived, and two more state police cars.

Jason briefed the ambulance crew on the driver's condition, then got out of their way. He was now more than a half hour late for his meeting with Mrs. Bates. He could probably leave the accident scene soon—as soon as the ambulance was on its way.

The medical technicians worked quickly to place a protective collar around the woman's neck and make their own inspection for broken bones and other damage. One of them commented, "She seems to have been pretty fortunate except for the head injury. If her car had an air bag, she might not have gotten that."

Then, with the help of one of the troopers, they carefully removed her from the car and placed her on a cot. She was strapped down on top of a flat board, and her head was blocked to prevent any movement that might cause further injury to her back or neck. When they had completed their work, the technicians stepped back and Jason got his first good look at his patient. It was a face he had seen only once before in his life, but it was a face he instantly recognized. Barbara Bates.

"Dr. Andrews?" The sound of the vaguely familiar voice threw Jason even further off balance. "Walt Briggs." The state trooper offered his hand.

"Hello, Lieutenant. How are you?"

"I'm fine, Doctor. You involved in this?"

"I was just driving by and saw the accident. I stopped to see if I could be of any help."

At that moment the trooper who'd arrived first at the scene walked up to them.

"What've you got?" Briggs asked.

"Pretty obvious hit-and-run, Lieutenant." The trooper flashed his light on the side of Barbara Bates' car. "You can see here along the door and front quarter panel where there's paint scraped off the other car, and the car's front wheels are turned into the bridge instead of away from it. What I figure happened is that another car tried to pass, then had to get out of the way of oncoming traffic and tried to squeeze back into the right-hand lane. The lady turned away from him and went right into the bridge.

"Only a couple of things that are kind of unusual," the trooper continued. "One is, a young man here, Mr. Jackson, says when he arrived at the scene, there was some guy leaning in the driver's side door, but he ran off. And when we searched the car, we couldn't find any identification, registration, anything like that. There was no purse or valuables—except the lady was wearing a watch and a couple of rings."

Briggs motioned for the other trooper to give him his flashlight, then began his own examination of Mrs. Bates' car. He looked closely where the two cars had collided. "Black paint," he said. "It's probably not going to be very helpful that the other car was painted black. Maybe we'll get lucky on the make. You check the license plates?"

"I called it in, but it's Maryland, so I haven't heard back yet."

"Barbara Bates," Jason hear himself say. "The woman's name is Barbara Bates. I didn't get a look at her face until just now when they finally had her ready to go into the

ambulance. Her husband was Hiram Bates, the congressman. I met him once at the clinic."

"How do you know Mrs. Bates?" Briggs didn't miss a
trick.

"Her husband died under strange circumstances—
possible suicide. I had seen him at the clinic shortly before his death and hadn't detected the slightest indication
of any suicidal tendency, so I met with Mrs. Bates to see
if I'd missed something. It was her opinion that her husband had been murdered."

"The police check that out?" Briggs wanted to know.

"I'm not sure anyone but Mrs. Bates thought it was
murder, but I do know that in addition to the local police,
she got a visit from the FBI." Jason let that sink in before
saying, "It gets even stranger.

"Mrs. Bates called me tonight, said she'd found some
doodling her husband had done on the back of an envelope that might have something to do with his death."

"Why'd she call you? Why not the police?"

"Actually, her first thought was to contact the FBI. She
said she'd left a message at the director's office. He was
out of town and was supposed to call her tomorrow. She
called me when she couldn't get hold of the director because one of the things he'd doodled was the name of the
clinic."

"What else did the good congressman doodle?"

"It was a list of names, Lieutenant. Political figures. I
frankly didn't pay as much attention as I should have because I thought I was going to see the list in an hour or
so. Mrs. Bates said she was visiting her sister near here
and wanted to show me the list before she drove back to

Maryland. I was coming to meet her when I came upon the accident."

Briggs turned again to the other trooper. "You find any envelopes, anything like that in the car?"

The trooper shook his head. "We found zilch, Lieutenant."

"We'll have to search the car one more time, also check the lady's personal effects at the hospital, see if we can come up with anything. Doc, you got any idea what that list might mean?"

"Not really, Lieutenant. Like I said, I wish I had paid more attention."

Jason gave Briggs his best memory of Mrs. Bates' address. Sorry, he didn't have a clue about the sister. He promised to think about the envelope and see if he could recall anything more. Briggs said maybe he ought to try taking that Psychoden drug. It might help his memory some. Then Briggs was on to other aspects of the investigation, and Jason was free to go.

Something new began to worry Jason as he headed home. The first thing he did when he got back to his place was to go inside and get a flashlight, then come back out to have a good look at his car. It didn't take long to find what he was looking for. Right there on the front quarter panel, just behind the bumper. Black paint.

Chapter Thirty-seven

"How are you today, Senator Albright?"

"Just fine, Doctor. Never felt better." Somehow, Jason wasn't surprised by the senator's response—or by his wife's reaction.

"Don't you *dare* listen to him, Doctor. He's as bad as ever. Wouldn't even brush his teeth if I didn't tell him to." If there was an ounce of sympathy or understanding in Lillian Albright's tiny body, it was very cleverly concealed.

Jason had spent a sleepless night, one minute telling himself that his own life was in danger, that he had landed in the middle of some anti-government plot; the next minute convincing himself that it was all just his imagination. He couldn't deny Barbara Bates' injury, but was it simple hit-and-run or attempted murder? The envelope had disappeared, but so had her purse. It could have been a simple theft, but by a man dressed in a suit? Jason had convinced himself that it was ridiculous to believe that there was any link between Mrs. Bates' automobile accident and the collision he'd been involved in earlier in the evening. The only common denominator was the black paint—a pretty thin thread to tie the two together.

The good news was that Mrs. Bates was out of surgery and seemed to be stable. Her neurosurgeon thought that her prognosis was reasonably good. Beyond that there was really no news at all. The police didn't seem to have any leads on the car that had hit Mrs. Bates. No envelope had been found. Her sister had confirmed that Mrs. Bates had had a purse with her when she left the sister's house. The purse was still missing.

All Jason had was a series of disturbing events stretching back over a period of several months. If they were all linked together by some terrible conspiracy, what was its purpose? He hadn't even begun to think about that.

For now Jason tried to sequester all those suspicions and worries somewhere in the back of his brain so that he could focus his full attention on the problem at hand. The senator and Mrs. Albright deserved no less than that.

"Why don't you go ahead and give him that Psycho drug right now," Lillian Albright suggested, "so we can find out what's wrong with him?"

Jason took a deep breath. "What works best, Mrs. Albright, is if I do the Psychoden interview alone with the patient. Having other family members in the room tends to be distracting." Another issue, which Jason chose not to voice out loud, was that under the influence of Psychoden the senator might verbalize something that he wouldn't want his wife to hear. "Why don't you go get a cup of coffee and have a seat in the waiting room? We'll have a talk after the interview is over."

She agreed, with some reluctance.

As soon as she was gone, Jason turned to his patient. "If you're ready, Senator Albright, we can go ahead and place the Psychoden patch."

"Ready when you are, Doctor." The senator's spirits seemed instantly raised by his wife's departure.

Jason quickly had the Psychoden patch in place, then waited a few moments for the drug to take effect before beginning the usual questions.

"What is your name, sir?"

"Hollis Horatio Albright," in that far-off Psychoden drone, "named after my maternal grandfather." The bit at the end was typical of the expansiveness patients tended to demonstrate while under the influence of Psychoden.

"When were you born?"

"January the thirteenth, nineteen hundred and nine."

"Where were you born?"

"Shelby County, Kentucky. On my daddy's horse farm."

"What kind of work do you do?"

"I do the people's work. I am a United States senator."

"Can you tell me what today's date is, Senator?"

There was no response. The senator merely stared into the distance as though he hadn't heard the question.

"What day of the week is it, Senator Albright?" Again there was no response. "Senator, when were you first elected to public office?"

There was no hesitation. "November the sixth, nineteen hundred and forty-seven. I was elected United States senator. It is the only public office I've ever held."

"What did you have for breakfast this morning, Senator?"

Once again there was no response. As Jason continued

the questioning, the pattern remained the same. Senator Albright could remember minute details of long ago experiences, but he had almost no memory of recent events. This made it extremely unlikely that the senator was suffering from depression or a psychosis of any type.

Remembering only remote events is typical of Alzheimer's disease. Patients can remember where they were born, but not where they were yesterday. They may be able to function reasonably well for months or even years in familiar surroundings, but put them in a hotel room and they may not be able to find the bathroom.

Jason did not look forward to sharing the news with the senator's wife. "There is no specific test for Alzheimer's disease," he told her. "It's what we call a diagnosis of exclusion. After we have excluded other possibilities, then we can be reasonably confident we're dealing with Alzheimer's. So I'll want to order a number of tests, which, quite honestly, I expect to be negative."

As he talked, he saw quite a remarkable change come over Mrs. Albright. Her voice softened. There appeared to be the beginnings of tears in the corners of her eyes. She began to comb her fingers through her husband's sparse hair as though she were smoothing it, but clearly it was a gesture filled with affection.

"What's going to happen to him, Doctor? Will he ever get better?"

"If this *is* Alzheimer's, then it's likely that he'll have some good days and some bad days, but over time his memory problems—and even his ability to care for himself—are going to get worse. How quickly that will happen, I can't say. It could be weeks or months." Jason felt compelled to state the obvious, "I think he's already at a point where he can't be expected to function as a senator, or even manage his own affairs."

"Is there any medication which might be of help?"

"Not for the underlying brain process. That's due to loss of the ability of his brain cells to function. Sometimes, when there is a significant element of depression—as there may be in the senator's case—giving the patient anti-depressant medication can be useful, but eventually the disease progresses."

The senator's wife received this information in thoughtful silence. "You know, Doctor," she said, "I thought he was just being moody, that he was mad at me for something." At least at one level, Mrs. Albright was actually relieved by the diagnosis.

"Part of his moodiness," Jason explained, "is his own frustration with his inability to remember things. You told me during your last visit that all he wanted to talk about was the good old days. There's a good reason for that. That's all he can remember."

Jason tried to demonstrate the senator's memory problem for his wife. "Can you tell me what day it is today, Senator?" Senator Albright seemed not to have heard the question. "What day is it today, Senator?"

"I'm not going to answer stupid questions like that!"

Jason turned to Mrs. Albright. "It's a way for him to hide his loss of memory." Then, turning back to the senator, "Senator Albright, I once heard a story about you, that you once read from the Bible for two straight days on the Senate floor."

That actually brought a smile to the senator's face. "I

knew those hypocrites wouldn't have the guts to stop me reading the Bible. I could have gone on for a month."

Jason's next question came unsummoned from the back of his brain. It was as though the two worlds that Jason was straddling suddenly collided and created a single shining star.

"Senator Albright, who is Gerald?"

The senator didn't hesitate for an instant. "That's a stupid question. Gerald Ford, of course. Thirty-eighth president of the United States. The only man ever to hold the office who hadn't been elected to either the presidency or the vice-presidency."

Chapter Thirty-eight

The apple that fell and struck Isaac Newton on the head could not have brought with it more revelation than Hollis Albright's mention of Gerald Ford's name. Suddenly, bits of the puzzle began to fit together. The significance of the code name "Gerald" was only one piece, but it was a very central part of the puzzle, and several other pieces fit into it very nicely.

Darkness had long since fallen outside the clinic. Jason sat at his desk, pretending to be hard at work on a stack of patient charts. His secretary had left nearly three hours ago. The janitor had come and gone. Jason had said that he was too busy to permit more than a cursory cleaning of his office. The janitor appeared to have no problem with that. Now Jason was left alone, waiting for the right time to make one more assault on the clinic's computer files.

Jason understood that Senator Albright didn't have a clue that there was a conspiracy afoot. Senator Albright couldn't tell you what color his socks were—without looking. Alzheimer's disease had deprived him of the ability to make new memories. Albright had simply looked back into his dusty file of old memories and come up with the

one association he knew. The name Gerald rang, only one
bell. Gerald Ford.

If the senator had stopped there, perhaps Jason would
not have made the connection. But Senator Albright had,
with typical Psychoden expansiveness, embellished his answer, reminding Jason that Gerald Ford had been *appointed*, not elected. The rest had been easy for Jason. No
heavy lifting required.

Since Herbert Allen's death the vice-presidency had
been vacant. Any day now the President would be nomi-
nating a replacement, to be confirmed by the Senate.
Hiram Bates' list, on the back of the purloined envelope,
showed that Bates was either part of the conspiracy or
had somehow stumbled onto it. According to his wife,
Congressman Bates had written his own name at the end
of the list and put a big circle around it, suggesting that
Hiram Bates had decided that he himself should play the
role of Gerald. The untimely death of Congressman Bates
suggested that others had not shared his view.

Jason tried to remember what other names Mrs. Bates
had said were on the list. Herbert Allen, for sure. The late
vice-president's name had been at the top, crossed out
many times. Senator Chandler, Rachel's brother, was also
on the list. Was it just above Hiram Bates' name? Jason
couldn't remember. But the appearance of the Chandler
name on the list only made Jason all the more suspicious
of Rachel.

And somewhere at the top of the envelope, Bates had
written "Marsden Clinic." Did that mean Arthur Marsden
was involved? Jason wanted to believe that he wasn't. He
wanted to believe that with Arthur Marsden, what you

saw was what you got. But sometimes Marsden seemed just too stereotypical, too much a caricature of the absent-minded professor. Marsden's long periods of distraction were punctuated by episodes of remarkable lucidity that seemed entirely out of character.

What about that supposed sham Psychoden demonstration that had made Rachel's boyfriend suspicious—the boyfriend who had then rather conveniently died in an auto accident? Had Marsden staged another fake Psychoden interview for Jason's benefit that day in his office? What was that all about? "Ask me anything," Marsden's note had said. If Arthur had thought that Jason was suspicious, he might have expected Jason to take the opportunity to get Marsden to incriminate himself. After all, under the influence of Psychoden, Marsden could tell only the truth, and Jason wouldn't need to worry that Marsden would remember anything after the interview. Perhaps Marsden had not been under the influence of Psychoden at all. He merely wanted Jason to think he was. Jason would ask probing questions, and Marsden would supply the answers he wanted Jason to hear. Because he believed Marsden to be on Psychoden, Jason would assume that Arthur had told him the truth. It was like cheating on a lie-detector test.

In the end, Jason decided he'd have to put a question mark beside Marsden's name. But Charles Talmedge was no question mark. Jason was prepared to believe nearly anything about Talmedge. *Necrophiliac of the Year* honors? That's our Charlie.

How was the Marsden Clinic involved? The obvious thing about the clinic was that it provided access to politicians of every stripe. They all came to the clinic. Then what? Jason's hunch was that the answer lay in those closely guarded computer files.

He looked at his watch: 8:30. Time to make his move. By this time of night, almost everyone would have left the clinic. If Jason waited much longer, the lateness of the hour would only serve to draw more attention to himself and arouse suspicion. He picked up the stack of folders from his desk, put them under his arm, and set off for the medical records room.

When he stepped from the elevator on the top floor, Jason was confronted almost immediately by a blue-blazered security man.

"Good evening," Jason said, putting on a smile that would have done the Cheshire cat proud. The man nodded but didn't speak. Jason could feel eyes boring into his back as he walked down the long hall toward medical records. Inside the records room, Jason took a seat at the table provided for doctors to review charts. He spread out his folders as though he were settling in for a long read, then sat down to wait.

The doctors' working area was maybe twenty feet by forty feet. Along one wall was a set of shelves filled with files. These were the files of recent patients. Most of them contained dictated notes that needed a doctor's signature. Once signed, the charts would be filed. The far end of the room opened into another, smaller room that was a secretarial area. The two rooms were separated by a divided door. The top half of the door was usually open, and the lower half was topped by a flat surface that served as a counter. In a corner of the doctors' working area was a small desk with a computer terminal on it. Jason found himself continually eyeing the terminal as he waited.

Nearly ten minutes passed before Jason heard what he was waiting for, the sound of muffled footsteps on the hallway carpet. Jason tried to appear startled as he turned, as though he'd been disturbed from deep concentration. The security man stood in the doorway, his hands clasped behind his back, a man fully aware of the awesome responsibilities of his office.

"You don't have any idea how to spell 'priapism,' do you?" Jason asked.

The man in the blue blazer shook his head slowly.

Jason put on an expression of frustration. "It's just that Senator Albright has had the problem continuously for the last forty-five years. I think they may have spelled it wrong here in his chart." Sighing heavily, Jason turned back to the chart. He waited for the sound of fading footsteps, then rose quietly and headed for the computer terminal in the corner of the room.

No luck. The keyboard was dead. The screen remained blank no matter what key he hit.

Jason moved quickly to the half door that opened into the secretarial area. Leaning into the other room, he saw a computer terminal tucked into a far corner. This time lady luck was on his side. Even from where he stood, he could see the cursor blinking at him from the monitor screen. The terminal had not been shut down. Jason took a quick look over his shoulder, then vaulted over the half door.

The monitor blinked a question at him: "Account name?" Jason typed in, "Bates, Hiram P." The computer gave him a choice of three different account types: Clinical, Business, Administrative. Jason chose "Clinical" and hit the return key. Instantly, he had access to Bates' entire clinical record.

Jason had no real idea what he was looking for, so he patiently scrolled through the entire computerized chart. When he got to the laboratory results area, there was nothing entered. Why? A battery of blood tests was part of the package. Jason had a vague memory of a conversation with Bates about blood tests. His impression had been that maybe Bates was afraid of needles, but the memory was too distant.

Jason exited the clinical record and pulled down the business record.

Interesting. The clinic's routine charges were listed, but under patient charges, zeros had been entered. Why would Bates have been evaluated for free? Sure, Bates was a powerful and important political figure, but so were most of the clinic's clientele. Why had Bates been treated differently? Jason attempted to pull up the final account, the one labeled "Administrative." The screen went blank except for a single word.

Password:

Jason swore under his breath. The file was protected by password entry. If you didn't know the password, you couldn't get into the file. Passwords could be anything, any length. It might not be a word per se, but rather a sequence of letters or numbers or both. *Aq.39**dt!q*, for example, would be an excellent password. If Talmedge had the IQ of a tuna casserole, Jason wouldn't be able to come up with the password in a million years.

Jason typed "GERALD" and hit the enter key. He was instantly in the file.

Unfortunately, the file was empty. Nada. Zilch.

Jason exited the file and opened a different account, Herbert Allen. He opened the clinical file and looked for something that might indicate why the vice-president had committed suicide. Jason had worried that some terrible test result had come back after the vice-president's clinic visit. Maybe Herbert Allen had found out that he had cancer and become depressed.

Nothing like that in the chart.

Jason moved on to the business file.

For whatever reason, Herbert Allen hadn't rated the free service that Congressman Bates had received. Allen had been sent an impressive bill, which had been promptly paid. Next, Jason selected the administrative account. He entered the Gerald password and hit the return key. Bingo.

The screen was immediately filled with biographical data. The first entries seemed innocent enough: date of birth, place of birth, parents' names and occupations, but much of the rest of the file read like a checklist designed to ferret out potentially compromising activities or behavior patterns. There didn't turn out to be very much of significance about the vice-president himself.

> Drug use: occasional alcohol
> Extramarital affairs: none
> Homosexual activity: none
> Illegal funding: none

The data filled several screens and included information on Allen's net worth, debts, activities during college, and so forth. There was similar data on his wife, all of which was essentially uninteresting, as was the data on the Allens' daughter. Then came the data on their son:

> One son, Herbert, Jr. Drafted and went to Vietnam at the insistence of his father. Son wanted to flee to Canada. Son reported missing in action, presumed dead one year later. This is still the official story. However, former CIA director informed Allen that strong evidence existed that son went voluntarily to Soviet Union and cooperated in anti-American activities. That was twenty years ago. No additional data available.

"Hey! What do you think you're doing?" The security guard had returned.

Jason hit the escape key. The screen was instantly blank. "Just trying to get one of these damn computers to work. You have any idea how to pull up the patient files?" He tried to make his voice as nonchalant as possible.

"You're not supposed to be in there."

"Sorry," Jason said, "the terminal in the doctors' area was dead, so I thought maybe I could get this one to work. No luck." He got up and opened the door, letting himself out of the smaller room. "I guess I'll just have to come back in the morning. Any idea how early someone will be here who could help me?"

The guard shook his head.

Jason filed his charts on the shelf under his own name, then wished the security man a good evening and headed for home.

Chapter Thirty-nine

Jason had spent another sleepless night. He understood that he was now in danger. The security guard would undoubtedly report Jason's unauthorized use of the computer terminal. Someone, probably Talmedge, would put two and two together. Jason had every reason to believe that he was dealing with people capable of murder.

But it wasn't fear that had kept Jason awake. The solution to the puzzle was tantalizingly close. There were still some pieces missing, but it wasn't hard to guess their shape. Jason knew, at least at one level, what was going on. But what could he *prove*? Very little. Perhaps nothing. His case was still far too circumstantial.

The only potential hard evidence was the data in the clinic files. If Jason went to the authorities with what he knew, a judge might well decide that there wasn't even probable cause to issue a warrant to search the clinic's files. And if a search warrant was issued and Talmedge got wind of it, those computer files could be erased in an instant. Then there would be no evidence whatsoever.

So for now Jason had to content himself with brooding over the facts already at hand and trying to come up with some way to find more evidence. What did he know so far? First of all, he knew that the clinic's computers contained files that had no business being there. Someone, presumably Talmedge, was collecting potentially compromising data on clinic patients. Jason assumed, but did not know for certain, that there were many such files, perhaps one for each patient.

Second, he knew that Vice-President Allen had resigned and then killed himself. It was not unreasonable to assume that blackmail, related to his son's activities, had led to the vice-president's actions.

Hiram Bates was dead, probably murdered. The envelope he left behind suggested that Bates had tried to place himself into position to succeed Vice-President Allen. Maybe Bates had tried to use a little blackmail himself, and it had cost him his life. His wife's discovery of the envelope had placed her life in jeopardy. The one good piece of news in all this was the hospital's report that Mrs. Bates was now awake and alert and making steady progress. Maybe she'd still get a chance to take her children on that cruise.

Jason doubted that Talmedge was the kingpin of the conspiracy. That made no sense. Talmedge must be working for someone else, some individual or special interest group that stood to benefit from having someone they could control in the vice-presidency.

And once you controlled the vice-presidency, your man was only a heartbeat away. Gerald Ford hadn't only become vice-president without a popular vote, he subsequently became president—and again without a popular vote of any kind. American democracy, which at times seems so strong, is in reality so very fragile.

The phone on his desk rang, startling Jason out of his thoughts. It was Helen, one of the denizens of the top floor whose only responsibility, as far as Jason knew, was to obtain blood samples from the clinic's patient's—which was exactly what she wanted from him.

"It's for insurance purposes," she explained.

"I don't understand," Jason said, trying to control his annoyance.

"We have to do these periodic screening tests," Helen explained, "for hepatitis and so forth. Our insurance company requires it."

Jason looked at his watch. He had a meeting with Marsden in five minutes and a full schedule of appointments to follow. He told Helen as much.

"We really need to have the blood as soon as possible, Doctor. I'm afraid we've let it slip too long already."

Jason couldn't imagine there was any real urgency, but he said he would stop by at the end of the day, after his last appointment. He hung up the phone and headed for Marden's laboratory, already late for his meeting.

As it turned out, Jason needn't have hurried. Marsden was huddling over one of his notebooks, deep in thought. Jason knew from long experience that it was best not to disturb Marsden until his mind returned to the real world. He seemed to have no sense of time or scheduling. Those who wanted to work with him had to learn to live with his idiosyncrasies.

Rachel was on the phone, sounding very exasperated. "But you just took samples a few weeks ago."

Jason's ears perked up. What was Helen up to?

"O.K.," Rachel said, "when do you want me?" She was submitting but not very happily. She hung up the phone with a loud sigh.

"What's up?" Jason asked. He tried to keep his voice even. It was impossible to be near Rachel and not feel the pain of her betrayal of him—of them.

"That was Helen," Rachel said, "wanting more blood. She says the lab lost the sample I gave them a few weeks ago, and the tests have to be repeated. Apparently some insurance people are going to go over the clinic's records tomorrow after the dedication ceremony. Helen says that Talmedge has been going over everything to make certain all is in order." If Rachel felt any pangs of emotion over the change in their relationship, she was doing a good job of concealing it.

"I'd forgotten all about that damn dedication ceremony," Jason said. "If it's any comfort," he added, "they're after my blood too."

Rachel didn't appear to be comforted. She sat down heavily at her desk and started to shut down the little portable computer that was resting there.

"Is that your portable from home?" Jason asked.

Rachel nodded. "We still can't get rid of the virus in my desktop computer. We've got some anti-viral software on order. If it doesn't get the job done, we'll just assume all the data on the hard drive is lost. It probably is anyway."

Jason smiled at that.

"What's the matter?" Rachel had the tone of someone who thought she was being laughed at.

"You really do have a virus in your computer."

"Of course," she said, "what did you think?"

"I thought you didn't want me to use your computer."

She gave him a strange look and shook her head. "Why would I care if you used my computer?"

Jason shrugged and wondered what other things he had misjudged. "There are a lot of strange things going on around here," he said.

"You can say that again," Rachel said, rather pointedly. Was she referring to their breakup?

"Who keeps track of the Psychoden drug supplies?" Jason asked.

"I do—now," Rachel answered. "A couple of months ago I became suspicious that some of our drug supply was missing, but Arthur had been in charge of maintaining the supply records—so you can imagine it was impossible to know anything for certain. Anyway, I started keeping my own backup records. We're losing about a gross of Psychoden patches a month. What would anyone want with Psychoden patches?"

Jason knew, of course. It was just one more piece of the puzzle. "Did you mention the missing drug to Arthur?"

"Yes, but not surprisingly he wasn't very interested. He'd only complain if he went to the cupboard and couldn't find any."

"Good old Arthur," Jason said. But he couldn't help worrying that it was more than that.

Rachel stood and closed the top of her portable computer. "I'd better get going. I told Helen I'd come right over." For a fleeting moment her eyes caught Jason's, and they shared once again the old intimacy.

Jason felt a moment of panic. He had to do something.

He picked up the tiny mini-cassette tape recorder from her desk. "You better put this in your pocket," he said. "Apparently they're disappearing all over the clinic. Talmedge sent out a memo saying he was going to start charging us for them."

Rachel gave him another look, but absentmindedly slipped the cassette recorder into the pocket of her clinic coat. "Like you said, Jason, there are some mighty strange things going on around here."

Jason watched as she left the laboratory. He felt more than a little guilty to be using her. But she should be safe. Rachel had very little knowledge of Jason's suspicions. And she had no idea that the cassette recorder was turned on.

Chapter Forty

Jason waited patiently for Rachel to return to the laboratory while Arthur Marsden continued to do the mental equivalent of space travel to Pluto. Fifteen minutes became twenty and then thirty. Relax, Jason told himself, she's not in any danger. It was what he truly believed. Still, when Rachel finally returned, Jason felt a very strong sense of relief rush through his body.

"You're still here?" Rachel's expression was slightly quizzical.

Jason nodded toward Marsden. "Arthur's still off in his own little world. You get your blood drawn?"

"I guess so."

"What do you mean?"

"You know how it is up there. They have you lie down on that comfortable couch, put on the headphones, and listen to the pretty music. You never know if you had any blood drawn or not."

"You've been gone for nearly forty minutes."

"Really?" Rachel said. "It seemed more like ten." A frown drifted across her face.

"May I see your cassette recorder?" Jason held out his

hand. Rachel gave him that same look she'd thrown at him when he suggested she take the recorder with her.

Jason rewound the cassette, then fast-forwarded through some dictating Rachel had been doing. Finally, after some back and forth maneuvering, he found what he wanted.

"Just lie down here." It was Helen's voice. "This won't take a minute. Pull up your sleeve. That's it. Let me get this tourniquet on."

"Jason!" Rachel made a quick grab for the recorder, but Jason pulled it back out of her reach.

"You were spying on me!"

"Not really, Rachel. Just hold on for a little while. This is important." He turned the recorder back on.

Several minutes elapsed during which no voices were heard on the tape. Jason kept the cassette running, real time. The next voice they heard was that of Charles Talmedge.

"Can you hear me, Rachel?"

"Yes," Rachel answered in a very distant voice, "I can hear you."

"Jason, what's going on?" Rachel wasn't certain just exactly what she was listening to.

Jason shut off the recorder. "It's Psychoden. Everyone who gets blood drawn up there undergoes a Psychoden interview at no additional charge."

"That bastard!"

"Precisely," Jason agreed. "He asks all sorts of questions. You know how Psychoden works. The patient can't keep anything secret. Whatever Talmedge finds out he can then use for blackmail or political leverage."

"I can't believe it!"

"It gets worse, Rachel. I'll fill you in after we hear what Talmedge is after." Jason started the cassette once again. Once again they heard Talmedge's oily voice.

"I want to know about your boyfriend, Rachel. Is he trying to cause problems for the clinic?"

"I don't have a boyfriend."

Jason and Rachel exchanged glances. Jason knew that the question was too general anyway. People on Psychoden did much better with very specific questions.

"I'm talking about Jason Andrews," Talmedge continued on the tape. "Did you two break up?"

"Yes."

"Why?"

"He's mad at me. I don't know why."

Jason reached over and gave Rachel's hand a squeeze.

"Is Dr. Andrews upset with something at the clinic, Rachel?"

"He doesn't like the clinic."

"Why is that?"

There was some hesitation before Rachel responded. "He doesn't like that he can't see his patients' charts. He doesn't like all the security people around all the time."

"Does he think there's something illegal going on at the clinic?"

"No."

"Rachel, is there anything you know about Dr. Andrews that you think he might not want me to know?"

Again, there was a pause before Rachel answered. "He doesn't like you. He thinks you're an asshole. He wouldn't be surprised to hear that you had won a Pederast of the Year award."

Neither Jason nor Rachel could help laughing.

She said, "Well, it's true."

On the tape, Talmedge now sounded angry. "O.K., Rachel, what are Dr. Andrews' sexual tastes? What's the most bizarre thing the two of you have ever done sexually?"

Rachel's recorded voice started an answer, but Jason turned off the recorder.

"I think we both know the answer to that," Jason said.

Rachel smiled and arched an eyebrow. "You and I might not have the same definition of bizarre."

Jason popped the mini-cassette out of the recorder. "I think we've heard enough. I'll just hang on to the evidence for now." He looked around. Marsden was still off in never-never land. No one could overhear them.

Jason began to share with Rachel what he thought was going on.

"Why didn't you tell me any of this before?" she wanted to know.

"As it turned out, it's a good thing I didn't," Jason said. "In the last half hour you would have told Talmedge everything you knew." He added gently, "Not your fault, of course. Under Psychoden you wouldn't have had any choice. I was also worried about the computer-virus thing. I didn't want to believe you were protecting Talmedge, but there was no way to be certain."

"You could have trusted me," Rachel said. There was genuine pain in her voice.

"I'm sorry, Rachel. I designed a little test for you, and I'm afraid you didn't pass it."

"What test?"

"I told you that I was planning to leave the clinic and asked you not to tell anyone. It only took about twenty-four hours for me to get called into Talmedge's office and asked about my plans."

"I swear I didn't tell Talmedge, Jason. Someone else must have."

"I didn't tell anyone else I was planning to leave," Jason said. "You must have told *someone*."

Rachel's face colored deeply. "Just my brother. I knew I could trust him—I thought I could. I thought he might be able to help you find a spot at the NIH. I don't know how Talmedge found out."

"I do," Jason said. "Your brother came to the clinic and had blood drawn." Once again a light went on in Jason's brain. "You remember that supposed seizure he had? That was probably a reaction to Psychoden."

"You mean . . ."

"I mean he doesn't have any secrets from Talmedge anymore. Talmedge just hooked up to your brother's brain and sucked out whatever information he was interested in. Just as he's done to every other politician who's come to the clinic."

"What are we going to do, Jason?"

"I have some ideas. I think, for now, you're still completely safe, Rachel."

"What about you?"

"I'm O.K. too, for now. I'd like for you to do something for me, Rachel. It will get you more involved in all this, but I think we've got almost all the evidence we need to blow this thing wide open."

"Whatever you want, Jason."

"What I'd like you to do is be right outside the front door of the clinic at five o'clock tonight in your car, with the motor running."

"What are you going to do, Jason?"

"I'm going to have my blood drawn."

Chapter Forty-one

When the phone on his desk rang, it was Helen again. "You haven't forgotten that you need that blood drawn, have you, Doctor?"

"No, I haven't forgotten. I'm just very busy. I'll be up around five o'clock—unless you want to put it off till tomorrow."

"Five o'clock will be fine."

Jason looked at his watch again: 4:35. His last patient had canceled, information he hadn't shared with Helen. His day *had* been busy, but now he finally had a few moments to think. Jason now understood more and more of the conspiracy, but he still had very little in the way of proof. What he really wanted to know was: *who was pulling Talmedge's strings?*

Talmedge was in this thing up to his eyeballs, there was no doubt about that, but this game was ultimately being played at a much higher level. What was the objective? Sheer, raw power? That was a possibility, but if that was the goal, Jason imagined that there wouldn't be a list of possible Geralds. Any person *that* power-hungry would undoubtedly want to play Gerald himself. So there was probably some narrower focus, some special-interest group that wanted to get a stranglehold on some aspect of government policy.

Jason immediately thought of the oil lobby, because of Talmedge's connection to it and because so many powerful, wealthy individuals were involved in oil, and finally because government control was exercised in so many areas: tax policy, drilling rights, tariffs. Big oil would love to control the government and already spent millions of dollars each year—legally—in its efforts to influence favorable legislation. So oil was one possibility, but there were others that were equally likely. The ability to control international arms deals, for example, would be worth billions.

Jason realized the potential list was endless. In addition to those with purely financial interests, there were any number of individual fanatics and groups with extremist social views that might want to promote their own agendas. Jason realized he wasn't going to be able to reason this thing out. He was going to have to do some more investigating, and he was just beginning to get the first inklings of how he was going to do it.

He checked his watch one last time: 4:50. Time to go.

Jason had tried to think through in advance everything he needed to do. He didn't want to have to start improvising in the middle of things. As he walked into the blood-drawing salon, the first thing he did was check the doorknob. Just as he thought, it was locked so that no one could accidentally interrupt while "blood drawing" was in progress. Helen stood with her back to him, leaning over the mahogany bar that served as her supply cabinet.

"Hello," he said.

Helen started slightly, but seemed to have regained some of her composure by the time she turned. "Dr. Andrews, I was beginning to think you were avoiding us."

"Why would I do that?" Jason asked. And who do you mean by "us"? he thought to himself.

"Just take off your sports coat and have a seat on the couch. Lie down if you like. I'll be with you in a second."

Jason watched as she turned to check her equipment one last time, then walked across the room to shut the door to the main hallway. The heavy door closed with a muffled click, and Jason wondered for the first time—a little late now—if the door was locked from the inside as well as the outside.

Jason had always been impressed by the room. It had all the trappings of a plush, comfortable den: thick carpeting, overstuffed furniture, paneled walls, thick draperies. Ostensibly, all this was to abet patient comfort and relaxation, but Jason now understood that the amenities served another purpose. The room was totally soundproofed.

For the first time Jason noticed a second door to the room. The paneling on the door blended almost perfectly into the wall. Where did that door lead? Jason tried to visualize in his mind the layout of the clinic's top floor. He couldn't be absolutely certain, but the second door probably led to Talmedge's office.

"Put these on, Dr. Andrews." Helen was offering him a set of headphones. "Just lean back, shut your eyes, and enjoy the music. I promise you won't feel a thing."

"That's okay," Jason said. "I'm a big boy. Just give me one last cigarette. I don't need a blindfold." He couldn't be certain where the Psychoden patch was. The headphones were a strong possibility.

"All right, Doctor, have it your way."

Forgoing the headphones didn't seem to faze Helen, which meant there was only one other place the Psychoden patch was likely to be. Jason watched as she came toward him with the tourniquet. He noticed that she was very careful about how she handled it, almost as though she was afraid of it.

"Let me have your arm, Doctor."

He gave it to her, sleeve rolled up. Helen wrapped the tourniquet above his elbow. It was a flat rubber strap, about an inch and a half wide, which fastened to itself with Velcro. Jason noticed that Helen hadn't fastened the tourniquet nearly tight enough to shut off the venous circulation. That wasn't an accident.

"Make a fist for me a couple of times, Dr. Andrews, so we can fill up those veins."

Jason made a couple of halfhearted fists and waited. He didn't feel anything yet, but by the time he did it would probably be too late. He noticed that Helen was just standing there. She didn't seem to be in too big a hurry to draw any blood.

"Something's wrong, Helen. I'm starting to feel sick. I think I'm going to throw up."

Helen started to reach for the tourniquet, but as she did Jason stood up, blocking her reach. Once on his feet, he began to feel light-headed, as though he might faint. Jason blinked his eyes slowly, trying to clear his vision.

"I'm going to try to make it to the bathroom," he told her, though frankly he wasn't certain he could. His legs felt like they were made of lead. They didn't want to move. Jason ordered them to, but they seemed to have a mind of their own.

He managed to make it to the door, pulling the tourniquet off his arm as he went. As he reached for the knob, a haze was beginning to fill the room and the walls were beginning to undulate.

The door was locked.

He was trapped.

Talmedge was going to ask him questions, and he would tell Talmedge everything he knew. Talmedge, or one of his associates, would kill him. Rachel, too.

Jason tried the knob again.

This time it turned—the door hadn't been locked at all. He pulled it open. He was in the hallway. The bathroom was at the far end. He was still woozy, but he didn't seem to be getting any worse. His legs were cooperating better.

Jason turned as he walked and saw Helen standing in the doorway. "I'm okay," he called back over his shoulder. Then he put his hand over his mouth and picked up his pace. He didn't look back again until he got to the door of the men's room. A quick glance told him she was still watching. He went in.

Jason's head was clearing quickly now. He took some deep breaths. He worked the muscles of his arms and legs to increase the circulation. Psychoden didn't stay in the system long once the patch was removed. He looked at the tourniquet in his hand, turning it over. There was a small round patch on the inner side. Not much doubt what a chemical analysis of that patch would reveal.

Now came the tricky part. He had been in the rest

room for about thirty seconds. Helen wouldn't be sure what to do. She might go talk to Talmedge; she might not. Jason was betting that she wouldn't just stand in the hallway watching the men's room door. If she did, there was nothing he could do about it. If she didn't, he and Rachel would gain a lot of time.

Jason put the tourniquet safely in his pocket and opened the door. The hallway was empty. In less than ten seconds he was across the hall and into the stairwell, taking the steps two and three at a time on his way down to the first floor. He opened the lobby door and walked calmly out of the clinic's front entrance. Rachel was waiting patiently in her car.

"Am I glad to see you," he said as he opened the door.

"Where to?" she asked.

"Baltimore," he said. "I'll explain on the way."

Rachel gave him that look again, the one that said at least one of them was crazy, but she pulled the car quickly away from the clinic's front door and headed for the main entrance to the grounds.

Chapter Forty-two

Helen wasn't sure what she should do. So for a while she did nothing. The only time anything like this had happened before was when Senator Chandler had come to the Clinic. That time she wasn't even in the room when it happened. Talmedge had called her back into the room and told her just to stand there; don't say anything. He'd do all the talking. She had been terrified when Dr. Andrews started to ask her questions. Now here was Dr. Andrews with something wrong with him. This job was getting stranger and stranger. Helen was thinking very seriously about getting back into secretarial work.

When Helen had first applied for a job at the clinic, that was what she wanted, secretarial work. But for some reason Talmedge had taken an interest in her application and told her he had in mind a completely different line of work for her. That was when he suggested this blood-drawing thing. She said she didn't know a thing about drawing blood and, besides, it sounded kind of icky. He said it paid twice as much as being a secretary. She said she'd give it a try.

What she had worried about most when she started her

job was causing pain to another human being. That was something she just couldn't stand to do. But Mr. Talmedge said don't worry, we've got this little bitty tranquilizer patch on the tourniquet. The patient doesn't feel a thing. Well, it certainly made her feel a lot better. The other thing, Talmedge said, don't ever mention the tranquilizer to anyone. It's kind of a trade secret. If it works, we may be wanting to patent it.

Well, that worried Helen some, but not as much as what happened next. Talmedge had this idea that while the patient was under the tranquilizer, he could ask them some questions. How did they enjoy their visit to the clinic? Did any member of the staff treat them badly? Stuff that the patient might otherwise be reluctant to talk about. Mr. Talmedge said, since it involved personnel stuff, she should go through the little door and wait in his office until he knocked.

At first that worried Helen a lot. She thought maybe Talmedge was one of those pre-verts, like those dentists you were always reading about in the newspapers, the ones who gave you the gas and then gave you the business.

But after more than a year Helen hadn't seen one shred of evidence of any sexual impropriety, so she didn't worry about that anymore. Right now she just hoped that Dr. Andrews was okay. She figured he would just come back to the blood-drawing salon as soon as he felt better. When he didn't return, she marched herself right on down to the men's room and knocked on the door. No response. She knocked again, then opened the door just a crack.

"Dr. Andrews?" Nothing. She opened the door a little

farther. "Dr. Andrews!" Still no answer. "Is anyone in there?" By this time she could pretty much see more of a men's room than she had ever cared to see, and could pretty well tell it was empty. By the time she got back to the blood-drawing room, Talmedge was waiting for her.

"Didn't Dr. Andrews show up?" he asked. He already looked angry, and she hadn't even told him what had happened yet.

"Well, yes, sir, Dr. Andrews was here, but he got sick and ran out." Helen hadn't felt this nervous since her first day on the job.

"Where is he now?"

"Well, sir, I'm not sure. He ran down to the bathroom, but he doesn't seem to be there now. Maybe he's in his office."

"When did he get sick, Helen?"

"Right after I put the tourniquet on him." She could tell that Mr. Talmedge was growing angrier, and she still hadn't told him the worst part. She watched as Talmedge looked around the room, carefully scrutinizing the beautiful mahogany bar that she used to set out her equipment.

"Where's the tourniquet, Helen?" Talmedge's face was red. He was grinding his teeth and making the muscles on the side of his face stand out.

"I don't rightly know, Mr. Talmedge. When Dr. Andrews left, he was still wearing it."

In some ways his reaction wasn't as bad as she had feared. Talmedge didn't say another word. He just turned, went back into his office, and slammed the door.

* * *

Talmedge tried to remain calm. He grabbed his phone and punched in Jason's office number.

"This is Mr. Talmedge. Is Dr. Andrews there, please?"

"I believe he's gone for the day, Mr. Talmedge," the receptionist answered. "He was to have some blood drawn, and then he said he was going to go home. I'd be happy to take a message for him."

Talmedge hung up and called Security. "This is Talmedge. I want you to find Dr. Jason Andrews for me. Search the entire building. When you have him, bring him to me. It's possible that he is suffering from a reaction to a drug. He may be belligerent. Use force if you have to."

There was nothing for Talmedge to do now but wait. Half an hour later, there was still no sign of Andrews. Talmedge had no choice but to make the call. He had never used the direct, emergency number before. The phone was picked up on the third ring.

"Mr. Ambassador," Talmedge said, "I think we may have a problem."

Chapter Forty-three

Rachel and Jason never actually made it all the way to Baltimore.

Jason had imagined a narrow escape from the clinic. He had visions of screeching tires and packs of blue-blazered security men in hot pursuit. None of that happened.

Rachel drove. Jason sat beside her, constantly looking behind them and giving Rachel frequent, random instructions to turn here, turn there. After twenty minutes it was apparent that no one was following them.

"It looks like we're in the clear, at least for now. We just need to find a hotel or someplace to spend the night where we won't be discovered—even by accident," Jason told her.

"What kind of girl do you think I am?" Rachel asked him. But she smiled.

They drove into Washington, then out the George Washington Parkway to Maryland. They found a hotel just off the Beltway and checked in, using Jason's real name and a credit card. There was no way, Jason reasoned, that he and Rachel would be found that night—unless some government agency was involved in the conspiracy and took part in the search. Jason believed that was highly unlikely. Still, although he had thoughts of calling the FBI that night, in the end he had decided against it.

What worried Jason was quite simple: if *he* could crack this thing wide open, why couldn't the FBI? They had supposedly been on the case for months. The FBI director himself had personally visited Mrs. Bates shortly after her husband's death. At Senator Chandler's party the director had claimed to be suspicious of the goings-on at the clinic, but as far as Jason could tell, there had been no action. And most disturbing of all was something Jason now remembered from his last conversation with Barbara Bates. She had attempted to call the FBI director the day of her accident. She had left some sort of message for him. Somehow, someone had known where to look for Barbara Bates that night. Could it have been the FBI?

All of those concerns evaporated, if only for a little while, as soon as they were in their hotel room. Jason put out the Do Not Disturb sign and threw the dead bolt. When he turned, Rachel was standing in the middle of the room, watching him. At least for now the threatening outside world was locked away. They were safely hidden. For Jason the sensation that crowded out all others was a feeling of intimacy, of being once again alone with Rachel. He gave her what he hoped was his most alluring smile.

"I was going to ask you one question."

"What was that?" she said.

"The night I came by to collect my things at your house, as I was leaving, what was Talmedge doing there?"

"It was as big a surprise to me as I'm sure it was to you,

269

Jason. The man had never been to my house before. He came by without calling. Basically, I think he really wanted to know if I had any idea what you were up to." She paused, then got that look again. "Jason, you didn't think there was something romantic going on between that despicable man and me? How could you?"

Jason had a ready answer: "Because I'm stupid. That's really the key to understanding me, Rachel. Once you accept the fact that I have the IQ of a cantaloupe, everything else pretty much falls right into place."

He walked across the room and put his arms around her, held her as tightly as he could. They began to kiss.

On both sides there was a certain amount of what economists refer to as pent-up demand.

"Jason?"

"Hmm?"

"What are we going to do?"

The room was now completely dark. The clock on the bedside table said 10:30.

"I don't know," Jason said. "I was thinking room service."

The answer earned him a playful punch in the ribs. "I'm serious," Rachel said. "Isn't it time to turn this over to the police or somebody?"

"What would I tell them?"

"The same thing you told me."

"I certainly wouldn't want them to have the same reaction you had."

"What do you mean?"

"A bunch of policemen, all they can think about is how fast they can get their clothes off."

Another punch in the ribs. "I'm serious."

"So am I. Ouch!"

Rachel sat up in bed and turned on the light. She looked down at him. He looked up at her. Rachel pulled the sheet up tightly under her chin. "Your privileges are officially cut off until I get some answers."

"The problem is, Rachel, I don't have any real proof of *anything*."

"What about all those computer files?"

"First of all, I know about only one file for certain. I assumed there are other files, but I don't know that for a fact. Second, how long do you think those files would remain unerased if Talmedge thought he was about to be exposed?"

Rachel shrugged. "It's a chance you'd have to take."

"The other idea I've had is that maybe that wouldn't be such a bad thing if all those files were erased."

"What do you mean?"

"Think what may be in those files. The private thoughts of our nation's most public figures. Personal confessions. Revelations of mistakes made years ago. Some of it, maybe, should be known, but most of it is probably nobody's business."

"Wouldn't the government be able to keep it all secret?"

"Since when has our government been able to keep anything secret? Information leaks are a way of life. Just think what the press would do once it heard about those files. They'd smell blood in the water and go into a feeding frenzy."

"I guess," Rachel said, "that's part of the risk of being a public official."

"In case you've forgotten, Rachel, one of those public figures is your brother. Another is your father. And you and I aren't public officials, but I bet we've got files in Talmedge's computer. I had blood drawn when I first came to the clinic. I'm not worried about myself, but I probably talked about some of my ex-wife's problems. She doesn't deserve to have her personal affairs become a matter of public record. Just think of all the other wives, children, friends of public figures, or clinic employees who might have their private lives opened up to public scrutiny. Look what Herbert Allen did when he thought someone was going to reveal his son's actions. How many Herbert Allens do you suppose are lurking in those files?"

"I'm sorry, Jason. You're right, of course. I just hadn't thought it through. What other proof *do* we have?"

"An envelope. An *alleged* envelope with an *alleged* list on the back. *If* Mrs. Bates ever gets her memory back, she could testify to that. We have the tourniquet with the Psychoden patch on it. That's the only hard evidence we actually have in our possession."

"Still, Jason, you could take what you have to the authorities. They could pick up the investigation from here. At the very least, Talmedge would have to stop what he's doing. He couldn't do any more damage."

"I think you're right about that, Rachel. We could stop the hemorrhaging. Talmedge would have to close up shop, but we'd never find out who's really behind this. Talmedge is a pawn, a rook at most. There's someone or some group behind him."

"Any ideas?"

"It could be almost any powerful special-interest group. They'd have to be well financed. I'm sure Talmedge is charging them plenty."

"Could it be a foreign government?"

"Sure." It was a possibility that had been gaining momentum in Jason's mind. "Can you imagine? A foreign power controlling the White House?"

"What *are* we going to do, Jason?"

"I have an idea. I'll need your help." He didn't really want to involve Rachel further, but he couldn't see any way to avoid it. "What I think we should do is give Charlie Talmedge an opportunity to confess."

Chapter Forty-four

By eight o'clock the next morning, Jason and Rachel had checked out of their hotel and were on the road.

Rachel had called her brother at their family home in Virginia the night before. At Jason's instruction, she had deliberately kept the conversation short and to the point. They couldn't be certain, Jason said, that the senator's phone wasn't tapped. And Jason had another concern that he didn't share with Rachel.

"Hi, Rob," Rachel said to her brother, "I wasn't sure if you would be in Virginia or D.C. tonight."

"I drove down this evening because of the dedication at the clinic tomorrow. Where have you been?"

"I went out to dinner. Why?"

"Charles Talmedge called, said he'd been trying to get hold of you."

"Please don't tell him you talked to me, Rob. I'm afraid he's developed sort of a romantic interest in me. I'm trying to discourage him as best I can."

"Oh, God."

"What time are you going to the clinic in the morning?"

"The dedication is at nine-thirty, so I suppose I'll leave here at nine. I've arranged for a limo to take me to the clinic and then back to Washington—so I can get some work done on the way."

"I'll see you at the clinic, then, in the morning."

Jason didn't tell her until after she'd hung up the phone that he thought it would be a good idea if they drove to the family estate in the morning and hitched a ride with the senator in his limo. "It might be safer," Jason told her, "than driving to the clinic by ourselves."

When they arrived at the Chandler estate, the limousine was waiting out front, motor running. They waited in their car for the senator to step outside. When he did, he was all smiles.

"We thought we might as well just ride in with you, Rob, if that's O.K. Jason's car is already at the clinic."

"Sure, fine. The more the merrier." If Senator Chandler had any sinister thoughts they were well concealed.

The ride to the clinic was uneventful, mostly small talk. An additional security point had been set up at the main entrance, apparently because of all the dignitaries who were expected for the dedication. Their chauffeur rolled down his window and said, "Senator Kennedy," to the general amusement of everyone in the back of the limousine. None of them wanted to embarrass the driver by correcting him. They were waved quickly through. So much for security.

There was a crush of people in front of the new research wing, milling around, greeting people they knew. It looked to Jason as though half of Washington had decided to put in an appearance. Hardly anyone noticed Senator Chandler when he emerged from the limousine. No one paid any attention at all as two unknowns, presumably aides to the senator, stepped out behind him.

Jason and Rachel slipped quickly into the building. Once inside they separated. Jason squeezed Rachel's hand and gave her a kiss on the cheek. She started off for her lab while Jason headed for the clinic's brand-new auditorium. He was able to stand inconspicuously near the back of the auditorium next to a group of congressmen talking shop. As far as Jason could tell, no one had noticed him. So far, so good. All he had to do was wait for the festivities to begin at 9:30. He only hoped that things were going as smoothly for Rachel.

At exactly 9:30, Rachel turned on her desktop computer for the first time in more than three weeks. She took a deep breath and logged onto the clinic's mainframe. She tried to enter patient files, but data was disappearing faster than she could pull it up. The virus was loose. Within minutes the clinic's files would be decimated, all data would be gone. Some of it would be important medical data, but that could be retrieved from hard-copy originals that were warehoused. The business data would be gone forever, so would Talmedge's "administrative" files.

Rachel left her computer on and went across the lab to fix herself a cup of coffee. Nothing to do now but wait.

Simultaneously, pandemonium had broken out in the clinic's administrative offices. Computer screens were going blank throughout the building. No one could access data.

"You'd better call Mr. Talmedge," someone said.

"Can't," was the reply. "He's at the dedication."

As 9:30 approached, people began to take their seats in the auditorium. Talmedge was still walking the aisles, glad-handing the visiting dignitaries. There were senators, congressmen, at least one Supreme Court justice, the governor of Virginia. All in all, Talmedge had outdone himself with the guest list. The new research wing would give an additional boost to the clinic's prestige, securing once and for all its eminence in neuropsychiatric research. The auditorium was to be the site of future national and international conferences.

Jason remained poised in the shadows, waiting for just the right time to make his move. He saw Arthur Marsden on the stage with some other physicians and researchers from the clinic's staff. There were still a few empty chairs up there. Presumably one of them was intended for Jason.

Finally, Talmedge led the governor of Virginia onto the stage and showed him his seat. Then Talmedge took his place at the podium, flicking the microphone a couple of times with his finger to make certain the sound system was working properly. The audience quieted itself. It was time for Jason to act.

He walked swiftly down the aisle, smiling as he went, as though nothing were amiss. Talmedge didn't notice him until Jason actually stepped onto the stage. As their eyes met, Jason put on the broadest, friendliest grin he could muster. Talmedge appeared confused. He just stood there, like a deer caught in headlights, watching Jason approach.

Jason extended his hand. If he smiled any wider, his face would crack. Talmedge shook the hand uncertainly, but Jason wasn't finished yet. With his free hand Jason cupped the back of Charles Talmedge's neck and pulled him forward in a warm embrace. The audience watched in silence, then someone clapped, then the entire audience began to clap at this remarkable display of affection for Charles Talmedge, director of the Marsden Clinic, the man whose foresight and hard work had made today's dedication possible.

Jason continued the embrace for as long as possible. Talmedge had at first tried to pull back, but Jason held him firmly. Talmedge could not escape his grasp without an obvious struggle.

Talmedge's resistance served only to increase his heart rate, thus increasing the rapidity with which the drug entered his system. As the applause died down, Jason turned to the audience. Talmedge stood passively beside him.

"I am Dr. Jason Andrews," Jason announced. "I'm working here at the clinic on a year's sabbatical from the Harvard Medical School, where I am a professor of psychiatry." Again there was applause. "I have been working with Dr. Arthur Marsden, the clinic's founder, on a drug he has discovered called Psychoden. I am certain many of you have heard of this exciting drug.

"Psychoden allows us to explore the patient's mind, free of any hindrance from the patient's own conscious or subconscious inhibitions. In short, in layman's terms, under the influence of Psychoden the patient is compelled to tell the truth as he or she knows it. The patient cannot be coy or deceitful. When we ask a question, the patient answers it with complete candor. After the drug is withdrawn, the patient has no memory of the session during which it was administered. All of this is potentially quite useful in psychotherapy."

There was some murmuring and nodding of heads in the crowd. The monologue had been largely a ruse to buy time, to make certain that Talmedge was fully under the influence of Psychoden before Jason proceeded.

"What Mr. Talmedge would like to tell you about today," Jason continued, "is some independent research he has personally been conducting at the clinic with Psychoden. Now, how many of you in the audience today have had blood drawn at the clinic? Please, raise your hands." There was a general rising of hands. "What you do not know is that when you had your blood drawn—up there in the clinic's luxurious blood-drawing salon--you were placed under the influence of Psychoden."

There was loud murmuring now from the audience, a tone of anger. Some fidgeted nervously. Jason surveyed the crowd and saw many well-known faces. His eyes locked briefly with those of a man seated near the back. The man's face rang a disturbing bell, but Jason couldn't quite place him. As Jason watched, the man left his seat.

Jason held up his hand to quiet the crowd. "Please, if I may have your attention, this will only take a moment." Jason had a very definite agenda. He wanted Talmedge to confess unequivocally to what was going on, and then Jason had just two more questions. Who was Gerald? Who was Talmedge's master? Then the show would be over.

"Mr. Talmedge," Jason asked in a stage voice, "what did

you do once patients were under the influence of Psychoden up there in the blood-drawing salon?"

"We asked them questions."

"What kinds of questions?"

"All kinds. Whatever we could think of. Were they queers? Did they have extramarital affairs? Did they accept bribes?"

"Why did you ask those questions?"

Talmedge didn't hesitate. "So we could blackmail them."

There was a general uproar in the auditorium as various dignitaries wondered what information Talmedge might have on them. Again Jason asked for quiet. Just a few more questions.

"Mr. Talmedge, where did you store the information you obtained from these patients?"

"Why, in the clinic's computers."

"Anywhere else?"

"Only in my memory."

Just a couple more questions.

"Mr. Talmedge, you have a plan that is code-named Gerald. Could you tell me what position your man Gerald is to assume?"

"He will be the next vice-president of the United States."

"And, Mr. Talmedge, who have you picked to be the next vice-president of the United States?"

The hushed crowd waited breathlessly for Talmedge's response and focused its attention entirely on the stage.

The next few seconds unfolded in slow motion for Jason. First he saw movement at the back of the hall. A man was pointing at Jason. No, wait, the man had a gun. Jason saw several flashes but heard no sound. Then the man was gone.

Jason felt no pain. There was only the sensation of warm blood flowing slowly down the side of his face.

Chapter Forty-five

Charles Talmedge was dead before his body hit the floor. He had sustained mortal wounds to the head and chest. Jason immediately removed the Psychoden patch from Talmedge's neck and began cardiopulmonary resuscitation, but it was hopeless.

Meanwhile, the auditorium erupted in chaos. There was yelling and screaming, people ducking for cover, others jamming the exits in an effort to escape. When it became apparent that there was no immediate threat of additional violence, some of the politicians began to think about what might be lurking in those computer files. They turned their attention back to Jason, who was still among the group of doctors attempting to resuscitate Talmedge.

Remarkably, it was Arthur Marsden who intervened. "Can't you see that Dr. Andrews has been shot? He needs immediate medical attention." Marsden took Jason by the elbow and led him off behind the stage and out a side door, then up a back elevator to Marsden's laboratory. In the elevator he gave Jason a quick examination.

"Just as I thought," Marsden said, "nothing but splattered blood from Talmedge. You feel all right?"

"I'm fine, physically. This isn't the way I planned for this to turn out."

Rachel was waiting in the lab. On seeing Jason, her face immediately registered shock. "My God, Jason!"

"I'm okay." He gave her a quick report of what had happened, then tilted his head slightly at the computer. Rachel nodded her head in response. Jason sighed. At least something had gone right.

Jason hesitated only briefly, then filled Marsden in on what he knew of the conspiracy. Marsden looked crushed. There could be no doubt that he was hearing all this for the first time.

"I feel responsible," Marsden said. "Psychoden is like a child of mine. I brought it into the world, and it turns out to be a serial killer. It never occurred to me that the drug had this kind of abuse potential." The day's events had been like a slap in the face for Arthur Marsden. His mind had been suddenly forced to focus on the real world for a change.

Jason turned to Rachel. "I hate to ask you to do this, but if either Arthur or I go downstairs we'll be swarmed by reporters and politicians. I imagine the police have taken charge downstairs by now. Would you mind going down and finding whoever's in charge and letting them know—confidentially—that I'm up here? I'm pretty sure they'll have a few questions for me."

Rachel was quickly off, leaving Jason alone with Arthur Marsden.

"You thought I was involved, didn't you?" Marsden said. "That's why you didn't tell me about any of this." His tone was matter-of-fact, not accusatory.

"I certainly never wanted to think that you were involved, Arthur. Besides, all this seemed a bit too, I don't know, practical for you." Jason managed a weak smile. "You were always much more interested in the esoteric, neuropharmacologic aspects of Psychoden than in its practical application. But I've been pretty paranoid about all this. At one point I even suspected Rachel."

Marsden shook his head. "In my heart I always knew that Talmedge was no good. I never should have trusted him. It was just too easy to let him manage things so I could focus on my research."

"Not your fault, Arthur."

When Rachel returned, she had two policemen in tow, the ubiquitous Lieutenant Briggs and a Sergeant Browning.

"I think I'll just assign someone to follow you around, Doc," Briggs said. "It seems like you're pretty much involved in anything that goes down within a hundred miles or so of here. It'd save us a lot of time."

Everyone introduced themselves and found chairs. They were likely to be at this for quite a while. "And when we're done," Briggs said, "the FBI is gonna want to talk to you."

"You wouldn't believe what a zoo it is downstairs," Rachel said. "Politicians are down there, saying they won't leave the building until they have their files in hand. I heard a newspaperman offer a secretary a thousand dollars for the file on a Supreme Court justice. The secretary said if she was in that business—which she wasn't—she'd already been offered ten thousand for the same file." Rachel shook her head. "It looks like no one is going to have anything to worry about, though. Apparently the clinic's entire computer system just imploded. All the data seems to be gone."

"Funny, isn't it," Briggs said with more than a hint of suspicion in his voice, "that the system would go down at exactly the same time you're putting on your little dog-and-pony show with Talmedge?"

Jason tried to sound philosophical. "Maybe it's for the best. The information in that computer was nobody's business. It was too sensitive to risk letting *anyone* have access to it."

"You could trust the Department of Justice," Briggs said.

Jason shook his head. "Imagine you're in the political party that doesn't control Justice. You think you're gonna want them to have your innermost secrets on file? Just ask the politicians hanging around downstairs what they think about that. That's why they're still here. Their worst fear is that the Department of Justice will get those files. Then the newspapers will get them for free."

Briggs took out his notebook. "I think we better just start at the beginning, Doc. Tell me everything you know."

And Jason did. Everyone in the room hung on every word.

"In the end," Jason said, "I just didn't think I had enough to take to the police. I had lots of suspicions but very little evidence. It made sense to let Talmedge confess, and I wanted plenty of witnesses around when he did it. This morning seemed like a perfect opportunity. I didn't expect anyone to shoot him. I'm very sorry about that."

"Don't feel too sorry for Talmedge," Briggs said. "Sounds like he was guilty of a bunch of stuff. Maybe treason. Maybe murder—or at least complicity. I just wish he was alive so we could ask him a few pertinent questions."

"I seriously doubt he ever would have told you anything," Jason said.

"We could have put a tail on him. See where he led us."

"I thought about that. Then I wondered how many ticking time bombs like Herbert Allen are out there. I worried that by the time I had convinced the authorities that there really was something going on, someone else just might be dead. Not to mention that we might have a new vice-president by then."

Briggs considered that for a moment, then he asked, "Anyone here get a look at the shooter? It seems like everybody in the auditorium had his eyes on Talmedge. No one we've talked to seems to have seen anything else."

Everyone shook their heads.

"I sort of got a look," Jason said. "It was a man. A big man. He was back in the shadows. I thought he was pointing his finger at me. Then I realized it was a gun and figured I was the guy who was going to get shot. It never occurred to me that anyone would shoot Talmedge. Hell, he was one of them."

"Talmedge was about to take *them* down with him," Briggs said, "Whoever *they* are." The lieutenant appeared thoughtful for a few moments, then asked, "Does the Bates woman's accident tie into all this?"

"Maybe," Jason said. Then he corrected himself. "Probably. You remember that envelope I told you about? Whoever ran her off the road was probably after that list."

And at that moment a realization came to Jason. "I know who the shooter is. I mean, I don't know *who* he is, but I know what he looks like. I don't know why it didn't hit me immediately. Today was the third time I've seen him.

"The first time I saw him was at the National Gallery. Rachel and I had gone there for the afternoon. The guy was clearly following us. The next time was the day of Barbara Bates' accident. I had an accident too. I thought it was my fault—it probably was." Jason told them about trying to turn his car around on that desolate country road. "I imagine that he was just following me again. He was probably as surprised as I was when we had the collision. But I can recall that face now. It's the same one. And, Lieutenant, his car left some streaks of black paint on my car. They're still there if you want to check them out.

"The last time I saw the man was today. He was sitting in the auditorium for a while, then he was suddenly gone. He left his seat before the shooting started."

Briggs had his pen and notebook back out. "Tell me as much as you can about him."

"He's big, over six feet, probably six two or six four. His weight is probably well over two hundred pounds. I would guess he's around forty, sandy hair, slightly receding hairline. Every time I've seen him he's been wearing a dark suit. I have two impressions of him from the car accident. One is that he has big, powerful hands—something about the way they looked on the steering wheel. And the other thing, he's got nerves of steel.

"After our cars collided the first time, he was as close to me as you are now. I saw his face clearly. He seemed completely composed, totally in control. No pain. No fear. Like this kind of thing happened to him every day.

"I remember when I was in the operating room as a medical student one time, and a patient's aortic aneurysm burst. Blood everywhere, the patient's blood pressure went to zero. I was scared to death, but I'll never forget that surgeon. It was the same thing. No panic. Just maximum concentration and a calm, methodical approach to the problem. The patient did fine. Anyway, this guy was like that."

"Sounds like a pro," Briggs said. "Not too surprising that he would be. This is a high-stakes game they're playing. We'll want you to look at some mug shots tomorrow, but I doubt you'll find him. The really high-priced talent is never in the books. That's one of the reasons they're so high-priced."

Briggs collected phone numbers and addresses from everyone. He asked Jason not to leave town without letting him know. They would probably need to talk to him some more.

Jason looked at his watch. It was just after one o'clock. He felt as if he'd been on call for thirty-six hours. He needed a rest.

But just then the door to the laboratory opened and two men in suits entered. Something about the way they carried themselves instantly reminded Jason of Walt Briggs. He knew they were policemen of some stripe or other.

"Dr. Jason Andrews?" the taller man asked.

Jason nodded.

"We're from the FBI."

And Jason began his story all over again. From the beginning.

Chapter Forty-six

The FBI's primary concern was the national security angle. It was clear they were trying to figure out a way to bring the murder under their jurisdiction, but so far hadn't been able to manage it. One of them asked Jason quite hopefully if he thought the killer looked like a foreigner.

"You're going to have to help me with that," Jason replied. "What exactly does a foreigner look like?" It had already been a long day. Jason was going to have to work very hard at controlling his temper.

Half the time one or the other of the two FBI agents was on the phone taking a report from some other agent or relaying information elsewhere. The interruptions were frequent and time-consuming. Michael Cordova, the director of the FBI, had been in San Francisco but was jetting back to Washington. They were constantly in touch with his office so that updates could be forwarded.

The man who had introduced himself as Special Agent Matthews hung up the phone and turned to Jason. "You're coming to Washington with us."

For Jason, it was the last straw. "Look, you rude bastard, if you would like me to assist further in your investigation I will, within reason, but I expect you to show me the same respect that I show you. I don't like being ordered around, and I don't like being treated like a criminal. So let's discuss what we can do in Washington that we can't do here. If we don't come to an understanding, I'm going to shut up and let you talk to my attorney. Then *you'll* get an opportunity to see what *real* rudeness feels like." Jason had in mind a friend of his who was a professor at Harvard Law. Having that guy go against you was like having a pit bull in your shorts.

"I'm sorry, Dr. Andrews." Matthews sounded convincingly contrite. "I guess we're all under a lot of strain. What I should have said is that the President would like to speak with you at the White House as soon as we can get you there."

The President actually sent a helicopter to pick Jason up. It landed right behind the clinic and took him directly to the White House.

Jason had been very uncertain about leaving Rachel. "You could be in danger," he told her.

"How could I be in any danger," Rachel said, "when I don't know anything?"

The biggest danger for Rachel, the FBI man said, was hanging around Jason. Jason could identify the killer. Jason was the one they would be after.

In the end Jason had to agree with them, but he did exact a promise from Rachel that she would spend the night at her family's estate, so she wouldn't be alone. Rachel told him he was behaving like a typical macho male, but she did acquiesce. Only, she said, to humor him.

Jason's flight lasted just over half an hour. He decided that White House Air was probably the most convenient form of travel in existence. Still, he wasn't convinced it was worth the cost. These days, anyone who served as president automatically paid a terrible price. They came into office with such high hopes and left stooped and bloodied.

Like most Americans, Jason had never been inside the White House before. He was dutifully impressed. He had a few minutes that he could have used to gather his thoughts before being ushered into the Oval Office, but mostly he felt like sleeping. He was at least very close to being asleep when he heard his name called.

"Dr. Andrews, if you would come this way, please."

Jason hadn't given a lot of thought to who might be in the Oval Office. The President, he assumed. He hadn't expected the entire upper echelon of the national security apparatus.

The President, who was already standing when Jason entered the room, offered his hand. "Dr. Andrews," he said. It was a rather noncommittal greeting. Then he said, "We're trying to decide whether we should thank you or throw you in jail."

"If those are my choices," Jason said, "I should probably state right up front that I do have a definite preference."

The President gave just a hint of a smile and began to introduce the others in the room. "I understand that you have already met Mr. Cordova."

The FBI director gave Jason an almost imperceptible nod. "If you're interested," the director said, "my vote was to throw you in jail."

Always nice to know where you stood, Jason thought.

The President gave a slight frown and went on with the introductions. "These other gentlemen," he said, "are Mr. Martin, the CIA director; Mr. Conn, my chief of staff, and General Simpson, the National Security adviser." Jason nodded to each in turn. The men seemed somewhat less than thrilled to meet him. Perhaps, Jason told himself, they're just shy.

The President indicated for Jason to sit and took a seat himself in his favorite chair. "I've invited you here, Dr. Andrews, over the nearly unanimous objections of my senior advisers." Given the warmth of the reception he'd received, this bit of news came as no great surprise to Jason. "It appears that we are caught up in the middle of one of the greatest crises the United States government has ever had to face," the President continued. "I want to hear a firsthand account of what's going on. You're the only one who can give me that. So, start at the beginning and tell me what you know. I've cleared my calendar. Take all the time you need."

For the third time that day Jason told the story from beginning to end. He was weary of it, but with repetition his retelling of events had grown more efficient. The President's advisers rarely interrupted. They took copious notes. When Jason finished, the President chose not to wade in immediately himself. "Any questions?" he asked of his advisers.

There was a pause, and then the FBI director commented, "So, Dr. Andrews, let's see what we have. You say that the clinic's files were filled with personal data which was used in a blackmail conspiracy, but now those files have mysteriously been erased. You claim that Charles Talmedge was running the plot, and now he's dead. The evidence for the 'Gerald' portion of the conspiracy consists of an envelope which you have never seen, and which Mrs. Bates can no longer remember."

"She suffered severe head trauma," Jason interrupted. "She's probably forgotten many things. That's quite typical of that kind of injury."

"What are you saying, Michael," the President asked, "that none of this ever happened? That there never was a conspiracy?"

"I'm prepared to believe that Talmedge was in the blackmail business. I think his actions may have resulted in some resignations and decisions by various politicians not to seek reelection. But when you start to talk about somebody trying to appoint their own man to the vice-presidency, well, I think the evidence gets a little thin." Cordova paused to let everyone consider this before he added, "One thing that *is* likely is that Dr. Andrews' interference may have ended forever any chance we had of getting to the bottom of this." Cordova's anger was evident.

"I knew," Jason said, "that I could do things the FBI wouldn't be permitted to do. I could search those files without a warrant. I could question Talmedge under the influence of Psychoden. I'm sorry that he was killed. I had no idea that might happen. The files I'm not sorry about. There was information there that no one had a right to see. Patients' most intimate thoughts, most closely guarded secrets. What we do know is how quickly those files were able to disappear. Also, without Psychoden I think it is likely that Talmedge would have said nothing. In short, if I hadn't acted, I think you might have had much less information than you have now.

"We all know," Jason added, "the consequences of my actions. What you are failing to consider is how much worse the situation might be had I failed to act."

The President seemed to be content just to listen. He did pick up one loose thread. "This Helen person, the one who was supposed to be drawing blood at the clinic, have we talked to her?"

"Yes," Cordova said. "It appears that she didn't have any knowledge of what was really going on. We'll question her further in the morning. She's agreed to take a lie-detector test."

The President considered this, then asked, "Dr. Andrews, what do you think Talmedge's goal was? Why would he want to do all this?"

Jason shook his head. "I didn't really know the man well. He seemed to be mostly interested in money. I'm sure he was doing this for someone else."

"Who?" The President posed the million-dollar question.

"I have no idea. Someone with a lot of money and an ax to grind. It could be an American or a foreigner—could even be a foreign government."

After a moment's reflection the President asked, "Are there any additional questions for Dr. Andrews?"

There were none.

The President thanked Jason for coming and said that if he would return to the area where he had waited before, the FBI would meet him to make further transportation and security arrangements.

As soon as Jason left the Oval office, the President turned to Cordova. "As it stands, we now have only two remaining potential nominees for vice-president, the attorney general and Senator Chandler. I want a full investigation of any association they may have had with Talmedge or his clinic. Repeat the background checks on both of them.

"I have full confidence in the attorney general, but for now I feel she must be out of the loop for the remainder of this investigation. You understand, Michael. You report to me on this. No information flow whatsoever to your boss." Cordova nodded. "I'll tell her myself," the President added, "so there won't be any question.

"Senator Chandler represents a different problem. Half a dozen House and Senate committees are going to want to launch their own investigations. Everybody on the Hill is scared to death about what might have been in those files and what might still leak out. We can't keep them from holding hearings, but we won't cooperate. We give them nothing. This is a clear national security issue. You can use my name. I'll take the heat.

"Now, Michael, what about Talmedge's associations?"

"Since he's been at the clinic, his political associations have been pretty much across the spectrum. He's schmoozed with the left, the right, and everybody in between. Prior to that he was closely associated with petroleum interests, both domestic and Middle Eastern."

The President turned to Hal Martin, the CIA director. "What have you got on his Middle Eastern connections?"

"Several countries. It's all old stuff. We've had his name for about six hours now. We should start getting reports back from our assets on the ground in the Middle East sometime tomorrow."

"Let's keep working at it from both ends," the President said. "We'll have to repeat the background checks on both candidates, this time looking for any relationship to Talmedge, oil interests, the Middle East, and so forth." The President was briefly lost in his own thoughts. Then he asked, "Anyone have anything else?"

There was no response.

"O.K." He checked his calender. "We meet here again at one o'clock tomorrow afternoon."

Chapter Forty-seven

The man they knew only as Smith had seen operations unravel before. When that happened, you cleaned up as best you could and cut your loses. Smith understood that. He wondered if the Arabs did.

Once Talmedge started to talk, the toothpaste was out of the tube. There was no way you were going to coax it back inside. If Talmedge had lived, the entire operation would have been revealed. So there was no question that killing Talmedge was the right thing to do. Smith's problem wasn't who he *had* killed. His problem was who he *hadn't* killed.

He hadn't killed Jason Andrews. There simply hadn't been time. Then, Talmedge had been his first priority. Now, Jason Andrews was.

Smith told himself maybe he was wrong; maybe Andrews wouldn't remember him. Then he said, listen to yourself, you're hearing a dead man talking. If the doc didn't recognize you at that moment, he's remembered you by now. He looked right into your eyes. There's a picture of you somewhere in his mind.

Smith felt his chin. Only twenty-four hours' worth of

stubble so far, but already he looked different. He had skipped breakfast this morning, the beginning of a diet. With a beard and carrying thirty pounds less weight, he would no longer be recognizable from the description of his appearance at the clinic. Especially if the one man who had any real cause to remember him was no longer among the living.

For now, getting to Jason Andrews was not going to be easy. Andrews was being guarded too closely. So the direct approach was out. But Smith had a pretty good idea how he could get the doc to come to him.

Smith was driving yet another rental car. They'd tried to give him a red one, but he said gray or black—or no deal. So he was driving a gray Crown Victoria four-door. He liked the big American V8 engine, not one of those whiny little foreign jobs.

The Arabs wanted a meeting. Smith didn't know what their plans were, but he knew what his were. Retirement. The operation was over. Smith had taken a very large personal risk when he eliminated Talmedge. Now he expected to be compensated appropriately. The Arabs would complain. They always complained. But in the end they had no choice. Smith knew too much. They would have to pay, and then Smith would slip off into retirement in the Caymans.

It wasn't exactly blackmail that Smith had in mind. His knowledge acted as a sort of insurance policy, to keep the Arabs honest. They would pay. And then Smith would eliminate Andrews. And then it was off to the Caymans.

The Arabs had picked a spot in the Maryland suburbs for the meeting. They were always very big on meeting in

Maryland. Smith figured it was because their embassy was in Washington and the clinic was in Virginia. That left Maryland.

Smith's instructions were to drive to the corner and stop very briefly. His contact would climb in on the passenger's side. It would only take a few seconds. This wasn't the way they'd ever wanted to do it before, so he was cautious. He had scouted the location in advance and come up with a plan.

Smith parked his car several blocks away and walked to a sandwich shop within sight of the corner. He found a window seat and waited. A few minutes before the meeting time, the contact arrived. The princeling! His Excellency the bastard. Smith could see no one else. Not even a bodyguard.

Smith shook his head, thinking of the time he'd wasted taking precautions. If the Arabs were up to anything, the dictator's "nephew" wouldn't be allowed within a hundred miles of the place.

Ten minutes later, Smith was braking the car at the corner to give the kid a chance to hop in, but the kid was in no hurry. He sauntered over to the curb, slowly opened the door, then made a great show of carefully arranging his topcoat around him before he sat down.

Smith stomped the accelerator, throwing the kid back against the seat. The forward momentum of the car slammed the door.

"You're late, Smith!" The kid was furious. As always, he pronounced it Smythe.

Smith gave him a look. "Do you think they'll make me

stay after school and clean erasers?" What the kid needed was a good smack.

"Turn here!"

Smith gave the kid another look to let him know his patience was being tried, but he made the turn. "Where are we going?"

"Just do as I tell you."

Smack. Smith didn't do it, but he thought about it. Just one quick one to get the kid's attention.

"That was a very stupid thing you did," the kid said.

"Which thing was that?"

"Killing Talmedge. You're a very stupid man, Smith." Smythe.

"I guess I should have just let him stand there and tell the entire story. Then the U.S. Air Force could use your uncle's palace for bombing practice."

"You should have stopped Andrews *before* any of this ever happened."

"The doc was Talmedge's responsibility. I don't work for Talmedge."

"You work for me, Smith." Smythe.

Smith gave him the look again. "Was there a coup I didn't hear about?"

"You don't like me, do you, Smith?"

Smith ignored the question.

"I think you're a racist, Smith."

Again Smith ignored him.

"Turn here!"

The kid loved to give orders. They were well out into the Maryland countryside now. What was the kid up to?

"Where are we going?" He started to slow the car.

"Not much farther."

Smith saw something flash. He looked over: the kid was pointing a tiny, silver-plated pistol at him. Probably a .22. It looked like it was probably designed to be carried in a purse with a matching makeup kit.

"What the hell is this, kid?"

"Excellency! You will address me as Excellency!"

Smith ignored him.

"Say it!"

"Do any of the adults back at the embassy know what you're up to, Excellency?"

"You will pay for that, Smith. I was going to offer you a quick, painless death. Now, I assure you, you will die very slowly."

It was probably the first accurate statement the kid had made. A .22 could kill quickly with a point-blank head shot, but the kid was pointing at his side. Smith knew a lot about killing. That was his business. A .22 has no stopping power. Smith could still kill the kid *after* he pulled the trigger. Unless the kid got lucky and hit a really big artery, Smith probably wouldn't even feel the effects of the bullet for minutes or even longer. That didn't mean the bullet couldn't kill him. It would just take a little while.

"You're no longer of any use to us, Smith." The kid was yammering on, trying to screw up his courage. "You are a liability only."

"I think we're both finished, Excellency," Smith said.

"What do you mean?"

Smith gave a nod of his head off to the right. "It's the FBI."

The kid actually looked.

Instantaneously, Smith's right hand left the steering wheel and delivered a ferocious blow to the front of the kid's neck. Smith could feel and hear the cartilage give way, obstructing the airway. As the kid slumped, Smith crashed two more blows in rapid succession into the back of his neck. There was a small cracking sound, then one final exhale of breath, then nothing.

Smith pulled off the road and stopped the car. In a few seconds he had transferred the body into the trunk. Then he turned the car around and headed for the cabin.

Chapter Forty-eight

Smith had instructed the ambassador to come alone but knew that he would not. The ambassador was a coward. And the ambassador must surely know that Smith did not intend for him to survive.

Still, the ambassador had few options. He could hardly go to the U.S. authorities for assistance. At the same time, his own government would hold him responsible for the safety of the dictator's "nephew." The ambassador had of course never wanted the nephew to come to America. He had argued against it, but one could not argue too strenuously with the dictator. So now the problem child was his responsibility.

Smith had promised a simple deal: the return of the nephew in exchange for a large sum of money. He assured the ambassador that the kid was O.K., but he offered no proof. The ambassador was in no position to make demands. Smith assured him that if he didn't cooperate, the kid would be returned to the embassy by parcel post. A package a day for a month. The ambassador had no choice. He could either try to deal with Smith or go back to his own country with the blood of his president's heir on his hands. It would be much better to attempt to deal with Smith.

But Smith knew that, no matter what, the ambassador would not come alone.

Smith had bought the property many years ago under another of his many names. He built the cabin himself. The place was so isolated that no one was likely to happen upon it by accident. He had never brought another living soul here. He had never encountered so much as a hunter or backpacker in the neighboring woods.

The only way to approach the cabin by car was via an overgrown logging road. The only other access was through miles of woods. Smith had mapped out escape routes in each direction. He had rehearsed various escape scenarios hundreds of times, day and night.

There was a point of high ground on the property from which Smith could see a good portion of the logging road and a couple of miles either way of the county highway that bordered the property. It would be very difficult to take him by surprise, and he would know if another car was following. He had warned the ambassador of this and of the consequences should he fail to heed the warning.

But he knew that the ambassador would not come alone, so he watched from the high ground until he saw the ambassador's car, the Crown Victoria he'd been instructed to rent. There was no other car in sight, which meant that the ambassador had someone in the car with him.

Smith watched as the car passed near him. The ambassador appeared to be alone. Then Smith cut through the woods to come up behind the ambassador as he parked in front of the cabin. The ambassador did not see him until Smith was standing beside the car door with a 9mm automatic pointed directly at the ambassador's head. Without saying a word, Smith motioned for the ambassador to get out of the car. He put a finger to his lips to caution the ambassador not to speak.

The ambassador reluctantly pulled himself out of the car. Then Smith used him as a shield, keeping the ambassador between him and the car as he inspected the backseat and floor areas.

"O.K.," Smith said, "where's the money?"

"In the trunk. It's all there." The ambassador offered the keys to Smith. His expression was quite hopeful.

Smith shook his head in disgust at this evidence of ineptness. He leaned into the car and fired a single shot through the backseat cushion. There was a sharp cry of pain from inside the trunk.

Smith changed his aim by about a foot and fired again. This time he heard a muffled groan. He fired again. Nothing.

He shook his head disappointedly at the ambassador. "Open the trunk. If there's no money inside, you're going to join your friend, and I'm going to park the car somewhere in bright sunshine."

The ambassador was terrified. "Don't worry, Mr. Smith. Your money is in the trunk. All of it. Don't worry." He slowly opened the trunk.

"Were you planning to go to the opera?" Smith asked. Inside the trunk was the body of the embassy's cultural attaché. He had been shot once in the upper thigh, once in the chest, and once in the head.

"He demanded that I bring him along," the ambassador pleaded. "He threatened me."

Smith knew better. The attaché was a professional. He would have known instinctively that hiding inside the trunk was tantamount to committing suicide. The ambassador was the one who had done the threatening.

Fortunately for the ambassador, he had brought the money. Smith counted it carefully. When he finally got around to searching the ambassador, he found a small pistol and a knife. He took them away but wasn't particularly worried one way or the other. The ambassador lacked the courage to use them.

Next, he assigned the ambassador to burial detail. Two graves, he told him.

"I knew that I couldn't trust you," the ambassador said.

"And I could trust you?" Smith said.

It wasn't until the ambassador was finished digging that Smith showed him the body of the princeling, and the ambassador understood that, at least for now, he was getting a reprieve.

The ambassador had enjoyed a very long career in his country's diplomatic service. During that time he had undoubtedly been privy to many state secrets. Smith understood the value of such knowledge, and he intended to invite the ambassador to share what he knew. If the ambassador was reluctant, there were ways to encourage his cooperation, but the old ways were crude and unpleasant. Within the next day or so, Smith intended to have at his disposal much more sophisticated, much more modern means.

Smith had one more loose end to tie down, and then he could focus exclusively on his retirement plans.

Chapter Forty-nine

The clinic was a shambles. At first no one seemed to be in charge. Arthur Marsden tried his best, but it was his lack of administrative skills that had opened the door for Talmedge in the first place. Jason and Rachel stepped in to fill the vacuum.

Ironically, it was the blue-blazered security forces who were initially their most useful allies. Once it became apparent that they had no knowledge of or involvement in Talmedge's scheme, Jason was able to put them immediately back to work. The clinic grounds were crawling with reporters. All four major networks had set up satellite dishes so they could broadcast directly from the clinic parking lot. No area of the clinic property was secure.

But as soon as Jason gave them their marching orders, the security people cleared everyone out. No one was admitted without proper credentials. The FBI and police backed the clinic's security people one hundred percent. The clinic was private property. They had every right to control access. And incidentally, it made their investigative work much easier.

The clinic's staff were advised to stay home. They

would be called in as needed and issued new credentials. The clinic's finances were uncertain, but if money was found to be available, they would be paid until they received formal notice of severance of their employment. Jason warned those not directly involved in the research end of the clinic's work that they would be well advised to begin looking for alternative employment. Fortunately, in the health care industry employment was usually readily available.

When asked about the clinic's financial status, Marsden said he didn't have a clue. Talmedge had taken care of all that. Jason recommended an emergency meeting of the clinic's board of directors. They were clamoring for information anyway. Some had already resigned their positions, hoping to distance themselves from the mess the clinic had become ensnared in.

Jason said they needed to have a plan ready to present to the board, and he made a few suggestions. First of all, they had to hire an outside accounting firm to give them an objective assessment of the clinic's financial status. Second, it seemed obvious that, at least for now, all patient-care activities should cease. It wasn't as though patients were likely to be beating down the clinic's doors anyway. It was safe to assume that the clinic's political patient base was gone forever.

What about research? Marsden wanted to know. Jason thought that all funded research projects could go forward. In fact, if the clinic was to survive, it was likely to be as a research institution with limited or no patient-care responsibilities. To Arthur Marsden that sounded like one hell of a good idea.

Jason tried to convince the FBI and the state police that he didn't need them to baby-sit him twenty-four hours a day. They didn't agree.

"If it was purely a question of your own safety," Special Agent Matthews had said, "we'd just back off. We'd think you were stupid to resist our efforts to protect you, but in the end we'd just back off and let you sink or swim on your own. But it's not only your personal safety that we're concerned with here. You are the only known witness to a very important crime. Also, the crime you witnessed is linked to an even bigger crime, a conspiracy to topple the government. So for now we have to insist that you cooperate."

Jason realized that Matthews had a point. For now he could put up with having the FBI around. But he balked at Matthews' other request.

"We simply can't protect you adequately at your apartment," Matthews said. "The place is impossible to secure. It would be best if you let us take you to the FBI Training Center at Quantico each night. You'll be safe there."

No way, Jason said. That was going too far. He offered a compromise. Since he was spending all his time at the clinic anyway, he'd just stay there at night. There was no shortage of beds. It was practically like staying at a hotel, and right now it was about as secure as the Pentagon. Matthews agreed.

Which left Jason free to worry about Rachel.

"I'm going back to sleeping in my own bed tonight," Rachel said. "There's no reason why I can't."

Rachel had made up her mind, and Jason knew there was nothing he could do to change it. "Just be careful," he said. "I'll be here if you need anything. I can be there in ten minutes with half the law enforcement agents in northern Virginia."

"You're the one who needs to be careful, Jason. The bad guys are after you, not me."

That's what all the law enforcement people kept telling them. The only danger to Rachel was Jason. The best thing he could do would be to stay away from her. Reluctantly, Jason agreed.

Rachel was happy to be back in her own place. Her parents' house had been home once, but now this was home. She was comfortable here. She felt safe here.

The first thing Rachel did was take a long, hot shower. Then she slipped into an old bathrobe and went down to the kitchen to see what was in the refrigerator. She was able to piece together a pretty decent chicken sandwich that she washed down with a glass of chardonnay. She poured herself another glass, trying to take the edge off. She felt restless.

Dusk was approaching, but there was still plenty of light outside. What she really should do is go for a walk, burn off some of her excess energy. She ran back upstairs and threw on a warm sweater and an old pair of jeans, then back downstairs and out the back door.

It was a beautiful evening. Not too cool. The sun was going down but the sky was still blue. There was a full moon and you could already see a star or two. Planets, probably, she reminded herself. That's probably Venus over there. Or Mars. Which was it?

There was a large brick patio behind the house and beyond that an expansive lawn that sloped gently downward. There were numerous trees and plantings, but nothing yet in bloom. At the bottom of the hill was an old springhouse where she could remember playing as a little girl. It had seemed so very far from her parents' house, across the broad pasture and up another hill.

Rachel started out toward the springhouse, then stopped, thinking she heard a car. Something told her to be cautious. There was the sound of a car door slamming, then nothing.

She worked her way around the corner of the house, behind some bushes, slowly moving forward, trying to keep herself hidden. A dark late-model sedan was parked in front of the house. She moved just a little closer, and she could see a man standing at her front door. He was a big man, well dressed. He was probably in his middle forties.

There was nothing about him that ordinarily would have set off any alarms. If she had been inside, she would have answered the door, maybe talked to him through the door first, to see who he was. But outside she felt very vulnerable. Something warned her to hide.

She started to slowly, quietly back away. A twig snapped. She saw the man turn his head. Did he see her?

Rachel started to move more quickly now. She ran from tree to tree. She looked back and saw the man coming around the corner of the house. She broke into a run, no longer looking back, no longer seeking the protection of each tree as she came to it.

She practically dived around the corner of the springhouse. She tried the door. It was locked.

Rachel listened. She heard nothing. In one direction was her house and the intruder, in the other her parents' estate and safety. But her parents' house was across that great expanse of pasture. Open country. She would be visible, and she had no confidence that she could outrun the man in the open. Her only chance was to hide.

At the far corner of the small building there was an old willow tree and beside it a bush. Rachel crawled in between the tree and the bush. She curled up, making herself very small. And she waited.

At first she heard nothing. Then she heard footsteps. Unmistakable footsteps. They were slow and steady. The man was in no hurry.

Suddenly Rachel felt very cold. She was shaking. Her hands felt like ice. Her breath was coming in staccato bursts. She could feel her heart pounding.

And then he was there, standing over her. She saw the gun in his right hand. With his left he slowly pulled back the branches of the bush to expose her. From where she hid, curled up on the ground, he looked like a giant. She knew it was hopeless. No one would even hear the gun. No one would even look for her until tomorrow. By then her body would be as cold as the night.

"Dr. Chandler?" The voice was deep and masculine, but friendly.

Rachel tried to answer, but she had no voice of her own. A hand reached toward her. It seemed more an offer of assistance than a threat.

"I'm sorry if I scared you, Dr. Chandler," the deep voice said. "I just saw someone running from the house and had no idea who it was. I'm Special Agent Buford Ferris, FBI."

Rachel felt all the air go out of her in one great big sigh of relief. She was still shaking. Her heart was still pounding, but at least she was safe.

"I'm sorry," she said, "but could I see some sort of identification?"

"Sure can, ma'am." He pulled out his wallet and flipped it open.

By the dim light she could just make out that he was exactly who he said he was: Buford Ferris, Special Agent, Federal Bureau of Investigation.

"I feel like such a fool," she said, accepting his hand and pulling herself up.

"No, ma'am," he said. "You're right to be cautious. A lot of strange stuff has been going on."

They started to walk back toward the house.

"What was it you wanted?" Rachel asked.

The man hesitated a moment. "I was trying to give you a moment to catch your breath," he said. "Actually, there is a problem—at the clinic. It's Dr. Andrews."

"Jason! Is he all right?"

"He's going to be fine. Just a flesh wound."

"He's been shot?"

"I'm afraid so. Like I said, we think he's going to be fine. He wanted to see you, so they sent me to get you. Security at the clinic right now is tighter than ever. You about have to be in the company of an FBI agent to get in."

They hurried back to the car. He opened the passenger-side door for her, and Rachel climbed in. Dark was falling quickly now.

Ferris started the car and slammed it into reverse. With

a screech the car backed around. Then he threw it into drive and the tires screamed forward. He hardly braked the car at all at the end of the driveway. He made a hard left turn, and the rear tires protested loudly as they slid sideways out onto the main road.

The man is in such a hurry, Rachel thought, he's turned in the wrong direction. He was driving so fast, all in the wrong direction. They were losing valuable time.

And then she realized that he hadn't made a mistake. It wasn't something that she reasoned out. She just suddenly knew the truth. She reached for the door handle. They must be going seventy miles an hour, but she had to risk it. There was nothing there. The door handle had been removed. She wanted to cry.

"I'm such an idiot," Rachel said, mostly to herself.

The man didn't look at her. He didn't change expression. But he answered. "There was nothing you could do. You were coming with me no matter what you did. This way you didn't have to suffer any pain."

"Where are you taking me?"

"You'll find out. And tomorrow your boyfriend will be there too."

Rachel thought she was going to be sick. Jason! She looked around, desperately seeking some way to escape. Should she try to grab the wheel? The man was twice as big as she was. He seemed to read her mind.

"You can't get away, so don't even try. I don't want to have to hurt you. Don't worry. You're going to be fine. I only want your boyfriend."

Rachel wasn't even thinking about herself anymore. The man's plan was obvious. Jason was too well protected for him to get to, so he was using her as bait. She would be used to lure Jason to his death, And, only as an afterthought, she understood that her own death was as certain as Jason's. His only crime had been to see this man's face. Now she had seen it too.

Chapter Fifty

The man they called Smith said simply, "I've got Rachel Chandler."

And Jason instantly believed him. Rachel was so far only a few minutes late, but he had already called to check on her. There was no answer at her home.

"What do you want?" Jason asked. His tone conveyed complete surrender. Smith would get whatever he wanted.

"I need you to bring me a few Psychoden patches, Doctor. When I get the patches, you and the Chandler woman will be free to go."

Jason knew better than that. "What do you want the patches for?" He was only stalling, trying to clear his thoughts and come up with a plan.

"That needn't concern you, Doctor."

"How do I know that Rachel is all right?"

"You don't."

"How do I know that you even have Rachel?"

"Just trust me, Doctor."

"I'm not doing anything until I know you have her and that she's all right." Jason tried to muster his most convincing tone.

"Would you rather I send you a finger or an ear?" Smith said. "Or perhaps some larger part?"

"Don't hurt her!" Jason tried to sound tough, but even to his own ears his voice sounded pleading.

"Just do as I say and you'll both be fine."

Jason knew that was a lie, but he had no choice. His only chance to save Rachel was to play along.

"How many Psychoden patches do you want?"

"I think about a hundred should do it." Smith had been giving this some thought. His first idea had been to just use the drug on the ambassador to get as much information from him as possible. Whatever he learned from the ambassador could be used as a sort of insurance policy. If the ambassador's government came after Smith, he would leak the information. Then he thought, hell, some of the information might have resale value. Other countries might be willing to pay for it. Which immediately led him to realize how useful a personal supply of Psychoden might be. If Talmedge could do it, why couldn't he?

"O.K., Doc, enough fooling around. From now on you're on the clock. You've got one half hour to get the Psychoden and drive to the first pay phone. No police. No FBI. There's no way they can get to me without me getting enough warning to give Rachel Chandler a very painful death. You'll never see her alive again if you try anything. You understand, Doc?"

"I understand." Not only did he understand, Jason *believed* every word Smith said.

Smith gave him the location of a pay phone. It was in a shopping mall not far away. Then the phone went dead. If Jason hurried, he had enough time—just. That was clearly an important part of Smith's plan: don't give Jason time to think, which implied to Jason that if he just thought hard enough, he could beat Smith.

A gun, Jason thought. If only I could get my hands on a gun. But that was Smith's game. What chance did he have of beating Smith at his own game? Think, Jason! Think, dammit!

Jason looked at his watch. Two minutes already gone. He was in his office at the clinic. When he opened the door and stepped into the outer office, the first person he saw was Special Agent Jackson, the FBI man who had been assigned to him for the day.

Jackson stood. "Are we going somewhere, Doctor?"

"Up to the lab for a little while. I have some things to do up there."

They headed off together for the lab. Jason tried not to appear as though he was in a hurry. One thing was certain, he wasn't going to involve the FBI. He'd been suspicious of them from the beginning. Mrs. Bates had trusted the FBI. And Smith surely knew that Jason was being guarded by the FBI. That didn't seem to bother him much. Think, Jason.

By the time they arrived at the lab, Jason had a plan. All he needed was a few minutes alone at the back of the lab. He found Special Agent Jackson a seat near the door and warned him that he might be working on his research for a couple of hours. Jackson said that would be fine. He'd brought a paperback to read. A few minutes later Jason slipped out the lab's back door and down a rear stairway.

Security at the clinic was geared at keeping people out.

No one cared who was leaving the grounds. For Jason it was simply a matter of walking to his car and driving out the main gate. The guard gave him a nod as he passed the security gate. Jason smiled back. When he was questioned later, the guard would remember having seen Dr. Andrews leave. By then, for better or for worse, Jason would be long gone.

The phone was already ringing when Jason arrived at his first destination.

"Hello."

"I was about to hang up, Doc. What kept you?"

"I came as fast as I could. I had to go to the lab to pick up your Psychoden." Jason was standing in the middle of an indoor shopping mall. It was nearly empty at this time of day.

"Here's the way this works, Doc. I'm going to give you a series of locations. Each one will have a pay phone. I'll call and tell you where to go next. Remember, I'll be watching you. You better be alone. And don't try to make any phone calls, either. I see you make a phone call, it's over for the girl."

Jason looked around. As near as he could tell, no one was paying any attention to him, but the man could be out there, watching, right now. All he could do for now was cooperate and pray that Rachel was unharmed.

"Listen, whoever you are, I'm going to do everything exactly as you tell me. So don't hurt Rachel. Please."

"Here's your next stop," the man said, and he gave Jason directions to a public park many miles away.

Jason carefully wrote down the instructions, then asked the man to repeat them.

"You're stalling."

"No, I'm not. I just can't afford to get this wrong."

The man repeated the instructions, and Jason wrote them down again.

The scenario was repeated again and again. The settings became increasingly rural. Jason's car was frequently the only one on the road for long stretches. The man who had kidnapped Rachel Chandler would have ample opportunity to make certain Jason was alone.

At one stop, just as Jason was walking back to his car, the pay phone rang again. Jason answered, there was a pause, and then the click of someone hanging the phone up at the other end. The man was making certain, Jason reasoned, that Jason wasn't making any calls to tell anyone where he was. The man must be counting on Jason's having been too afraid or just not having had time enough to set anything up with the authorities.

After several stops it all became quite routine. It would have been boring if the stakes hadn't been so high. All he could think about was Rachel.

Now he was looking for a narrow, unmarked road. The voice said he would be approaching a state park camping area and that there would be lots of children around. The phone was near the shower facilities. Jason thought he followed the directions precisely, but something had to be wrong. The farther he drove into the woods, the more convinced he was of his mistake.

Damn it! He was wasting precious time. He was going to be late. Should he turn around or risk driving deeper into the woods?

Jason rounded a final turn and saw a cabin. Two late-model Fords were parked out front. This was no camping area. He threw the gear shift into reverse and looked back over his shoulder. That's when he saw the man with the gun. It was a man he recognized. This was now the fourth time he had seen him.

Jason turned off the engine. The man was motioning for him to get out of the car. All Jason could think about was the cabin. Rachel was in there.

'Is she all right?" Jason asked. "You didn't hurt her?"

"She's fine. You'll see her in a minute." The man spoke very softly. Jason wanted desperately to believe him.

He had Jason put his hands on the car and then searched him very methodically. If Jason had had a gun, or a radio transmitter, or a pencil the man would have found it. The man handcuffed Jason, hands behind his back, then asked, "Got anything in the trunk?"

Jason slowly shook his head.

The man fired three shots in quick succession through the backseat cushion into the trunk.

"Now, let's open the trunk," he said, "and see what we've got."

Chapter Fifty-one

The trunk was empty.

"Got any bugs hidden on the car?"

Again Jason slowly shook his head.

The man took some kind of electronic device out of his pocket and spent several minutes sweeping the entire car for bugs. All he found was the bottles containing the Psychoden patches that Jason had placed on the front passenger's seat. When the man was satisfied, he stood back and shook his head in disappointment.

"You know, Doc. You're stupider than I thought. You should have at least tried *something*."

"Can I see her?" was all Jason said in response.

The man motioned with his head for Jason to start toward the cabin. Inside, Jason found Rachel in tears, but otherwise appearing to be okay. One leg and one arm were handcuffed to a straight chair.

"Jason! I thought he'd shot you!"

They kissed and tried to comfort each other as best they could given their handcuffs.

"When I heard those shots," Rachel said, "I just assumed you were dead."

For the first time Jason noticed that there was a fourth person in the room. The man sat on a bed, eyeing them with a mixture of arrogance and contempt. At first Jason assumed he was a second captor; then he noticed the handcuffs. The man appeared to be of Middle Eastern descent.

"You came alone?" the man asked.

Jason shrugged.

"Then you are a fool." The man turned his head to the wall. These Americans were not worthy of his gaze.

Their captor found this performance amusing. "Meet your patient, Doctor. He likes to be called 'Mr. Ambassador,' but I call him Buttface. I think it fits him perfectly. Incidentally, he's the reason you're in this mess. He wasn't content to blackmail a couple of congressmen, maybe a senator or two. If he'd stopped there, he could have had enough clout to influence some important votes that affected his country, maybe even controlled some important committees.

"But, oh no, old Buttface here kept getting greedier and greedier. He saw a chance to blackmail the vice-president. Then the VP offs himself and Buttface figures, what the hell, he'll just slide his own man into the slot. And do you know what they had planned for me next? As soon as their man's in the vice-presidency, all I have to do is shoot the President. Simple as that. Right, Buttface?"

Buttface remained aloof and uncommunicative.

"Doc, why don't you ask old Buttface if he brought anyone with *him*?"

Jason thought he saw the ambassador recoil slightly from the remark. It registered, somewhere in the back of

Jason's mind, that he now knew almost the entire story. There was only one major piece missing. Jason had nothing to lose, so he asked, "Who's Gerald?"

The ambassador turned his head back toward Jason and beamed a self-satisfied smile, but said nothing.

"Don't worry, Doc," their captor said. "As soon as we put that patch on him, he'll tell you. In fact, I'd kind of like to know the answer to that question myself."

The ambassador turned to the man he knew as Smith and smiled once again.

For a moment it looked as though Smith would hit him, but then he seemed to change his mind. He picked up one of the bottles and took out a Psychoden patch.

"Might as well get started," Smith said. "Just put this right on Buttface's neck, do I, Doc?" He stuck the patch on the ambassador's neck and said, "Now what?"

Jason didn't really want to cooperate, but there was no point in needlessly irritating their captor. The only useful thing Jason could do right now would be to prolong their ordeal for as long as humanly possible.

"You need to wait five or ten minutes," Jason said. "Then I usually start by asking a lot of straightforward, unthreatening background questions: where was he born, how old is he, that kind of thing."

So they waited. And then Smith began a long litany of questions aimed at probing the most closely held secrets of the ambassador's homeland. He asked about secret military bases and atomic energy projects, about germ- and chemical-warfare development. He asked about the country's involvement in various terrorist bombings and assassinations. The list went on and on. In another setting Jason might have found it all quite fascinating.

Jason tried to comfort Rachel as best he could. He whispered, "Did he hurt you?" She shook her head no.

Rachel's right wrist and left ankle were cuffed to the chair. If the arm and leg had both been right or left, she might have had some mobility, might even conceivably have been able to swing the chair as a weapon, but this way she couldn't defend herself at all. Jason still had his hands cuffed behind him. He could move, even run, but he had no illusions that he could ever pose a meaningful threat to their captor. Maybe if he had taken up kick-boxing . . .

The cabin was small and rustic. Heat was provided by a wood stove. There was a stack of small logs and kindling that might serve as a weapon if you had a free hand. Rachel had a free hand.

The interior of the cabin consisted of a single room, perhaps twenty-five feet on a side. There was an indentation in one corner, a small, walled-off area with a door. When she saw Jason looking at it, Rachel mouthed the word "bathroom." There were windows on each side and a front and back door. Outside, in every direction, all Jason could see was woods.

The furnishings were sparse. There was a single wooden table with four straight chairs. A kerosene lantern sat on the table. There was a bed in one corner. A single, more comfortable-looking armchair pulled up next to the bed was occupied by their captor. His back was to them. He was either very careless or very confident of his abilities. Jason thought about the possibility of Rachel's sneaking up behind the man and hitting him on the head with a small log. She'd have to drag the chair—and hit him left-handed. There was no way she could pull it off, even with Jason kicking for all he was worth at the same time.

And then, suddenly, it was over. The man was talking to them.

"I guess that's all the questions I have." The obvious implication was that he no longer had any use for any of them.

"You didn't ask about Gerald," Jason said.

"Oh, yeah. Right. O.K., Buttface, who's Gerald?"

The ambassador just continued to stare off into the distance.

"I think you'll have to ask this question a little differently," Jason offered. He walked across the room, desperately trying to think of some way to shift the balance of power. He looked out the window. Nothing. He looked at the ambassador. The man was under the influence of Psychoden. He was of no use.

Smith stood as Jason approached. He was a huge, powerful man.

"Mind if I ask him the question?" Jason asked.

Smith shrugged. It made no difference to him.

"Mr. Ambassador," Jason said, "you are aware of a plan to replace the vice-president by a man who is known by the code name Gerald?"

"I am," the ambassador replied in that far-off Psychoden voice.

"What is the real name of the person who is known by

the code name Gerald?" Jason was attempting to be very precise with the question.

Once again the ambassador appeared unable to come up with an answer.

Jason tried again. "Mr. Ambassador, do you know who was picked to be Gerald?"

This time the Ambassador had a simple answer. "No."

"Was *someone* picked to be Gerald?"

"Yes."

Jason was trying to understand what was going on here. "Who picked the person to be Gerald?"

"Mr. Talmedge, of course."

Jason sighed. Talmedge was a dead end. "Does anyone else know the identity of Gerald?"

"So far as I know, only the president."

"The President! The President of the United States knows who Gerald is?"

"Oh, no. Only the president of *my* country knows who Gerald is. At His Excellency's request, Mr. Talmedge communicated the name directly to him."

The implications of this last statement stunned Jason. He now understood why the ambassador had smiled so complacently when he was asked about Gerald earlier. Whatever they did to him, the ambassador had the satisfaction of knowing that they would never find out who Gerald was.

For a few moments Jason had completely forgotten about Smith. That now changed very quickly.

"I think we've learned just about all we're going to learn from our friend here," Smith said, mostly to himself. He was now once again holding a pistol in his hand. "I think it's time to take that patch off the ambassador's neck so I can do what I have to do."

Jason looked at Smith. He was too far away for even a desperate kick at the gun. Jason could lunge at their captor, but Smith would simply shoot. There was nothing to be gained by that kind of mindless heroism.

"It would be a kindness," Jason said, "to leave the patch in place."

"If the shoe were on the other foot," Smith answered with a sneer, "I can assure you that the ambassador's people would have no such sympathy for you." But he considered it for a second and then said, "Have a seat, Doc."

Jason hesitated while he carefully considered his options one last time. Was there anything he could do?

Smith answered the unasked question. "Just have a seat, Doc."

Jason turned and started across the room. Rachel had tears in her eyes. He could offer her no real comfort.

The sound was unbelievably loud. And there was a blinding flash of light. Jason was thrown to the floor, his head aching, his ears ringing. Unable to hear. Unable to see.

His mind tried desperately to make sense of what was happening. The man hadn't shot the ambassador at all. He'd shot Jason! In the back of the head, the occipital lobe—that accounted for the flash. But wait, he wasn't dead. Not yet. So there would be more. And then he heard a shot, and then another. Understanding came very slowly.

Rachel!

Chapter Fifty-two

"Doc! Doc!"

Someone seemed to be trying to get his attention. A hand roughly shook his shoulder. The ringing in his ears would not stop. Jason struggled to get to his knees. *Rachel.* He knew he had to protect Rachel. But he was totally disoriented. It would be several minutes yet before his mind began to comprehend what had actually happened.

A stun grenade, Lieutenant Briggs said.

Smith had heard something or sensed it or seen it—something. He had started firing almost before the grenade exploded. The police had no recourse but to return fire. Smith was dead. Everyone else was fine.

Jason managed to get to his feet and find Rachel. They were both still handcuffed, so she could only throw her free arm around Jason and clutch him closely to her. Rachel cried. Jason tried to be strong for her.

Black-uniformed members of the state police SWAT team were everywhere. Someone found some keys and began unlocking handcuffs. Jason was finally able to give Rachel a real hug.

"How?" she asked as soon as she was able to trust her voice. "How were they able to find us?"

"I left a trail," Jason answered.

"That's a pretty smart fellow you've got your arms around," Briggs said. "And pretty lucky, too," he added with a relieved smile. "There's one hell of a lot of places this plan could have gone wrong."

"So *tell* me," Rachel said. Her voice was getting stronger now.

"When I got the call saying he had you"—Jason nodded his head toward the body under the sheet—"I called Lieutenant Briggs and told him what was going on. There wasn't time to set anything up. That was deliberate, of course. We couldn't use any sort of electronic communication. There just wasn't time.

"And he said he would be watching me. That was the whole purpose of having me go from place to place answering pay phones. I could be watched to make certain I was alone and that I wasn't making any phone calls on my own.

"So what I did, I just wrote down the instructions to the next phone and left them for Lieutenant Briggs. He followed about ten minutes later, figuring the bad guys would be gone by then and no one would see him."

"What I was afraid was going to happen," Briggs said, "was that I would show up at the phone and there would be no note and no Dr. Andrews. I was afraid that once they thought Dr. Andrews was alone, they'd just swoop down and nab him."

"What would you have done then?" Rachel asked.

"Well, we'd tried to keep a rolling perimeter going, a series of cars in the area on parallel routes so we could seal off a large area if we needed to. We also had a helicopter ready to go. But it was a lot easier this way. That last note you left, Doc, I knew you weren't going to any state park."

"I was beginning to wonder where you were," Jason said. "I could just imagine one of my notes blowing away or someone else finding it."

Suddenly, Rachel gave Jason a disapproving look. "You might have told me what was going on."

"I'm sorry, Rachel. There just wasn't a chance. I couldn't risk arousing his suspicion that we were up to something. Besides, just think how disappointed you would have been if I had promised you that Lieutenant Briggs was on his way and in the end he decided not to come after all."

Rachel gave him only the tiniest smile

"What's the story on the Arab?" Briggs asked. "I tried to talk to him, but I'm not sure anyone's home at his house."

"Take a look at his neck," Jason said.

Briggs squinted back across the room. "Psychoden?"

Jason smiled and gave what he knew of the ambassador's history. "If you want to ask him any questions, I imagine you'll find him most cooperative."

"Maybe we ought to wait till the FBI shows up," Briggs said. "They're supposed to be on their way."

"There's one other thing," Rachel added. "I heard Smith and the ambassador talking last night about some bodies that they buried yesterday. I'm not exactly sure where, but they can't be too far."

Briggs didn't look terribly pleased at this latest bit of

news. Finding a couple more bodies was probably not going to *un*complicate his day any.

"Can we go outside now, Lieutenant?" Jason asked. "I think we could both use some air."

"Sure, but don't go far. I'm sure the Fibbies are going to have lots of questions when they finally get here." He looked at his watch. "It's after noon. They should be waking up any time now."

Rachel and Jason walked out into the cool Virginia afternoon. The air smelled of pine, fresh and clean. It was invigorating.

"Well, at least it's over," Rachel said.

"Not exactly," Jason replied.

"What do you mean?"

"Who's Gerald?"

Chapter Fifty-three

The President was angry and made no attempt whatsoever to conceal it. "So, what you're telling me," he fumed, "is that one of my two remaining potential nominees for vice-president, one of two of the finest people I have ever known, may be an operative of a foreign government."

"It is a possibility," said Michael Cordova, the director of the FBI, "that I cannot exclude. The background checks have revealed absolutely nothing—except of course for Senator Chandler's apparently rather distant relationship with Charles Talmedge and his sister's closer one. The attorney general comes out entirely clean."

"What about all those damn computer files at the clinic?" the President wanted to know. "Anything new there?"

Cordova shook his head. "All gone. Someone introduced a virus that wiped out the entire system."

"Any idea who?"

"It's possible that no one at the clinic deliberately sabotaged the data. This virus has gotten into other government and university computers. On the other hand, Dr.

Andrews has stated openly that it's just as well that the files disappeared."

"I can't entirely disagree with that," the President said.

"It is also true," Cordova added, "that both the senator and the attorney general have been patients at the clinic. It is probable that there *were* files on both of them— unless one of them was a co-conspirator. According to Dr. Andrews, there was no file on Congressman Bates despite the fact that he had been through the clinic for his annual physical. Knowing what he knew, it appears that Bates deliberately avoided having his blood drawn."

"Whatever else Bates was," the President said, shaking his head, "he was no fool."

Silence filled the Oval Office while the President considered his options. Cordova waited for the President to speak.

"One of those two has to be Gerald," the President said. "Either I appoint one of them and take the ultimate risk, or I reject both of them and deprive the country of the best candidates for the job." The President thought for a few moments about all the others who had politely refused to be considered for the nomination. Presumably they had been blackmailed. He thought of his old friend Herb Allen, who had taken his own life rather than allow *something* to become a matter of public knowledge. Even the President didn't know what that something was. There were lots of crazy rumors floating around, but no one knew for certain—except Jason Andrews, and the doctor wasn't telling. Jason said he wasn't about to reveal a secret that Herbert Allen had killed himself to keep hidden.

"I suppose I have no choice," the President finally said.

"I'll have to begin to consider a new batch of nominees."
It wasn't a happy thought. After the attorney general and
Senator Chandler, the President was left with a bunch of
second-tier candidates.

Cordova shifted uncomfortably in his chair. "I feel obligated to point out, Mr. President, that may be just exactly what the conspirators wanted you to do. It is just
possible that their Gerald has not yet made it onto the list
of potential nominees."

"Expletive deleted," the President said. "What do you
suggest, Michael?"

"The only idea I've been able to come up with is, well,
it's sort of a live by the sword, die by the sword kind of
thing."

"Let's have it."

"Well, sir, this Psychoden drug that has caused all this
trouble, it does seem to work. From all that I have heard,
it's better than any lie-detector machine we've ever had."

"You mean, give this drug to potential nominees?"

"I'm not talking about some big fishing expedition
here," Cordova said. "I'm talking about a set of questions
agreed to in advance—by the candidates. All we would be
looking for would be whether or not they were involved in
the conspiracy. It would be clearly stated at the outset
that there would be no probe of their personal lives. We
would tell them the questions before they consented to
the test."

"And what if they refuse?" the President wanted to
know. "Gerald's not going to agree to submit to something
like this."

"What you do then would of course be entirely up to

you, Mr. President. Obviously, it would look quite suspicious for one of them to refuse."

The President didn't have to think about it for long. "I won't do it," he said. "What kind of a precedent would this set? Can you imagine? All key government appointees now having to submit to this new standard. It's un-American. I simply won't do it."

Cordova wasn't surprised at the President's reaction. "My first thoughts were the same as yours. Then I tried to look at it in as unemotional a light as I could. It's not as though lie-detector tests aren't used routinely right now, both in the government and in private industry to investigate employees in certain sensitive positions.

"We've all learned to accept that modern life requires certain infringements on personal liberty. People traveling by air must submit to searches both of their luggage and their persons. In the workforce, more and more employees are subjected to mandatory drug testing. The list goes on and on."

But the President shook his head defiantly. "I won't do it," he said. "I simply won't do it."

Chapter Fifty-four

Jason's initial reaction to the FBI director's proposal was identical to the President's. No way. Expletive deleted.

What was the difference, Cordova wanted to know, between this situation and what Jason had done with Talmedge?

If you need to ask, Jason had replied, all the explaining in the world is not going to help you understand the difference.

But in the end both Jason and the President had been persuaded. They very foundation of American democracy was being threatened. It was their duty to insure, beyond the faintest shadow of doubt, the integrity of the vice-presidency. They could not permit any lingering suspicion that the person who occupied the office of vice-president—a person who would be only one assassin's bullet removed from the presidency—was an agent of a foreign power.

This was the point the President came back to again and again, as though he were still trying to convince himself.

They were assembled in the Oval Office: the President,

the Director of the FBI, the attorney general, Senator Chandler, and Jason. The President had deliberately kept the list of those present to a minimum.

"I think that you cannot imagine," the President told them, "the amount of soul searching I've had to do. This may ring hollow to you, but there are no two people in government in whom I have greater confidence than the two of you. I've known you, Charlotte," he said to Attorney General Moran, "for many years, and I've always counted you among my closest advisers. And, Senator, though you and I have not had the same personal relationship, we've worked together for nearly ten years. I've always admired your integrity and forthrightness.

"So, I guess what I'm doing here is, I'm apologizing for what I'm asking of you. I'm almost ashamed that I have to do it. I would not do it for a lesser cause than the security of the United States of America."

The senator and attorney general were each handed a list of the proposed questions. "I cannot absolutely promise," the President said, "that if your answers are either ambiguous or suggest you have been involved in the conspiracy, that under those circumstances I would not want to ask related, follow-up questions. I will guarantee each of you that there will be no fishing expedition into your personal lives. We are only interested in matters directly related to this Gerald conspiracy. If either of you enjoys making sausage out of orphans in your spare time, that's your own affair. For our purposes here today, we're not interested and we're not going to get into it.

"Now, before either of you agrees to our plan or decides to leave the room, I want Dr. Andrews to say a few words about this drug and what you'll experience and side effects and so on."

"I should probably start by pointing out," Jason said, "that each of you has undoubtedly already been exposed to Psychoden. You've both been to the clinic. I assume that Talmedge had files on both of you.

"In your case, Senator Chandler, this is especially relevant. The episode that you experienced at the clinic, which was thought to be a seizure, was almost certainly a reaction to Psychoden. This type of reaction causes no long-term harm and is not dangerous. I would expect to be able to prevent it by giving you a type of antihistamine that we use to treat these reactions when they occur. You'd receive the antihistamine before the Psychoden patch was placed."

Jason went on to discuss the drug at length just as though he were obtaining informed consent from a patient. Then he asked if they had any questions. They did not.

"I guess that's it, then," the President said. "Once again, I apologize to each of you for having to ask this question. Would you be willing to submit to this test?"

Neither the senator nor the attorney general showed the slightest hesitation.

"I believe," Jason suggested, "that it would be best to begin with Attorney General Moran. That way I could go ahead and give the senator a dose of Benadryl to protect him from having another reaction."

So it was decided. A short while later the attorney general of the United States was under the influence of Psychoden and answering the usual routine questions.

"What is your name?"

"Charlotte Moran."

"Where were you born?"

"Houston, Texas."

And so forth. Then, finally, "Attorney General Moran, when did you first become aware of the Marsden Clinic conspiracy to blackmail certain political figures?"

"Three or four days ago. The day of the Talmedge shooting."

"Prior to that time, had anyone mentioned to you the possibility that the Marsden Clinic was involved in any illegal activities?"

"Mr. Cordova, the FBI director, had mentioned his suspicions, but he said he had no proof."

"When did you first become aware of the plot to place an agent under foreign control in the vice-presidency?"

"Yesterday. Mr. Cordova briefed me on the kidnappings in Virginia and told me the whole story."

There was just one more question on the list, and Jason fully expected it to be the most revealing.

"Attorney General Moran, are you now under any threat of blackmail by anyone for any reason?"

Her answer was swift and definite. "I am not."

The men in the room exchanged glances. They had agreed that there would be no other questions. The attorney general had passed the test. The President appeared especially relieved. Charlotte Moran had been his protégé. For her to be implicated would be particularly painful, both personally and politically.

Jason removed the Psychoden patch from the attorney general's neck. He had assumed that she was Gerald, perhaps because he didn't want to consider the possibility that Rachel's brother might be involved. Now the focus was on the senator, and Jason worried about the effect all this would have on Rachel. He was sorry that he himself was involved, that the responsibility of breaking the hard news to Rachel would fall to him.

Most likely, Jason comforted himself, the senator was not a willing participant, merely a victim. Like so many others.

"Shall we ask the senator to come in?" the President asked.

"We need to wait a few more minutes," Jason said, "for the attorney general to fully recover from the effects of the medication."

What Jason could not understand was why Senator Chandler had agreed to submit to the Psychoden interview in the first place.

Chapter Fifty-five

The President was on his feet congratulating his attorney general as soon as the effects of Psychoden began to wear off. "You did fine, Charlotte. No problems. I hope you'll forgive me for putting you through all this."

She was very gracious. "I understand that you had no choice, Mr. President. I have nothing to hide."

He led her off through another door, some sort of secretarial office, Jason presumed, to await the testing of the senator. When the President returned, he signaled Jason that it was time to bring in Senator Chandler.

Jason found the senator in a comfortable chair, his head bowed, his eyes closed. He was sound asleep. The Benadryl could be partly responsible. The drug could be mildly sedating. Still, you had to admire the man's coolness, given what he was about to face. Jason tried not to feel sorry for him.

"Senator Chandler," he said, gently touching the man's shoulder, "you're on."

The senator awoke with a start. "Sorry, I guess I must have dozed off."

"The Benadryl probably had something to do with that, Senator."

"Please, call me Rob. I understand you're practically part of the family." The senator certainly seemed unconcerned, cheerful even.

Jason managed a weak smile in response. Under the circumstances it was difficult to imagine pursuing a more familiar relationship with Robert Chandler.

Inside the Oval Office the mood was somber. Everyone had reached essentially the same conclusion. Senator Chandler was Gerald. Case closed.

What Jason felt mostly was sadness, especially for Rachel. When he looked at the President, Jason saw disappointment. Cordova, on the other hand, could not conceal his contempt.

The senator appeared to notice none of this. "I'm ready whenever you are," he said with a smile.

Jason placed the patch on Chandler's neck, and they all waited while he drifted off into that Psychoden twilight that all patients went to. After a few minutes, Jason took a deep breath and began.

"What is your name?"

"Robert L. Chandler."

"Where were you born?"

"Charlottesville, Virginia."

"What do you do for a living?"

"I am a United States senator representing the commonwealth of Virginia."

The usual litany. Then, at last, Jason had no choice but to ask, "Senator Chandler, when did you first become aware of the Marsden Clinic conspiracy to blackmail certain political figures?"

"The day of the Talmedge shooting. I was there, you know. It was terrible, just terrible . . ."

"Prior to that time, had anyone mentioned to you the possibility that the Marsden Clinic was involved in any illegal activities?"

"At one point my sister said something to me about your suspicions, Dr. Andrews, that there was something going on. She didn't really seem very concerned, so neither was I."

"When did you first become aware of the plot to place an agent under foreign control in the vice-presidency?"

"Yesterday. My sister Rachel called last night to let me know she was all right. She told me all about the kidnapping and the plot."

There was only one question remaining on the list. "Senator Chandler, are you now under any threat of blackmail by anyone for any reason?"

There was a hesitation, as though the senator didn't quite understand the question. Jason was about to pose it again when the senator spoke.

"No, I am not, nor have I ever been."

Jason was momentarily stunned. They were finished. Both potential nominees had passed the test. Most of all he felt relief for Rachel. Jason turned to the President. "I guess we're done," he said.

But Cordova was on his feet. The scene had awakened the prosecutor in him that was ever present just beneath the skin.

"Hell, no, we're not done." His voice was much too

loud for the room. "I've got a few questions that the senator is going to have to answer!" He made his way across the room to stand beside Senator Chandler.

Then the President was on his feet. "There will be no more questions," he said very firmly.

Cordova turned toward the President in disbelief.

"I understand your prosecutorial zeal, Mr. Cordova, but we made a solemn promise to these people. They're here without counsel, and they're allowing us to trample all over their civil rights. They did this because they trust us. I will not betray that trust.

"As far as I'm concerned," the President said, "both Senator Chandler and Attorney General Moran have passed this test with flying colors. There is absolutely nothing to suggest that either of them had any part whatsoever in the conspiracy or that either is being blackmailed to cooperate with the conspiracy. Our investigation here is over.

"You can go ahead and take that patch off the senator, Dr. Andrews, and I don't care if I never hear of that damn drug again."

Jason quickly removed the Psychoden patch. He had no desire to see Cordova take advantage of Senator Chandler. The President was right. Enough was enough.

While they waited for Chandler to recover, the President went to look for the attorney general. When they returned, the President did not speak until Senator Chandler confirmed that he felt back to normal.

"I want to thank you both," the President said with evident sincerity, "for participating in this test. I hope that such a thing will never again be necessary in this country.

Your answers confirmed for all of us, once and for all, that you've taken no part in this treachery." Both the attorney general and the senator gave small, relieved smiles.

"I intend to make my announcement tomorrow," the President continued, "as to which of you will be my nominee to become vice-president. I would only emphasize at this time that a president could not hope to have two more outstanding candidates. Both of you have glittering careers ahead no matter what choice is made tomorrow."

With that they all stood. The President warmly shook the hands of the potential nominees. The meeting was over.

Until Jason spoke.

He almost didn't want to. It was as though he couldn't help himself. The last thing in the world he wanted to do was to be responsible for the downfall of Rachel's brother, and yet he couldn't just stand there and watch this happen. He told himself that he might actually be doing one of the potential nominees a favor.

"There's something else," Jason said, "that I feel obligated to mention. Perhaps there's another question that needs to be asked."

All eyes were suddenly on Jason.

"You're not thinking," the President asked, "of doing any more questioning under the drug, are you?"

"Oh, no," Jason said. "I just want us to think about one last thing."

"I suppose everyone ought to get comfortable then," the President said, taking his seat once again.

The others followed the President's lead. Only Jason remained standing.

"I've been thinking," Jason said, "about Herbert Allen. He was freely elected to the vice-presidency and clearly not part of any conspiracy. But he made the mistake of going to the clinic, and while he was there they opened up his mind and searched until they found something they could use. What they found was so explosive, so potentially damaging that they thought they could use it to control the vice-presidency and, perhaps eventually, even the presidency.

"They were right about the devastating impact of the information, but they were very wrong about the vice-president. He would never have cooperated with them under any circumstances. In the end he chose to take his own life rather than let the information become public and humiliate his family.

"But this started Talmedge and his friends thinking. The vice-presidency was vacant. In theory, the opportunity still existed for them to control it. It seems to me they had three options. The first was to place some willing confederate in the job, some co-conspirator. Fortunately, there aren't many of those around, but I do believe that Hiram Bates applied for the job.

"The second choice was to try to get someone into the job that they already had a death grip on, someone they were already blackmailing. We don't know how many people like that are out there. I think that probably a lot of the people they blackmailed simply left their positions rather than allow themselves to be blackmailed in place. We've seen an incredibly large number of surprise retirements over the last two years.

"Today we've already explored these two possibilities

with Senator Chandler and Attorney General Moran. We know that neither of them was part of the conspiracy, and we know that neither of them is being blackmailed, but there is a third possibility that we haven't yet explored."

The silence that filled the Oval Office was total. All eyes were fixed on Jason.

"Attorney General Moran and Senator Chandler," Jason continued, "both of you have visited the Marsden Clinic. Both of you had blood drawn. We must assume that Talmedge took that opportunity to suck out of your brain anything that he thought might be of the slightest use to him. We therefore must assume that anything you knew, you shared with him. You could not have prevented yourselves from doing that.

"I want to make this as clear as I possibly can. You have no secrets from Talmedge and his associates. If there was anything, anything at all in your memory that might be used to blackmail you, we have to assume that it will be used. I'm not talking about some little, subtle thing. It would be something *very* big. Something that might force you to make the same choice that Herbert Allen had to make: will you betray your country, or will you instead take your own life?

"If you have something like that hidden in your brain somewhere, you—and everyone else—would be much better off facing it now. And there's one more thing, and I can't emphasize this too strongly. The thing, this horrible knowledge that you may have tucked away, it may not be about you at all. It is at least as likely, maybe even more likely, that it is some terrible truth about someone you love. Talmedge may have believed that you would do anything to protect that loved one from being hurt, to keep that truth from becoming public."

Jason stopped. There was nothing more he could say. He felt his eyes being pulled toward Rachel's brother, almost afraid of what they might see. But Robert Chandler looked straight back at Jason without an ounce of guilt on his face. The senator turned his palms up and shrugged his shoulders. Whatever Jason was talking about didn't have anything to do with him.

Jason turned his gaze to the attorney general. Her eyes were cast down. She had grown suddenly pale. She was a picture of despair.

"I," she tried to talk. Her voice trembled. "I . . . I didn't think . . . of course . . . I mean . . ." She was devastated.

But as they watched, it was apparent that she was marshaling all her energy for what she had to do. She pulled herself to her feet and looked the President squarely in the eye.

"I'm so sorry, Mr. President. I would never knowingly do anything to harm you or to place my country in jeopardy. You will have my formal, written resignation within the hour."

And then, with a dignity which Jason would always remember and admire, Charlotte Moran walked gracefully from the room and out of public life.

Chapter Fifty-six

No president had ever made a more anxiously awaited address to the nation. Rumors of a government in crisis had spread rapidly throughout the land and, indeed, around the world. The White House was mum on the specifics of the President's speech, saying only that he would personally dispel many of the "silly rumors" that had caused so much needless concern across the country.

Jason and Rachel watched from their room in a downtown Washington, D.C., hotel. They planned to stay in Washington a few more days yet. For now, going home meant having to face the press, especially for Jason. They hoped that in a week or so, much of the furor would have died down.

"Would you mind turning on the TV, Rachel?" Jason asked. "I seem to have a cramp in my foot." He grimaced a little and massaged the foot for emphasis.

"Why don't you just use the remote?"

"I tried. It doesn't seem to work."

He watched as Rachel slid out from under the covers. "Don't look," she said.

"Wouldn't think of it," he replied, not taking his eyes off her for an instant.

Rachel poked the button on the TV set and then dived back under the covers. They curled up against each other while they waited for the President to come on.

"And now," the announcer said, "from the Oval Office in the White House, the President of the United States."

The President's face immediately filled the screen. It was a grandfatherly face, a face that America trusted. He was wearing a warm smile which served immediately to forestall the gloomy expectations of many of his countrymen.

"My fellow Americans"—the President looked straight into the camera as he spoke—"I am pleased to announce to you this evening my intention to nominate Senator Robert Chandler to be the next vice-president of the United States. The nomination will be sent to the Senate tomorrow, and I have every reason to believe that it will receive bipartisan support and speedy confirmation. Senator Chandler has had a long and distinguished career in the service of his country. . . ."

The President went on to chronicle the details of Robert Chandler's career and to emphasize how fortunate America was to have sons such as these willing to devote their lives to public service. Then the President's expression became more somber.

"Also, I must tell you tonight that I have, with the greatest reluctance, accepted the resignation of our attorney general, Charlotte Moran. When she first accepted the appointment four years ago, she warned me that she might only be able to stay in Washington for one term.

Some time ago she notified me of her desire to return to private life. I wish to express to Attorney General Moran the gratitude of this nation for her years of service. She brought to the office a spirit of uncompromising integrity that will leave a lasting imprint.

"I am pleased to announce this evening that I will nominate Mr. Michael Cordova to replace Attorney General Moran. Mr. Cordova is, as you know, currently serving as director of the Federal Bureau of Investigation. Prior to assuming that post, Mr. Cordova had a distinguished career as a federal prosecutor."

Then, once again in a more somber vein, the President turned his attention to the Middle Eastern coup that had dominated the evening news.

"I wish to emphatically deny," he said, "persistent rumors of CIA involvement in the coup and in the assassination of that country's president. The strained relations between our two countries are a matter of public record, but the United States is not in the business of overthrowing foreign governments. That having been said, we do wish to extend the hand of friendship to that country's new government and promise them our full support as they struggle to throw off the chains of dictatorship and move toward democratic institutions.

"Finally," the President said, "I wish to comment very briefly on the persistent, wild rumors surrounding the recent events at a clinic not far from Washington, D.C. One report claims that the clinic kept files on national political figures for purposes of extortion and influencing government policy. The FBI has made a full investigation, and I am able to tell you tonight that no such files exist.

"Further, the murder that occurred at that clinic, witnessed by so many dignitaries and members of the news media, appears to have been the act of a single, deranged gunman. The man later embarked on a spree of kidnappings and murders that involved both U.S. and foreign nationals. The gunman was killed in a shoot-out with law enforcement officers of the state of Virginia. The case is considered closed."

The President went on to admonish those who persisted in rumormongering and called upon the press to exercise discretion consistent with the best traditions of the fourth estate. He closed with his usual "Good night and God bless the United States of America."

Jason sighed and clicked off the remote control.

"I thought you said the remote didn't work." Rachel pulled herself up on one elbow so she could look Jason directly in the face.

He gave her a slight smile. "You don't believe everything you hear, do you?"

Epilogue

Four months later and Jason still came to the clinic every day. Same building. Same office. Everything was just the same.

And everything had changed.

The Marsden Clinic had risen yet again from the ashes of its former self and now appeared destined to finally become the thriving research center which Arthur Marsden himself had always envisioned. Of course, the go-go days of the luxury political spa era were gone forever. The movers and shakers came no more. But the money flowed in—now more than ever before—this time in the form of federal grants supporting Marsden's research.

Jason understood that the grant money was in part a bribe. Or, at the very least, payment for silence. The *powers that be* had decided it would be all for the best if certain things had never happened. It would serve no useful purpose for the American people to hear just how closely their government had flirted with chaos. "If a tree falls in the woods," Michael Cordova had said, "and no one is around to hear the sound . . ."

Arthur Marsden was already hard at work developing

Son of Psychoden, a drug with all the clinical benefits of Psychoden but without the abuse potential.

Of all the changes, the part Jason liked least was that he and Rachel were still shouldering all the clinic's administrative responsibilities. The part he liked most was that they were now together nearly twenty-four hours a day.

"I fear," he told her, "that I am becoming dangerously serious about you."

"I already knew you were dangerous," Rachel said, "but I had no idea you could be serious."

For Jason all that was missing was the opportunity to see a few patients. But how in the world could he ever get patients to come back to the Marsden Clinic?

In the end, he relied on word of mouth. He let a few colleagues know that he was once again available for consultative work. After all, he wasn't looking to start a booming practice. He just wanted a few patients to see, perhaps a couple of days a week.

And Jason was confident that patients would materialize eventually. All he needed was that first one, just to break the ice. Perhaps a referral from an old Harvard colleague. Or from Dr. Klein in Charlottesville. But, just as had happened so many times over the past several months, Jason's wildest imaginings did not adequately prepare him for reality.

His first patient was self-referred. A patient he'd seen before, but whose problems he'd barely been able to guess at.

And so it was that four long months after he thought he'd finally closed the door on Charles Talmedge and his erstwhile cabal, Jason found himself sitting face to face with Gerald. Herself.

She was nervous, as in their first interview, and Jason was struck once again by the remarkable discordance between the appearance of the woman now seated before him and the carefully scripted public persona of Charlotte Moran.

Now, of course, Jason had considerably more insight into the turbulence which lay just beneath the glass-smooth surface which the former attorney general presented to the world. That fateful White House meeting had revealed the existence of a dark secret, even though its exact nature remained an enigma.

Jason could imagine the overwhelming sense of helplessness she must have felt. This accomplished, self-confident woman had had the world at her feet. She might have become the first female vice-president, perhaps the first woman president of the United States. Then, with all the suddenness of a trapdoor opening beneath her feet, she was barred, instantly and forever, from holding high public office.

From the beginning Jason had imagined Gerald as the mastermind of the conspiracy, someone who sought the reins of power for himself. It was not until near the end that Jason finally tumbled to the possibility that Gerald might be a pawn instead of a king; that Gerald might be a mere marionette, held in place by blackmail, his strings pulled by someone far away from Washington.

"I needed to talk to someone," Charlotte Moran said, "and you were the only person I could think of."

Flattery, Jason thought, will get you nowhere.

"I'm sorry, that didn't come out the way I meant it." She paused, struggling to gain composure. "It's just that you're already privy to certain events which we've all sworn not to disclose. You and I can discuss things without breaking that vow." She paused once again, this time to thoughtfully consider a well-manicured fingernail. Then she said, "And I need to talk to a psychiatrist."

"I'm happy to help in any way I can, Ms. Moran." At this point in the interview, it was best for the therapist not to say too much. The patient had come here to talk, let her talk. Some dark secret stalked the former attorney general. It was, Jason assumed, about to be revealed.

But whatever was troubling her had not distracted Charlotte Moran from her usual meticulous attention to her appearance. Her hair and makeup were suitable for a fashion shoot. Her clothes might have been selected for a no-nonsense press conference, but nonetheless conveyed a subliminal sexuality that was not accidental.

"I'm sure you're wondering," she began, "like everyone else, what it was in my life that was so terrible it could force me to give up the vice-presidency."

Her eyes found Jason's, and she hesitated momentarily as though waiting for a response. Then she continued:

"That's been the worst part of all this for me, people like the President believing I must have done something horrible. He's tried not to show it, but I can feel how he has pulled back from me. He needs a margin of safety, some room for deniability.

"And Cordova is conducting his own private investigation over at FBI. He can't stand the thought that someone, somewhere might have broken a law and gone unpunished. Just between you and me, Cordova can look all he wants. He won't find anything."

Jason watched as Charlotte Moran once again studied her hands. She took a couple of deep breaths, obviously screwing up her courage for the revelation that was about to come.

"I had a brother and sister who were twins," she said, then quickly corrected herself. "I'm sorry, that didn't come out right, either. My sister Geraldine is still alive. I believe I told you that Tommy, my brother, died in a boating accident." Quite unexpectedly, she gave Jason a small smile. "I'm afraid we called them Tom and Gerri when they were kids. They hated it.

"Anyway, Geraldine was always—emotionally speaking—a little off balance. She was never a very happy child, always very jealous of Tommy. They fought constantly, and it was always Geraldine's doing. Or at least it seemed that way. Maybe that was part of the problem. Geraldine always said we picked on her. Perhaps we did. Tommy was the Golden Boy. Geraldine felt she was the ugly duckling sister.

But after Tommy died, Geraldine suddenly became his champion. Her life became sort of a living monument to his memory. She even began to insist that everyone call her Gerri. She used to *hate* that name.

"This fixation she has on Tommy's memory has continued all these years. It gets worse and worse. It's clearly way out of control. She's barely able to function in everyday life. He's all she talks about. Her apartment is filled with pictures of him and all kinds of Tommy memorabilia.

She's been to all the best doctors, in and out of institutions. Nothing seems to help.

"I've always looked after Geraldine as best I could, especially since my parents died. I pay her bills and see that she has food and clothing. So far as I know, I'm about the only person she ever talks to. She has no friends. My other brothers and sisters have pretty much given up on her. And I can't say that I really blame them. She's so difficult, always saying terribly hurtful things to people.

"It's just that she's so very fragile. The slightest little thing could push her over the brink, and there would be no chance of ever getting her back."

Charlotte Moran hesitated once again, marshaling her forces for the final assault. She had the beginnings of tears in the corners of her eyes. Jason waited, every faculty focused intently, not yet guessing where all this would lead.

"I'm sure it seems like I'm rambling pointlessly, Dr. Andrews, but I assure you, I'm not.

"That day at the White House, when you said that Gerald might not be part of the conspiracy but rather someone who the conspirators *knew* they could control through blackmail, when you asked if either Senator Chandler or I had something in our past that could be used against us—you even said it might not be something they had on one of us directly, but something about someone we loved. Anyway, I knew instantly that I was the one. I was certain what Talmedge had learned and how he would use it. I even wondered if it might be more than just a coincidence that they picked the code name Gerald. I mean, with my sister being Geraldine.

"You see, Dr. Andrews, the thing that only I knew, the secret which Talmedge discovered when he picked my brain at the clinic, was that my sister Geraldine *killed* my brother Tommy."

She was openly sobbing now, her shoulders rising and falling with each new sob. She tried to talk, "I'm sorry, I just . . ."

There was little that Jason could do. He couldn't just say that everything was going to be all right. He couldn't tell her that she was making a mountain out of a molehill. She'd just told him that her sister *killed* her brother.

So he waited. He offered Kleenex. He told her to take all the time she needed. They could even continue on another day if she preferred. Finally, she was able to go on.

"It wasn't murder. It wasn't like she was actually trying to kill him. No jury would ever have convicted her of anything—not even manslaughter.

"We were out in a boat, the three of us. Tommy and Geraldine started to quarrel, began pushing and shoving. They were only twelve years old. All of a sudden Geraldine had an oar and swung it at Tommy. It was all she could do to lift the oar, but it caught him squarely on the temple. If I close my eyes right now, I can still picture that moment like it just happened.

"Tommy fell into the water and sank like a stone. I dived in after him and kept diving till all my energy was gone. At the end, I couldn't even pull myself back into the boat. I almost drowned myself.

"Geraldine just froze. She couldn't move. She couldn't speak. It wasn't until after the funeral that she finally came out of it, and then she began her lifelong memorialization of Tommy.

"I never told anyone what happened. I thought it would serve no purpose other than to guarantee that Geraldine's life was ruined: *there goes the girl who killed her twin brother.* Like I said, Geraldine was psychologically fragile *before* Tommy died. I don't know, maybe I did the wrong thing. Maybe I should have told someone. But I was only fifteen myself when it happened. As time went on, it seemed to make even less sense to go back and relive the tragedy.

"But, of course, under Psychoden I must have told all this to Charles Talmedge. And I'm sure I expressed my deepest fear—that this would get out. Understand, I wasn't worried at all for myself, but that day at the White House I instantly knew exactly what Talmedge's clients would threaten to do. They would threaten to confront my sister with the truth. And that would have killed Geraldine. Literally."

Charlotte Moran was beginning to regain her composure. Her mascara had run all over her face, but the tears were drying up now. Her words were coming more evenly. There was only an occasional sniffle.

It occurred to Jason that it hadn't really mattered to Charles Talmedge whether confronting Geraldine with the truth would in fact have had a devastating effect. What Talmedge had learned through the use of Psychoden was that Charlotte Moran *believed* that the truth would kill Geraldine. Charlotte Moran's belief was all the blackmailer required.

"So that's why I'm here, Dr. Andrews. Not really for myself, but for Geraldine. Is there some way that you could help her, or is it too late now to use the truth to save her?"

Jason absently shook his head, not in response to Charlotte Moran's question, but at the remarkable ironies of life.

"There is a chance, I believe, Ms. Moran, that your sister could be helped. It's a small chance, but I believe it's worth a try. We have a drug that was discovered right here at the clinic, a drug with which you are quite familiar. . . ."

FEAR IS ONLY THE BEGINNING

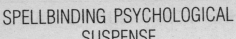